Emily

EDEN FRANCIS COMPTON

WITH RACHAEL FLANERY

This book is printed on acid-free paper.

Published by:
Level 4 Press, Inc.
13518 Jamul Drive
Jamul, CA 91935
www.level4press.com

Library of Congress Control Number: 2019943919

ISBN: 978-1-64630-056-3

Printed in the United States of America

Other books by Eden Francis Compton

Death Valley
Hedy
Catch and Kill
Anti Trust
Belle

Dedication

For my mom.

Author's Note

Emily's dialogue is her original words gathered from her poems, notes, and letters.

Prologue

In Winter in my Room
I came upon a Worm—
Pink, lank, and warm—
But as he was a worm
And worms presume
Not quite with him at home—
Secured him by a string
To something neighboring
And went along.

A Trifle afterward
A thing occurred
I'd not believe it if I heard
But state with creeping blood—
A snake with mottles rare
Surveyed my chamber floor
In feature as the worm before
But ringed with power—

The very string with which
I tied him—too
When he was mean and new
That string was there—
I shrank—"How fair you are!"
Propitiation's claw—
"Afraid," he hissed
"Of me?"
"No cordiality"—
He fathomed me—
Then to a Rhythm Slim
Secreted in his Form
As Patterns swim
Projected him.

That time I flew
Both eyes his way
Lest he pursue
Nor ever ceased to run
Till in a distant Town
Towns on from mine
I set me down
This was a dream.

—Emily Dickinson

Chapter 1

He is alone, surrounded by devastating headlines. His home office is dark. One dim lamp knocked on its side casts grim shadows on a desperate man. He sits on the floor in a mess of newspapers. When he shuts his eyes, all he sees are reporters thrusting their mics and cameras in his face. His last venture out ended in an ambush. He did not respond well. When your secrets are lies, it is impossible to come clean.

Teddy values his power too much to ever abuse it. Even now, past his prime, he knows exactly what to do to get what he wants from women. He's never needed to take it. He's rich. Talented. Famous. Brooding. Strong, but not threatening. He's handsome in an interesting way. His dark eyes, strong chin, and narrow, pointed nose all fit together well. He has a thick head of wavy brown hair with just enough gray sprinkled in to prove he's not vain. He is a master at walking a moral tightrope. It can get very thin, but he has yet to fall off. This is not a scandal detailing a shameful man and his devious desires. This lie won't get lost in hashtags. This is a different type of undoing. One juicy enough to rise above the noise and take everything from him.

He has to get out of there. He has to do something. He jams items from desk drawers into a worn leather bag and sprints from the safety of his home.

It does not take long to get out of the city. He can hardly see the yellow dashes on the road through the dark, a light sprinkling, and his dirty, cracked windshield. The wipers squeak and smudge with each pass; there isn't quite enough rain to make them useful. The old convertible top no longer closes correctly. Inside the car is damp from the drizzle and loud from the rushing air. Once gorgeous and vintage, his prized Porsche is now old and useless.

He doesn't know where he is or where he's going. He doesn't have a map. He has a gun. No one left him any tools to guide him, only the ones that could cause the most harm. His phone keeps buzzing as he speeds farther from home.

It's his son calling, or maybe his best friend, manager, and lawyer. Hard to be all three at once, but Philip has mastered his role over the years. Usually being the best friend takes the most work and leaves the most damage. It's okay, it's a job he gladly accepts and is overpaid to do. He wasn't prepared to be the lawyer, and that has left everything damaged beyond repair.

It's Teddy's fault. He blames himself for not insisting on mortgaging everything he owned to bring in a firm to snuff this out at the first spark. He trusted Philip. He trusted himself. He trusted the truth. All have failed him, and now he's here.

He spies a neon sign out of the passenger window. He pulls into the motel's banged-up parking lot, where there are more potholes than cars. He shuts off the engine and breathes in the silence. He's about to ring a bell, and he knows it can't be unrung, but he doesn't have another option. This is how it ends.

This no-name travel lodge, which looks like it caters to meth dealers and adulterers, is about to become famous. This is where they'll find him. This is where he'll take his last drink and write his last line.

It's raining harder now as he walks toward the office. He doesn't care, and he makes the trip slowly. His shoes fill with water. He feels nothing. A mercy he doesn't deserve.

The shabby lobby is the color of the insides of a garbage can. The young blonde behind the counter knows better than to make conversation with guests who check in this late. She's pretty with an unfortunate mole on her chin. She slides him the key to his room. *The* room. He hopes she's not the one who finds him. Or maybe he does.

His room is only a slight improvement from the lobby. The walls are freshly painted. The bed is covered with a burgundy quilt that looks like it itches, and the mattress has a dent in the middle. The carpet is flat. It's all perfect.

He dumps his bag out onto the bed and rummages through his supplies. He opens a bottle of vodka. He's never been picky, but he wishes his last drink was whiskey. He drains the bottle and searches for a pen. So far this isn't all that different from his usual nightly routine.

He stumbles to the dresser with pen and paper in hand. He loses his balance and kneels in front of the chipped plywood drawers. He writes.

He will have the last word. His final act will be the truth. Ink flows faster than he can think. He writes terrible things about that terrible girl. He writes words to stab and haunt her. You do not get to ruin a man and walk away from it. Take the only thing he has and not have to pay for it.

He writes about the things he's gotten right and even more about the things he's gotten wrong. He is too busy lashing out to say goodbye. He should. This will hurt Philip more than he knows.

He stops once he runs out of paper. He tries to keep going, writing on the dresser, but the pen can't dent the varnish. He pulls himself to his feet. He shuts his eyes. He waits a moment. Maybe, just maybe, when he opens them, he won't recognize the face in the mirror. This isn't him. This isn't who he is. There's another way out of this.

He opens his eyes and takes in his reflection. This is exactly who he is. Who he's always been. He puts down the pen and pulls the trigger.

It's raining. Again. The city is an overwatered plant. His lip curls up toward his left eye. This isn't his usual wakeup call of a dull booze-induced ache. This is a reckoning. His eye twitches open. He stumbles on all fours toward the bathroom. Not to throw up but to remove whatever has been jabbed into his temple. The pain coats him in a sticky sweat. He dry-heaves from the throbbing.

Weak arms grip the vanity, climbing toward the mirror. He hesitates when he gets to the summit. Once he looks, he can't unsee it. When he sees it: the knife, or the nail? Could it be wood or a pipe? He'll have to remove it. There are no bandages or even towels in the bathroom. It's a guest bathroom, and he never has guests.

An exhalation of courage. He holds his head up, rapidly blinking both eyes. Nothing. His hands fly to the spot of the phantom pain. Nothing. No weapon of mass destruction. No bump. No lumps. Not even blood. Just an imprint from the magazine he slept on.

This bathroom is getting smaller. Maybe he's getting bigger? Too big for these flimsy walls decorated with the most expensive and least practical wallpaper. The ornate mirror mocks his pain, his reflection revealing smooth untouched skin. He needs air. An open space to birth whatever creature has burrowed its way into his left temple.

He braces himself on the walls as he passes the master bedroom, where his wife is sleeping. A curled-up snail occupying a corner of the gigantic bed, still mostly made, and adorned with tasseled throw pillows. For decades she has lived deep in her shell, afraid of the salt her husband casually sprinkles. This little snail has sacrificed everything for self-preservation. You can't blame a creature for surviving, but you can forget it's there.

He grabs his keys from an ivory dish by the door. The table is cluttered with awards. Success has been such a given that he can't be bothered to showcase his trophies. Just something shiny to discard on the first available spot after coming home from a party.

Outside is gray and heavy. The sun is obligated to rise, but it is not interested in providing any warmth. Not for him. For a moment he forgets about the pain and panics, looking down to ensure he is dressed. Yes. To the early risers he's just another man in transit going from one bad decision to the next.

Is he dreaming? This feels like the in-between sleep. He walks through a puddle, soaking his shoe.

"Shit."

He's awake. His reactions are always much too big for minor inconveniences. This wet sock is a personal attack. If only there was someone with him to witness his tantrum. Someone like the little snail he could scare off with his fit. Without an audience, he simply mutters under his breath and limps to a nearby bus stop bench.

Miraculously, the flood in his shoe has stolen the spotlight from his pounding head. His face relaxes as he sits heavily on the bench. He's been awake for an hour, and his body has already gone through a marathon. What the hell did he do last night?

Forgetting is a common occurrence in the Maine household. Teddy Maine, our hero, drinks to forget. His wife, the little snail, sleeps inside her shell. His children have never had all that much to remember. Their lives have been make-believe from the start. They are grown and gone now but haven't gotten far. Family can be a blessing, a curse, or a cancer. Well, all three. The latter is often overlooked by greeting card writers, but true artists know how to profit from the pain of hanging from their family tree.

Teddy is a wizard at turning metastasized relationships into masterpieces. He has the money and awards to prove it. It's always about proving something. His father, the first to put the Maine name in lights, owned the world. Our Teddy dutifully continued the family business of telling stories. Plays, movies, and a failed Showtime series have built him a fortune and charted the course of modern culture. Undergraduates dissect his early works, and critics lavish fake praise on anything he touches. It's never enough.

Teddy sits like his father: legs spread, shoulders square. Built more like an athlete than a writer. His father was tan and charming. The universe couldn't give him everything, so when he lost his hair at an early age, he shaved his head. Teddy remembers that smooth tan skull acting like a beacon. Average people were desperate to be near him. He shone so bright they were bound to catch some of his light. It was too late when they realized the sun exists within a vacuum.

The charm that flowed through his body and radiated from his symmetrical crown attracted many lovers. Some men, some women. Some young. Many younger. For an artist, flesh was just another medium. Another tool he used to create his stories. There were no boundaries. When you're Zeus, the world is Mount Olympus.

Teddy never tried to compete with his father. He learned at a very young age that would be pointless. If his father was the sun, he was allowed to be the moon. Don't feel bad for him. Remember, the moon controls the tides. The moon makes pregnant women go into labor and lights the way for hunters at midnight.

Teddy can't think about who his father was without thinking about who he is now. Age is graceful for some but cruel to many. That magnificent melon is now shriveled and beige. It bobs on a feeble neck too large for its rusted frame. A booming voice now silent. A giant now compacted in a wheelchair. Watching a god crumble is uncomfortable. Perhaps that's why Teddy is happy to take care of him. To keep him close. Teddy has always excelled at making people uncomfortable.

When his brain is quiet, the space is often filled with thoughts of his father. Not fond memories of baseball or fishing, but a grainy slideshow of thick fingers and toothy grins. Melting ice in highball glasses, and his mother with her eyelashes smeared down her cheek.

"I know you."

A man, probably en route to his cubicle, stops and points with his latte.

"You're that guy."

It's time to go. Teddy mumbles, "Sure," as he attempts to slide past.

"Your face is in Times Square!"

"Yup." As he walks away, his foot squishes in wet wool.

"Hey, can I get a picture?"

Teddy spins around. He takes quick steps, invading this invader's space. "What's my name?"

"Huh?"

"What's my name?"

This worker bee was looking for a quick Instagram post, not a fight. He's not interested enough to remember his name. The way Teddy's eyes narrow warns him not to guess.

"Dude. Relax."

Teddy stares at him longer than necessary. The man shrinks under his gaze.

"Have a great day!" Teddy smiles as the man scurries past.

It feels nice. Smiling.

Chapter 2

A black sedan is parked outside the grand entrance to his high-class apartment. An unfamiliar deep voice calls out from it when he walks by.

"Teddy Maine?"

"Yeah?"

"I'm your ride."

Teddy leans into the open passenger window. "What?"

"Your boss, Philip, sent me."

"He's not my boss," Teddy corrects him as he gets into the back seat.

He must have forgotten a meeting. The car pulls out and heads downtown. He must have forgotten an important meeting. They rent a fancy office suite whenever a big deal is signed, or a pending lawsuit is settled.

Teddy squirms in the tan leather seat. He can't get comfortable. There's a lingering ache in his head. It feels permanent. His stomach churns, empty and queasy. This car ride in heavy traffic isn't helping. He cracks the window.

"You hot?"

"Need some air."

The driver rolls down the front windows. The incoming breeze blows a pile of dandruff and dead skin off his shoulders. White flakes hang in the air like snow. Teddy is horrified. He doesn't say anything, not because he's kind, but because he doesn't want to risk getting it in his mouth. He pulls his shirt up over his nose and mouth. When the car finally stops, he exits without a word.

He shakes off the imaginary filth as he rides the elevator to the twenty-seventh floor. The doors open to a bustling lobby. A pretty girl behind a glass desk greets him. She's spent a lot of time to make her hair look like she just got back from the beach.

"Hello, Mr. Maine. You're in conference room six."

Teddy nods and heads off to find Philip. He's eating at a thick glass table. He looks good in business casual. He has the build and complexion designed for a corner office. He's aged well and has enough money to attract women that are decades younger. His blue eyes may be more cloudy than bright these days, but they can still draw attention from across the room. Teddy always thought he looked like a human version of a golden retriever, but maybe that has more to do with him being such a loyal, dutiful sidekick.

"Can you believe this place?" The bottom of Philip's breakfast burrito falls onto the wrapper being used as a placemat. Teddy sits across from him.

"Free breakfast," Philip continues. "Beautiful women in the lobby. Fantastic coffee. Let's never go back to our shit hole." He takes a sip from a mug. "You're probably wondering why we're the only ones here."

Teddy's not. If the car hadn't been waiting for him, he would be at home sleeping. Or writing. But most likely drinking. He has no idea why they are downtown surrounded by glass. Staying quiet should get him his answer.

"I'm not keeping anything from you," Philip says. "I thought I'd try talking with them alone. You know, keep things breezy."

"Breezy?" Teddy has no idea what meeting he was cut out of.

"Light. Keep the feelings out of it."

Teddy nods his head like he knows what they're talking about.

Philip continues. "Really great news."

Teddy waits as Philip wipes his mouth. Is he stalling?

"What the hell is going on?" Teddy has lost his patience. With the morning he's had, it's amazing it's lasted this long.

"You hungry?" Philip holds out his burrito. Teddy is about to pounce. "Okay. Okay. Anyways. Really great news. Sonya is going to—"

Teddy jumps out of his chair.

"Sonya was here!"

"Calm down." Philip motions for him to sit.

"This is the meeting you had without me? Sonya and that bitch who are out to destroy me—"

Philip's tone is condescending. "Sonya and her client were here to discuss their alleged book."

"And?"

"It's going away."

"How?"

"I told you it was nothing. Who knows if it's even real?" Philip pauses and delivers the truth. "One of their sources backed out."

"So it's done then?" Teddy's anger is deflating.

"Done."

"Dead."

"Absolutely."

Philip did his job. He charmed, he threatened, and he got lucky. Maybe their injunction would have held up in court. Maybe not. He wants to believe Teddy. He does believe Teddy. He's glad he doesn't have to ask any more questions.

It was because of Philip that they were able to get a head start avoiding catastrophe. Sonya, a well-respected entertainment lawyer and former fling of Philip's, did them the "courtesy" of tipping them off about a client's new book. She was surprised when they threatened court. Teddy of all people should have been relieved. They had all known each other long enough to expect much bigger skeletons in his closet.

"Doth thou protest too much?" she'd cooed over drinks.

Sonya was smart enough to not take on a client who could be sued for libel. Her clever little author had only suggested Teddy was a fraud. She'd presented "evidence" and let the reader draw their own conclusions. The book was a study of toxic masculinity in the twenty-first century arts scene. What broke Teddy wasn't her suggestion that he'd stolen someone's work, but that he'd paid for it.

According to Kelsey or Hailey or whatever bullshit name her bullshit parents gave her, Teddy Maine did not write his first two plays. He bought them from his roommate.

The story started out true enough, if not a little trite. A young brooding prodigy pounded the pavement determined to do it on his own. He might share a name with his famous father, but his success would be all his. Of course, that was impossible. He could never truly get out from his father's shadow, but he was going to try. He was going to write plays that were brutal and unforgettable. Instead, he drank. He took pills. He snorted what he could and smoked the rest.

Teddy Maine cracked under the pressure. Kelsey contended that the weight of his name crippled his ability to finish anything. To start anything. He was a mirage in a desert of real talent. He couldn't meet his own off-off-Broadway theater's deadlines and was going to fail before he began.

Like a fable, the rich prince who had everything he ever wanted but not the one thing he desperately needed used an unsuspecting ordinary accomplice with an extraordinary gift.

Paul Sharpe was a nobody who happened to be roommates with an icon's son. Paul and Teddy met their junior year of college, shortly before Teddy dropped out. Paul was smart. Too smart. He made people uncomfortable. If he laughed, it was too loud and too long. He often joined the conversation two topics too late. He was always a little unkempt, though he was meticulous about keeping clean. Teddy liked having him around. He enjoyed studying the different ways his off-putting nature rippled through a crowd.

When Paul needed a place to stay in the city, Teddy was happy to host him. He took pride in being the one guy who would take his calls.

When his stay turned permanent, it was like having an old, nervous basset hound around.

Paul didn't think twice about helping Teddy, and Teddy didn't think twice about using him. Paul would be a quick fix. Just a boost to get him going. He gave him the ideas. Teddy was the big-picture guy and Paul filled in the details. As far as collaborations went, it wasn't that out of the ordinary. Except Paul's name was nowhere to be found. That was their deal. Paul, who was so used to getting nothing, took whatever he was offered.

The plays were certainly not Broadway-bound, but they created buzz and put Teddy on a path independent of his father. A path he continued to go alone. Paul's plays are often the marquee pieces in chronicles of Teddy's early work. The author graciously conceded later in her book that Teddy eventually found his voice with the help of many other unnamed co-authors.

Philip was surprised by the intensity of Teddy's reaction. The whole thing was just an expensive tabloid story. No one who mattered would believe it or care. But the more Teddy raged, the more he could believe it. Even if he didn't want to. If they couldn't stop the story, his next move was encouraging Teddy to lean into it. He took advantage of this guy once; he could do it again.

It's been ages since Teddy has written anything noteworthy. The theater has been doing seasons of remounts just to keep the lights on. No one is in love with Teddy's passion project du jour: a historical drama starring Emily Dickinson. He's been researching his way out of writing for at least a year. Philip often wonders if it will ever be finished or even started. Teddy hasn't let him see a word. He can be possessive of his drafts, especially in the early stages, but this time it is to the extreme. If there really ever was a Paul Sharpe, Teddy could use him now.

The whole book bombshell tossed Teddy off course for weeks. He's supposed to have a first draft to the theater's board in a matter of days. Teddy doesn't play nice with others and has been on perpetual thin ice with the revolving board members. This play determines how he retires. Does he go out on top, or is he pushed out the back door?

You would think he'd be safe at his own theater company, but that's not how progress works. Old, entitled men who drink too much and talk about the pretty girls in the lobby are on their way out of every institution. The theater world is not immune to this rapid changing of the guard. Having your name hung over the door doesn't save you anymore. His name could soon be the only thing he has left, and this book will take that, too.

The idea of giving anyone else credit was never going to fly. Teddy can't process any of this threat without becoming completely irrational. No matter what happens, Teddy is going to handle it badly. Hopefully, Philip has succeeded in blowing this off, and no one will have to find out just *how* badly.

"In light of our good fortune, take the night off," he tells Teddy. "We'll get steak. I'll have the girl out front make a reservation."

"A bit early in the day to think about steak."

"Bad night?" Philip is happy to be once again amused and annoyed by his oldest friend.

"I don't remember."

"Probably not great, then. Twenty years ago, maybe." Philip winks. He always needs to keep it light. Breezy. "Go home. Take a shower. I'll check in later."

Teddy nods. He wants to sleep for days. He's the worst kind of tired. Exhausted but wired.

"I'll call for a car."

"I'll walk." His voice is firm. Teddy doesn't want to risk another four-door gross encounter.

"Suit yourself."

Philip waves into the various glass boxes as they walk to the elevators. He stops and leans over the front desk to chat up the receptionist. Teddy hears her laughing as the elevator doors close.

The air outside is cool and damp. It feels good. Fresh. He doesn't remember being cold sitting on the bench earlier. The chill makes all the difference between feeling refreshed or moldy.

A city bus idles at the stoplight. It's impossibly loud. There's a gorgeous ad on the side for the Met's upcoming production of *The Magic Flute*. Teddy is transfixed by the rich, vibrant colors. The production design hasn't changed one bit from the last run that sold out over ten years ago.

Teddy had gone to opening night with his daughter, Elizabeth. He'd pulled a million strings to surprise his wife with tickets, but she had the flu. Or maybe it was one of the other children who were sick? Either way, he needed a date. Elizabeth wore one of her grandmother's beaded gowns. Her grandmother had given the collection to Teddy's wife, but she was much too practical to be bothered with playing dress-up.

The cool evening air tickled her bare arms like the cleansing caress Teddy is being treated to now at the bus stop. She was radiant. Glowing and shy. She must have been around fifteen. The dress was a smidge loose and sparkled with the same bold colors adorning the bus. He remembers her being a little embarrassed, which was unusual for his Elizabeth. But then again, a teenager who's just figured out popularity is often unusual.

Teddy never knew if his eldest daughter was going to crawl into his lap or spit "shut up!" in his face while slamming the door. A stop-motion montage of all the doors she slammed runs through his brain. Dark lines of mascara smeared over freckles. Vodka mixed with Lip Smacker heavy on her breath. Her young skin sticky like a Jolly Rancher candy. There she is, slamming the door over and over again. His wife blamed him for being too possessive.

The Magic Flute was a good night. Elizabeth was so excited. Teddy had spied in her journal a few days earlier about how "pumped" she was to go see some "Motzart." She was right, it sounds like there's a "T" in there. He couldn't wait to rub it in her face once she saw the program.

They floated through the lobby to their box seats. Old acquaintances marveled at what a fine young lady she had become. Teddy beamed with pride. He wasn't typically an old-fashioned or sentimental guy, but that night he felt like he was presenting his daughter at court and it was a huge success.

She squeezed his hand through the "Queen of the Night" aria. He had a scotch and she had ice cream during intermission. They danced and hummed around the apartment for weeks afterward. Things were good. For a little while.

Teddy rubs his temple as the bus pulls away. He coughs from the trailing exhaust. He digs in his pockets. The dull ache is getting sharper. He must have something. Lint. Change. Random pills to take the edge off. Blur the next round of memories. Keep the pain away.

He hustles through the crosswalk toward his block. Thankfully, he's already walked most of the way. He makes a stop at Chang's for coffee. He doesn't know the real name of the place. He knows Chang is the owner and the coffee is perfect. Chang is a good friend. He must have seen him hundreds if not thousands of times, and they have yet to say a word to each other.

Philip was nice to grant him the night off (maybe he *is* his boss). He has to work. He has to finish this play. He's so close to being done, but not as close as he's been telling Philip. He wants to spend his time thinking about Emily Dickinson, not writing about her. He can't admit the whole thing was a mistake now. Especially now. When he gets home, he'll find something strong to add to Chang's coffee.

Chapter 3

*I*n the daylight, his office is a charming space. Piles of books and papers hold the promise of another hit. Another play to titillate, entertain, and expose. A gracious scholar once credited him with holding a mirror to man's most complicated desires. Teddy just likes to tell secrets. A revival of his first breakout play, overflowing with these secrets, is currently paying for his youngest daughter's second master's degree.

Thirty years ago, the words flowed out of him. Only it wasn't *his* veins that he opened to fill the pages of his Tony Award–winning debut. He endeared himself to a group of survivors. Men who had found each other as they took on the Catholic Church. Men who, as boys, were abused by the people their families trusted most. Their growth was stunted by shame. The ones that survived to adulthood were shattered. There were no happy endings.

Teddy betrayed them. He told their secrets with unnecessary wit. Some reviews claimed the groundbreaking and layered tale was charming. What an impeccable talent to allow the audience to delight in such darkness! He cashed in on their broken spirits and paid no attention to what led him to their space. He had no interest in examining the wholeness he felt when listening to their specific pain.

The world has changed since *The Sins of Our Fathers* premiered. The controversy has been sadly played out. Still, actors begged, and producers flattered their way to an extended run off Broadway. Teddy's disinterest in the project has been highlighted by a few, mostly younger, mostly female, voices in the theater world. Reviews from previews have been so-so. Most skirt around the play and spend eight hundred words trying to fit this now square peg into a round hole. Most playwrights would be scrambling to make improvements before opening. Teddy couldn't give two shits.

There is one thing he cares about now. *Emily*. His work in progress. He's devoted years of his life to Emily Dickinson. First research. Now writing. He dreams of her. He lives with her words on the tip of his tongue. He is determined to give her the legacy she deserves. Of course, Emily Dickinson, the Belle of Amherst, doesn't need him to do anything for her legacy. But this isn't about scholarship. Her words are telling him something. Something everyone should know, but only he can hear.

His daughter introduced them. Teddy was never much of a reader, especially not a reader of Victorian poetry. When Elizabeth, his middle child, turned thirteen, she declared that henceforth she would only dress in white and speak in verse. It was fantastic. She swam against the current but always managed to be the first to shore, leaving a wake of confusion behind her. He loved watching her move through this world of boring people. They were one and the same. She handled it better.

It was on Christmas Eve when she was seven that he realized she was a gift the universe intended just for him. He didn't know what good deed he had done to deserve Elizabeth, but he was grateful for her every day. That year was no different from any other. The family celebrated at his parents' compound in the Florida Keys. A week filled with twinkling palm trees and green cocktails with sweet cherries on top. Teddy had never experienced a tropical Christmas until his parents moved south. He hated it. It felt like a lie.

By this Christmas, Elizabeth had peeked behind the curtain, taken the red pill, and knew the score. She liked being a kid all right, but she knew everything, and everyone, was pretty much bullshit. To witness a young girl cut a man down to his knees with just the tilt of her head was a spectacular sight to see.

The family was given matching Hawaiian shirts to wear to the beach extravaganza. Fireworks, roasted pig, and a mention or two of Jesus were on the agenda. Elizabeth came out of her room, a guest room used for hosting Playboy bunnies and Golden Globe winners, in a long-sleeved, blood-red velvet dress complete with an oversized black bow and white lace underskirt.

It was a bit tight and short. Something stolen from the nanny's dress-up bin.

Teddy lingered down the hall, listening to the argument that erupted between mother and daughter.

"Bitsy! People are waiting. We don't have time for this."

"Time for what? Let's go."

"Go back into that room and change."

"No." The little girl's defiance was a matter of fact.

"Excuse me?"

"No."

"Go put on the shirt your grandfather gave you right now." His wife was always on edge around the in-laws. She needed her daughter to be compliant.

"It's Christmas. On Christmas, it snows. It's cold, and you need a warm dress!"

"It's ninety degrees."

"Not where I am." Again, Elizabeth was stating a fact.

"Oh, for God's sake."

The battle ended with an eye roll and surrender. Trish retreated to one of the many guest bathrooms to fix her face. She rarely did things like curl her thin black hair or put on lipstick. A no-frills look worked with her simple face. Teddy didn't like it when she dressed up. He thought she looked like a clown, or worse, suburban. But here she was with a perfect bounce added to her usually flat hair, too much blush, and slightly uneven black eyeliner. She normally kept her surprisingly fit and curvy small frame deep undercover in sensible and forgettable clothes. Whenever they ventured to Florida, she managed to find a suitcase worth of form-fitting and skin-showing outfits. Teddy felt sorry for her. She was desperate for his father's approval.

That night, hot, humid air glistened on the exposed limbs of partygoers. Not Elizabeth. She created her own weather.

When it was time for family pictures, she was excluded. Teddy's father scooped up all his grandchildren but one. He held them close and whispered in their ears. He showered them with kisses and tossed them in the air for all his fans to admire. He juggled and tickled these beautiful creatures that he owned, all but one. Elizabeth sat in the sand, content as a clam, as the cameras clicked.

Teddy would be saved, after all. By this little girl in a red velvet dress.

The air conditioning is humming in his office, yet he has sweat through his shirt. It smells like Florida sweat. He smiles for the second time today. He must be working some serious toxins out of his system. He swears he can taste pork and sweet little cherries. There's a picture from that trip crooked on the bookshelf next to his desk. The cute handmade frame stands alone in a room drowning in wood and leather. They were in bathing suits. His son holding a fish. His wife holding a baby. Elizabeth holding his hand. He doesn't remember that day at all. Just the dress that never found its way back to New York.

The sun has moved and is now streaming through the blinds. How long has he been sitting daydreaming in his office? Whatever he did last night, he vows to never do it again. He's got to get to work. His first drafts are always pen and paper. His index finger has a permanent ink stain and thick callous. But right now, these stacks of chicken scratch and Victorian portraits are making him seasick.

More coffee will help.

On the trek to the kitchen, he passes by his sleeping wife. It could be days before he sees her awake. They live in a massive, modern apartment. The exterior, with its hint of historical significance, is misleading. Everything inside his residence is sleek and new. An expansive, open cube filled with sharp and cold edges. There's an occasional pop of warmth. A leather chair here. A tasseled pillow there. There's a smattering of indulgence. Intricate golden wallpaper here. Crystal and stained-glass bowls there. A stark-white front door opens into a marble, steel, and cement chef's kitchen. A huge dining table fills the space with a cold stone tabletop and plush embroidered chairs. A floor-to-ceiling gas fireplace and wall of windows makes for an impressive main living space. A narrow hallway that is often dark leads to the other secret spaces. Bathrooms. Bedrooms. His office. He mostly treads the square-tiled hall from the kitchen island to his office.

It takes a moment for his eyes to adjust to the flood of natural light in the kitchen. There's no cream. The contents of his fridge look like they belong to a college freshman. Butter will have to do. He'd be upset, but it is his fault. He's put the same empty bottle of creamer back on the shelf for days.

A buzzing takes root in his ears. He swats at nothing, and as quick as it started, the buzzing stops. Walking back down the hall, he pauses at another family picture. This one is large and formal. A proper photo from Augie's graduation. There's Nora, next to her mom, of course. Proud Augie holding his diploma, and Elizabeth in white, his arm tight around her waist. The two are smiling as if they are the only ones there.

The buzzing is back. Sharper. His coffee splashes from a sudden wince. What in the hell . . .

There's a fly trapped between the glass and the photo. It's hovering right over his smiling face. How did it get in there? How is that even possible? He taps the glass, and it stops.

"Trish!" He yells for his wife.

She can't hear him. He looks up and catches the bottom of a white skirt being shut behind a door.

"Trish?"

He goes to find her in that white skirt, but his attention is pulled back to the dying insect. The fly struggles and thumps into the glass.

It falls to the bottom of the frame, leaving a streak of brown down Teddy's body. He backs away, confused and disgusted. He goes to yell again but doesn't bother.

His office is quiet, the room no longer swaying after a shot of caffeine. He opens the desk drawer and pops more than the recommended dose of aspirin into his mouth, washing it down with buttered coffee. This might be a new low. He chuckles to himself. If he doesn't laugh, he'll cry.

He's in his safe space, his office, though the last few months of writing have been a chore. Each page is like picking off a scab. Now that he's to the final scene, it's the same scab over and over. The flesh gets hard, only to be opened and exposed again and again. It's never been like this. He's starting to worry a lot of people. One of them, his son, is calling for the third time today.

"Jesus, Augie. I'm working."

"Are you coming tonight?" His son's voice is kind but impatient.

"Where? Philip was going to check in later."

"Are you going with him? I can meet you there." Augie doesn't yet know they are talking about different things. That's been happening a lot lately.

"Going where?"

His son softens. Maybe his dad isn't avoiding something unpleasant. Maybe he doesn't remember.

"To the show, Dad. It's opening night."

"What? It's Wednesday."

"No, Dad." Augie's voice trails off.

It's not later in the day. It's tomorrow. Teddy's stomach flips; he's lost time. That's a recent phenomenon he's been secretly experiencing. He brushes the panic aside.

"It doesn't matter. The show opened thirty years ago."

"A lot of people worked really hard. This is a big night."

Saint Augie, always thinking of others.

"Wonderful. Yes." Teddy really isn't in the mood for a party.

Augie is quiet. He needs to play this right. "The board is going to be there. Big donors."

Teddy doesn't respond and chugs the last of his coffee. It's ice cold.

"Dad?"

"Fine!"

"The office is sending over a car."

"I need to work."

"Say you'll be there."

"I just did!"

"Love you."

Teddy doesn't respond. He rarely does. He nods.

Augie waits a beat for what he knows is a head bobbing on the other side of the city and hangs up.

"Dad." Augie is pushing Teddy toward the stage. They are crowded behind the curtain at his theater. "You have to say something." Augie is desperate.

Teddy takes a step back and looks up. How did he get here? When did he get here? Wasn't he just looking for a pen in his office?

"What am I doing here?"

"Just say thank you."

The theater is full. The play is over. While walking to the microphone, Teddy puts it all together. This is opening night of *The Sins of Our Fathers*. He's grateful he doesn't have to sit through it again. He keeps his speech short and sweet. He manages to get a laugh here and there. He can do anything on autopilot.

Fear starts to swirl in his stomach. Is this time jumping the beginning of the end? Is this what dementia feels like? How long until he is rolled around next to his father? He wants to be alone, but the party awaits. He should probably eat something.

Out in the lobby, Philip brings him a plate of finger food. Philip, his best (only) friend and agent, has taken care of him for decades. He doesn't like to ask questions, but Teddy's recent behavior is out of the ordinary, even for a guy who disdains ordinary.

"You good?"

Teddy nods and eats bacon-wrapped scallops two at a time.

"Great crowd. They freaking loved it." They didn't. Philip's biggest fault is his optimism.

"Does it matter?"

"Do you have a drink? Want a scotch?" Most people prefer Teddy after a few cocktails.

Philip gestures across the crowd to Augie, who brings over a drink. Here they are, Team Teddy, dedicated to making the world better through art. Summer homes and penthouses are an added perk.

At first, Philip thought it was a bad idea to bring Augie on. He had just graduated from law school, and he had hoped he would venture a bit further from the nest. He owed it to himself. He had been the calm in the storm for too long and deserved a break. Philip had the luxury of stepping back. He rarely did, but when Teddy got to be too much and things too complicated, and they did get very, very complicated, Philip could go home. Augie was already home.

"You good?" Augie unknowingly echoes Philip, which makes Philip smile. He doesn't have kids, and he's happy Augie is morphing into his Mini-Me. Augie is taller than his father, like Philip. His face is a softer version of Teddy's. He has his father's dark eyes and wavy brown hair, but looking at the three of them, you could assume any combination of relations.

"Why do people keep asking me that?" Teddy finishes his drink and holds his hand out to drain what's left of Augie's. "What's your mother doing here?"

The three men look over at Trish and Nora chatting in the corner. Teddy doesn't know his youngest daughter well. If Elizabeth was his, Nora definitely belongs to his wife. The two women often communicate without talking, and Teddy suspects it is about him. Nora is smart and kind. Beautiful and determined. All the things a father should want. But she isn't interesting like Elizabeth. Merely a passenger, like her mother.

Augie is confused. "What do you mean?"

"Why is your mother here?"

Augie and Philip exchange looks.

More and more people are communicating without words in Teddy's presence.

"She owns half the theater."

"I just left her sleeping at home."

"Mom was at the apartment?"

Nora comes over, interrupting them. She always looks like she just came inside from a brisk walk. Her cheeks are flushed, and her light brown, stick-straight hair is tucked behind her ears. She has a small frame like her mother and often covers herself in the same ordinary, modest clothes. Being thin and beautiful, she makes ordinary look on-trend. "Hi, Daddy." She dutifully kisses him on the cheek. "Nice show."

Teddy nods.

Nora, so gentle and good, shrinks when standing next to her father. It breaks Philip's heart. "How's school?" he asks. "You a doctor yet?"

"Oh, Papa P." She's instantly more comfortable. "You don't want me diagnosing you. And, no, not a doctor, a licensed therapist."

"What were you before?"

"A licensed feminist." Augie can't resist.

"Shut up!" Nora will always be the baby sister.

Teddy isn't listening. Doesn't appreciate these things he's built. His children are thriving adults fully in bloom despite their father only providing them shade and salt.

Elizabeth also no longer appreciates these precious family moments. She stands at the bar, looking at her phone. They're no longer speaking, but he's not surprised she's here. Like Augie, she's an entertainment lawyer, and she must rep an understudy or something. He's lost her three times. This has been the longest stretch without reconciliation.

The first time, she left him for popularity and the life of a teenage queen. The second time, for drugs, and this third time it seems she has left him for good. After a stint in rehab, she abandoned herself. She turned away from everything and anyone who used to matter and built a fortress of success and materialism to hide behind. None of Teddy's kids needed a career. Teddy didn't need a career. His parents made a fortune and a legacy that would have survived at least two generations. Elizabeth was going to write her own path. She had a talent that eclipsed the men in her family. All of it has been wasted now, wrapped up in a sensible charcoal-colored suit.

"I need to talk to your sister." Teddy walks toward the bar, leaving the puzzled crew behind.

Philip doesn't let him get far. "Ted . . . Teddy . . . hold up."

Teddy keeps his eyes on Elizabeth but stops to placate Philip.

"You sleeping okay?" Philip talks close, keeping his concern private.

"Don't do that. Don't *care* for me, Philip." He says *care* as if it's a dirty word.

"Right. You're strong like a bull. Is it done? The Dickinson draft? Martha and Jody want a copy."

Martha and Jody put up half a million dollars to produce Teddy's next play. His love letter that he can't finish.

"How am I supposed to work with all this shit going on?"

"This shit? You mean all these people celebrating and loving you? Come on, man. You know why you're my only client?"

"Because I make you rich, and you're lazy?"

"Because you write, Teddy. You write like nobody else. Ever. Not your father, not the hipsters coming out of NYU. You produce quality at a pace that is not human. And you've stopped."

"I'm sorry your next vacation will have to wait."

"That's not fair."

"It's been a weird day." More like days. He thinks about telling him, but there's no time. Elizabeth is almost done with her third drink. "The play is done."

"Really?"

"Nearly. I have to clean up a few scenes. Tell Maggie—"

"Martha."

"They'll have a script by the end of the week." He's done with Philip and walks away without fanfare.

Elizabeth's hair is short and perfect. Straight edges hit her collarbone and frame her tight face. Teddy prefers it long. Thick, long, and wild. Her nails are painted black. Her lips are dark and chapped. There is nothing welcoming about her appearance. She's still beautiful like her sister, but worn and tired. In heels, she's nearly as tall as Teddy. She turns toward him as he approaches the bar.

"We need to talk." Her voice is coming from deep underwater.

The pain from earlier is back. He can't walk. He hunches over in agony. She's not surprised. His hands press on his temples to stop the phantom blood from gushing. His eyes plead with her for help, but she doesn't move from her spot at the bar. Philip rushes over as he falls to the floor.

Chapter 4

"How was the show, Mr. Maine?"

He's in the back seat of a car. Another jump. He has no idea how he got here. His head isn't throbbing, though, and that's enough. He runs his hands over his temple. Nothing.

"I'm Charlie," the driver tells him. "Lou had the night off."

Teddy grunts.

"Don't worry, I'll get you where you're going." Charlie looks over his shoulder.

Teddy is embarrassed by how he recoils from his countenance. It's too long. His nose is off-center and surrounded by boils. There are pocks and bumps all over his face and knuckles. Teddy can only imagine that they run the length of his large frame.

"I can be hard to look at."

"No. No. It's been a rough day."

"Water?" Charlie reaches behind him with a bottle of water.

Teddy forces himself to grab it from his deformed hand. "Thank you."

They drive in silence. The city looks too quiet to be real. Teddy shakes his head. "I think I've lost it."

"Lost what, sir?"

"My goddamn mind."

Charlie laughs. It's loud and echoes through the luxury sedan. Teddy relaxes and sinks in his seat. He could sleep. Maybe that's all he needs. He wonders if Charlie would be agreeable to driving him around the city as he sleeps like a baby in the back seat.

"With you being an important person, the pressure must get to you."

"I'm nobody."

"Anyone who rides in the back is somebody."

Touché.

"I've never felt like this before. Weak. Stuck." Teddy feels safe confessing to a stranger.

"People, we're no different from fruit. We rot from the inside out. Something gets soft and bruised. Don't cut it off, and it spoils the bunch. Gets your kitchen all filled with flies."

"Sounds like you've had some bad apples recently."

Charlie erupts in laughter that makes the car shake.

"Secrets. That's the poison."

Teddy was initially relieved having a stranger to talk to. He's often surrounded by people who are there to listen. He just wants to talk to somebody who doesn't care. This is quickly going from helpful to cliché. Secrets. What's next, does he have to talk about his mother?

"So, what's the maggot in your fruit basket?" Charlie asks.

"Let me give you a tip. You'll want to streamline your metaphors." This time Teddy laughs, but it is neither loud nor genuine. "What is it? Poison, maggots, bruises . . ."

Lou doesn't talk much. Teddy makes a note to tell the office it needs to be Lou. He doesn't need some freak show getting into his business like this.

"Bet you're missing Lou." Charlie is a mind reader now.

"Just the quiet." Teddy goes to take a sip of water, and it burns his mouth. He yelps in pain and surprise.

"Everything okay?"

"The water . . . it's boiling."

Charlie doesn't respond right away. When he does, his voice is soft. "Must be scary. Losing your mind."

Teddy hands him the water. "I'm going to shut my eyes for a minute."

"Sure thing, boss. Can I get you another water?"

"No."

Who the hell is this guy? Teddy doesn't know what's pissing him off more, this stranger getting too familiar, or his use of random, mismatched *Chicken Soup for the Soul* metaphors. He keeps his eyes shut tight even though he's wide awake.

Thankfully, it's just a few more minutes to the apartment. Teddy tries to exit without conversation. As he heads toward the steps, Charlie rolls down the window.

"Watch out for those flies."

He turns and waves. Is this happening? Did that just happen? Teddy is grateful to be so annoyed. That feeling anchors him. Yes. He is here. Now. He just had to deal with another jackass. He had to suffer through another opening night. He counts his steps as he goes, willing his body not to make another jump. He's made it home. Alone. He can retreat to his office and Emily. Maybe he'll be able to do what he promised and finish the script. He doesn't care. He just wants to spend time with the person he loves. She'll understand what's happening. She'll know what to do.

Teddy has always been able to weave in and out of the worlds he creates. Writing saved him from a lonely childhood and fulfilled the family obligation of being a creative powerhouse. As he got older, it became more of a job and less of an escape. Until he met Emily. Is that why he can't finish? He's writing about something that matters to him. He doesn't want to lose her. He'll always have her poems. He can visit her anytime he wants. But everyone has those. He wants something special. Something more. Screw it. Maybe he'll never finish. Let the board remove him. Let producers sue him. This is bigger than all of them.

He doesn't remember turning the key in the lock. The door opens with a push. His wife must have beaten him back. She's always forgetting things like locking doors. He doesn't bother to look for her in the bedroom. He has to get to work. He'll finish. Make Philip happy. He deserves that. There isn't anyone else in the world who loves him like Philip does. He will give them this play, but he'll keep Emily.

He bounces down the hall. It's a new beginning. Without the trappings of the work, he and Emily can just be. He is her master, and she is his. Maybe he'll try his hand at poetry. She can guide him. His father always said poets were the only true writers. He can win another Pulitzer. That would be an award he would cherish. Another scene and then the rote task of typing. It will be done by morning.

At night his office is dark and soulless. Shadows fill the space. It's anyone's guess which lamp will turn on. Burnt bulbs linger, waiting to be replaced. Garbage cans overflow, waiting to be emptied. Stacks of paper that tower with promise in the daylight create cover for mice and earwigs in the dark. He's often huddled over the computer screen or writing by the light of his phone. Squeezing his eyes to capture light as he pushes out words. He flies to his desk. The day has brought him here. All of it. The pain. The walking dreams. Elizabeth. Elizabeth?

She was at the theater tonight. Right before he blacked out, she said they needed to talk. She hasn't needed anything from him in years. Should he call Philip? Augie? Let them know he is home safe? Are they worried? Why aren't they with him? He decides he never blacked out. All those people. They would have rushed him to the hospital. Nora would have insisted. For a moment, he wonders if the show opened tonight. He sways on his feet. He can't do this now. He needs to stay here so he can get to her. He doesn't want to blink and be in tomorrow. He wants to be in right now.

Something is different. Misplaced. His desk is out of balance. One side remains covered in papers. The other is clear. Nothing but a square outlined in dust. He runs to the desk, tripping and catching himself before his head strikes the corner. No. This isn't right. This is where he left his work. The work. The only thing that matters. His play is gone. Years of research. A year of mad scribbling . . . gone. He was so close to giving Emily what she needed. What *he* needed.

It has to be somewhere. He yells for his wife, who isn't there.

"Trish!"

Dread cripples him like a five-year-old who spilled grape juice on white carpet. This is really bad. None of the lamps are turning on.

"Goddamn it! Trish!"

The next lamp he tries sputters off with a flicker. He slams it to the floor. Back at the desk, he furiously turns each page of the remaining papers, searching. He tosses books off the shelf and throws open desk drawers. There's something in the bottom desk drawer that pushes pause on his panic. A gun. Not a special gun. Not a gun he knows how to use. An actor gave it to him as a closing night gift years ago. He sometimes holds it while he drinks in his office. He doesn't remember if it's loaded. Should he hold it now? He likes knowing it's there. He slowly pushes the drawer closed and collapses on the floor.

It's gone. The play is gone. He doesn't know what to do. He calls Philip.

"What time is it?" Philip sounds tired.

It's a good question. Teddy has no idea. It could be ten minutes or ten hours since they last spoke.

"It's gone."

"What?"

"The play."

"What play? Ted—where are you?"

"In my office—"

"Are you alone?"

"Of course—"

"Should you be? You've been—"

"I'm fine. Listen to me. There's no play."

"Buddy, you're going to get it done. I can ask Martha for an extension. No, I'll tell her there's going to be an extension. You can't stress yourself out like this."

"All of it is gone, Philip. Every page."

Philip is starting to understand. His tone shifts from concerned partner to disappointed father. "Teddy. Do you have a copy? Tell me there's a copy."

Teddy is now a toddler trying to get out of time out. "It was in my office. Like every time . . . you know . . . I write it out and then type—"

"Please tell me it's backed up."

"Backed up where?"

"On a fucking computer, Ted. We've made it to Mars, and you're still using a damn pen."

"I was going to—"

"Did you do any work at a coffee shop?"

"No. Just my office."

"Okay. Then it's somewhere in your office."

"Someone took it."

"Jesus Christ. Now we're in *The Thomas Crown Affair*?"

There is a pause where there normally isn't. Life is always easy with Philip. Teddy doesn't know how to handle his disappointment.

"Teddy." Philip waits for an answer.

"Yeah."

"This is serious. People's jobs depend on this. Your job depends on this. The board will vote you out."

"I'll fix it."

"You'd better. You wrote it once. Write it again." Philip softens, which eases the tightness in Teddy's chest. "Get some sleep. Maybe tomorrow . . . with a clear head . . . you'll find it. It's probably right in front of you."

Philip hangs up without saying goodbye. He could sense Teddy's emotions rising and did him the favor of leaving him to cry alone.

Teddy thinks about the gun. That's one way he can finish this quickly. He crawls back to the desk and opens a drawer. The middle drawer. He grabs a weathered book and strokes the cover. A picture of a young Elizabeth loses its grip as a bookmark and falls to the floor. Behind him, tacked to the wall, is the only verified portrait of Emily Dickinson. Her eyes shift down, watching him.

For a moment, he wonders if there ever was a play. Why would Teddy Maine write a play about Emily Dickinson? No one understands. He can't explain it. He'd quote a canned line or two from Augie. Or Philip would jump in with some rah-rah bullshit. The work started when Elizabeth went away. Is it because she reminds him of Elizabeth? Is she replacing Elizabeth? If he never started the play, then it's not missing. He doesn't need to write the ending. He can walk away from this. Agree that it was never going to work and quickly produce the hit everyone really wants. No one will lose their job. The theater isn't going anywhere. But he'll know. He'll know he failed. Again.

He opens the book to a random page.

Success is counted sweetest
By those who ne'er succeed.
To comprehend a nectar
Requires sorest need.

Emily's words comfort him. "You said it." He mumbles to himself. "Get your shit together."

It's only natural to be a bit dramatic, having spent your life creating drama. He hates when he lets it get the best of him. He stands and looks for a bottle. If there were a bottle left out, it would have been smashed during his recent tantrum. There's a suit coat hanging over the closet doorknob. He grabs two airline bottles of booze from the pocket.

Lately Teddy's emotions have been a rubber ball bouncing down the stairs. He goes from despairing to determined with one slug of booze. He downs both bottles for good measure. His body can't handle these benders like it used to. Another curse of getting old. Both his parents lost their sharpness prematurely. It didn't stop them from drinking. It won't stop him.

He has to write this play. He has to finish what he started, and he *did* start it. He wrote it once. He can write it again. He'll go back to the beginning and make it to the end this time. He's finished dozens of plays. Just freaking end it. He's gotten way too far in his head with this one. He opens his laptop, attempting to learn from his mistake. He pushes it aside and rummages for a pen, once again ransacking his desk. He grabs a cheap blue one covered in bite marks.

His hand doesn't move. The page is blank. The ball bounces.

"Goddamnit!" He throws the pen and storms out of the room.

He's heading for the bar by his fireplace. It's late. He's going to drink himself to sleep.

The room is a tunnel. She is the light. Emily stands, smiling. She is not the vulnerable vision of fantasy. She is his vision of truth. A long white dress billows over her porcelain frame. Hair the color of sunset is braided down her back. He walks toward her. With each step, his eyes get wider. His shoulders relax. His whole body is a smile. His skin tingles. They are feeling the same air. Their muscles are occupying the same space. This is new. This is real.

He's in her bedroom, only there's no hallway outside. No stairs, no walls, no building, no nothing. It's like looking over a cliff, but with no bottom.

"Emily."

She joins him in the center of their private universe. She formally introduces herself with a playful curtsy.

"I am small, like the Wren, and my Hair is bold, like the Chestnut Bur— and my eyes, like the Sherry in the Glass, that the Guest leaves."

Teddy grabs her around the waist. She doesn't resist, but she doesn't participate.

"You're beautiful."

She backs away from him quickly. She blushes as she agrees with his assessment. *"I know you're wrong, but I believe you're right. I've felt it myself."*

He takes a step, continuing to invade her space. The space shifts around them, and then they are standing in his office. He doesn't notice anything but her.

"What are you doing here?"

She knows exactly why she's there. He's not ready for the answer. She gets to play with him first.

"The riddle we can guess, we speedily despise."

She begins to pick up the mess and papers around them. He's embarrassed as her eyes scan his work.

"I'm . . . I'm writing about you." He spins around the room, drawing her attention to the random pictures and facts about her tacked to the wall. "I've spent years getting to know you."

She investigates a line of Post-It notes lining the door trim. She's not impressed. He's not the first to miss the mark.

"Those who know her, know her less the nearer her they get."

"I can't finish. I don't know how it ends." He studies his hanging scribbled thoughts next to her.

"To fill a gap, insert the things that caused it. Block it up with other and 'twill yawn the more."

She's judging him. He wants to wake up from this dream. This is a cruel way to go crazy. Exposed and a failure. She holds his hand, making amends. She's going to need to tread carefully.

"They have not chosen me. But I have chosen them."

She tours the room, taking in his take on her life. He follows her, picking up his mess, quickly trying to stash pages before she can read any more. She confirms and corrects his work.

"I was the slightest in the house; I took the smallest room. At night, my little lamp, and book, and one geranium."

"Did I get it right? Do you remember any of this?"

She laughs. It's a warm and full sound. *"If recollecting were forgetting, Then I remember not! And if forgetting, recollecting, how near I had forgot."*

"You hate it." It's rare that he throws himself a pity party, but this is a rare night. "Tell me the truth. It's all garbage."

"I'll tell you a truth. When Jesus tells us about his Father, we distrust him. When he shows us his home, we turn away, but when he confides to us

that he is 'acquainted with grief,' we listen, for that also is an acquaintance of our own."

She hands him a page. A fresh start. A new beginning. She's excited. *"My story has a moral. I have a missing friend."*

She waits for him to read it. It's his play, but better. This is all he needs. He quickly loosens his grip so his sweat doesn't blur the lines. He's found it, and he can't risk losing it again.

He's on the floor by the fireplace. He often wakes up in strange places. This time he was with it enough to at least grab a throw pillow. His head should be pounding. His joints and muscles should be stiff and bent from passing out.

He feels amazing.

He runs to his office. It's barely dark; it will be morning soon. He thinks he can finish the first act by sunrise. A wonderful, beautiful, brilliant dream gave him the jump start he needs. He's glad the play is gone. He's ready to write it now.

His dream. He hopes she comes to him again.

He writes as the sun comes up and moves to settle into a bright morning spot. He would still be working, but he's been interrupted by a visitor. He's having his second pot of coffee with a police officer he's never met. He's talking at a frantic pace. Philip lets himself into the apartment and joins them.

"Wonderful! Prince Philip has arrived! I'll get exhibit A." Teddy dashes off to his office.

"You wanted a welfare check?" The cop gruffly reports to Philip. "He ain't well."

"Thank you. I owe you."

"You said tickets."

"Yes. Yes. My office will send over two Knicks—"

"Courtside."

"Courtside. Tickets. Did you find any drugs? Should I take him to a doctor?"

"He's going on about some big heist. Some book. Emily Donaldson—"

"Dickinson."

"Sure. Someone broke into this penthouse and left with a stack of notes."

Teddy enters the room. "A script. They left with a script."

The cop takes out a notepad. "Have you discovered anything else missing? Money? Laptop?"

Teddy slams his new play down on the counter. "It was terrible, Philip. All of it. You were right. Complete trash."

"I never said that."

"Thank God it's gone."

The cop is confused. "Wait. Is it stolen or gone? Did you lose it?"

Teddy is dismissive. "Somebody took it. They did me a favor."

The cop does not appreciate having his time wasted. Even if it means courtside seats. "Somebody did you a favor by breaking into your apartment—"

Teddy is too loud. "Yes! It was garbage! What's so hard to understand—"

Philip interjects. Teddy might be working his way into an involuntary psych stay or an abrupt tasing. "Let's take a breath."

The cop slides the papers toward him. "So what's this?"

He's still too loud. "The play!"

"That was stolen?"

"No. She gave—" That was a big slip. He waves it off and tries again. "I started over."

He turns to Philip. "Almost done with Act One."

"Thank you, officer, for coming by. Appreciate you checking in on my friend."

Teddy is dancing around in the kitchen. Philip isn't successful at kicking the cop out.

"Why would somebody want it?" He's not convinced this is just a welfare check anymore.

Philip made a mistake involving a third party. "He's Teddy Maine."

Teddy stops moving. Philip has his back. It feels good. Solid and stable. He smiles at his oldest friend and embraces him.

The stranger is even less impressed than he was before. "Is that supposed to mean something?"

Teddy was teetering on the precipice of rage and is now slipping deeper into a manic frenzy. "This guy! I love it! You want a hug? Can I give you a hug?"

The cop backs up. This will get him out of there. He hands Philip his card, trying to keep his space from the frantic artist.

"Call me if anything else comes up . . . I guess."

Teddy walks them both to the door.

"Fantastic work. Thank you, sir, thank you. Don't worry about us at all! Treat yourself to a long lunch! Do you have a captain? Sergeant? Whatever they're called, I'm going to call them to sing your praises."

The cop forces a smile, nods, and walks away, hoping his day will turn around.

Philip lingers in the doorway, waiting until they're alone. "I called in a welfare check."

"I noticed."

"Last night, on the phone, I was worried." Philip takes a beat. "I *am* worried."

Teddy kisses him on the cheek.

"You're a good man, Philip. I love you."

Philip looks around for candid cameras.

"I've got it back." He triumphantly holds up his chewed blue pen. "Always had it. *Always*. No more remounts. No more rumors. This will be the best thing I've ever written."

Philip is worried he'll never be able to get out from under the weight of the book. The rumor.

"Don't put that much pressure on yourself. It doesn't have to be the best thing you've ever written. It just has to be done."

"Yes! Stop calling the cops on me and let me work. Go home. I have a play to write."

Teddy can be a hard person to be around. He can be moody. He can be negative and even sometimes cruel. He's often on something. Philip doesn't mind any of that. It's consistent. Interactions like this worry him most. What goes up must always come down, and Teddy isn't known for his soft landings.

Teddy waves goodbye as Philip makes his way down the hallway to the elevators. He slams his last cup of coffee and heads to his office. He can't remember the last time he felt this good. Young. Hopeful. He stops at the bedroom.

"Trish." She's slept through the morning's commotion. "It's going to be okay." He speaks quietly to not disturb her. He feels a softness for her that's been missing. She remains a stone.

He was not a good husband. He knows that. He was never interested in being anything different. At first, it was enough for her to share his children and his theater. He gave her moments of kindness that sustained her, filled her like a camel so she was safe to continue her journey through the desert. He picked her. He could have had any woman in New York, but he picked her. For a long time that was enough. She used to pretend to sleep. Now she stays far away.

He doesn't notice the picture in the hall. The one from Augie's graduation. The one that was buzzing. Dead flies are collecting at his feet. Forming a pile under the glass, working their way up his body. He should be more observant.

He dances into his office, giddy. He holds his worn pen like a triumphant battle sword. He flips it around in his fingers and gets ready to work. He's ready. Ready to work.

Nothing.

Okay. Don't panic. Shake it off. He reviews the last couple of pages.

He's nowhere near finished with Act One. Philip knows he always rounds up, but he has a lot of ground to cover.

"Shit."

He moves his brain in reverse, tracing last night's steps, the ones that brought him success. What was he doing . . . how did he do it? He didn't do anything. She did.

It was a dream. Right? It had to be. He's scared of the alternative.

His father's baritone voice hisses in his ear. "Pray you don't inherit your mother's weak mind. She's sloppy in her old age."

He wasn't wrong. There was something missing even before she got sick. This uncomfortable memory is from one of Teddy's last visits to the Florida compound. Seeing both his parents overrun by ordinary tasks was sobering. His father's moods turned on a dime. It was harder for him to get around, though he would never ask for help. Both his parents would forget what they were talking about midsentence. The beginning of the end was much harder to deal with than his father's current upkeep. Even his mother's passing was easier to handle than realizing where she was headed. Did they know they were slipping, losing control? Teddy is nearing that age. Is this when he starts to lose it?

Of course, it was a dream. If it wasn't, then this could be the start of his ending. He is not ready for that. He shakes off the unpleasant echo of his father and focuses back on the blank page.

He can't do it. She gave him the words, and she needs to give him more. Like a junkie, he only needs a little hit. Once he has his next fix, he'll be good to go. The truth is that he'd gladly give up his sanity for success. He will gladly start his descent into the abyss of old age if he can have this one last thing. He shuts his eyes and tries to conjure her up like a carnival psychic.

Will he be able to see her again? Does it have to be at night? Last night he was in such a panic. Is that how it becomes real? He's in a panic now, should he get drunk? Is that what's missing? How can he get to her? He walks away from his desk. The bottom drawer is open. He turns back and shuts it quickly. He could easily get discouraged.

If he wants this bad enough, she'll be there. If he needs her enough, she'll come.

He's in her bedroom. This isn't a dream. He doesn't know what it is, but just like before, he knows they are breathing the same air. She sits on a small bed with her sister, Vinnie, braiding her hair. It's an intimate moment. Teddy's mind races toward intimate things.

Vinnie was her caretaker in life and death. Filling Philip's role regarding Teddy, she spent her life trying to make sense of Emily. When Emily finally turned away from the world and wrapped herself in white, Vinnie remained her lifeline to the outside world. Vinnie encouraged simpler minds to believe simpler truths. This recluse chose her fate because of her wounded heart. White, a symbol of mourning over the relationships that could have been but never were. A spurned spinster who locked herself away in her tower gave people the story they needed.

Her father's friend, a much older, serious man, was the closest she ever came to marriage. Judge Lord. The women can hear his thoughts and start to reminisce and share Victorian gossip.

"Is it strange that I miss him at night so much when I was never with him?" Emily muses. *"My love invokes him as soon as my eyes are shut, and I wake warm with the want that sleep had almost filled. I dreamed last week that he had died, and one had carved a statue of him and I was asked to unveil it. I said that what I had not done in life, I would not do in death."*

Even without an invitation, he is confident in joining their conversation. "Why didn't you marry him?"

Teddy needs something to write with. His realities have weaved together. He crosses to his side of the world and grabs a pad of paper and his pen from the desk.

Emily is mildly annoyed by his intrusion. *"The gate is God's, and for his great sake, not mine, I did not let him cross."*

"It was never meant to be him." Vinnie is dutiful in her role as translator and mediator.

Both women come to him, crossing to his world, suddenly interested in what he's writing. He melts when they touch him. Emily coos into his ear. If he's going to demand her attention, she'll make it worth his while.

"The air was soft as Italy, but when it touched me, I spurned it with a sigh, because it was not him."

Teddy puts down the pen. The women circle him, wrapping him in their words like ribbons on a pole on May Day. They giggle like schoolgirls.

Emily begins. *"Don't you know that he was happiest while I withheld and did not confer?"*

Vinnie echoes. *"Don't you know that* no *is the wildest word we consign to language?"*

They take turns teasing him with their words. Moving their lips closer and closer to his face. *"To lie so near his longing, to touch it as I pass."* Emily's breath warms his neck.

He grabs her arm. They are playing a dangerous game. "You didn't say 'no' to everyone."

The women have tired of entertaining him. Emily strokes his cheek like he's a child. He bristles at the thought of her taking up a maternal space or, worse, using these visits just to play with him.

She proclaims, *"Royal, all but the crown. Betrothed, without the swoon."*

He's right. She didn't always say 'no.' She's referring to her onetime lover, Sam Bowles, another brooding and sometimes troubled writer.

Before they exit, Emily finishes with a slightly defiant tone. *"My Husband, women say, stroking the melody. Is this the way? . . . Here's what I had to 'tell you.' You will tell no other? Honor is its own pawn."*

They leave without looking back.

Teddy does not like how this feels, and he realizes she left without giving him what he needs. Was she just a tease? Another woman who abused her power? Maybe this partnership wasn't such a good idea. Bothered, he yells for his wife.

"Trish!"

It's time for her to wake up. This recent encounter has left him with an itch he can't scratch. He stomps to the bedroom. She's not there. The bed is perfectly made. An open suitcase waiting to be unpacked rests where her head should be.

"What the hell . . ."

It's his suitcase from a recent trip to Los Angeles. He returned home two weeks ago.

Chapter 5

He drinks alone in the kitchen. He doesn't want to see anyone right now. Not even her. The phone buzzes. A text from Augie. No doubt Philip has reported all his worries. Augie wants to meet for lunch. He should eat. He doesn't remember the last time he had food. Was it the party? When was that?

He has crashed hard from the high of being able to touch her. Being touched by her. He's sure it didn't happen. How could it have? He's embarrassed. A schoolboy whose love note was intercepted. Screw it. He downs his whiskey and heads out for lunch.

The last couple of days have been miserably linear. He didn't realize how good it felt going crazy until he became sane again. He wouldn't mind fast-forwarding through lunch. Aguie is not a disappointment, quite the opposite. He's a to-do list reminding all those around him how to become better. Teddy's task for today? Be nice and eat food. Augie has always looked up to his dad. It's a pressure Teddy does not appreciate. But here they are. Lives intertwined in every way.

There is enough whiskey in him to make the walk entertaining. He smiles at a small dog on a diamond-studded leash. A woman trying to soothe a toddler who dropped their treat. He's at the restaurant with time to spare. Teddy has a lot of faults but being late isn't one of them. He will get there first. No matter what happens, at least he was first. He banks a win before the game even starts.

The café chairs are woven and uncomfortable. Across the patio, a woman sits with her meaty thighs pushing through the geometric ropes. When she stands, she'll tug at her short skirt to cover up the waffle-iron indents. She is eating a salad with too much dressing. Teddy, unlike the woman's date, is slightly repulsed by the amount of ranch that is missing her mouth. Must be tourists. Good for them, taking a bite out of the Big Apple.

Teddy's mood has flipped from sour to gracious. He can't stay mad at Emily. Discovering her Victorian exploits absolved him from his own indiscretions. What a time to be alive. Buttoned up from head to toe, fearing the fire and brimstone, and all the while swapping wives and collecting whips. Teddy is convinced Emily had many lovers, her brother's wife, Sue, being a most-loved notch on her belt, her brother a sweet, if not scientific, experimentation. It was silly of Teddy to feel threatened by Judge Lord, an old man, and Sam, a one-night stand.

Teddy has had many affairs. Some with his wife's blessing. Some without. Some with her participation. Others in secret. The secret ones were always more fun. Just as Emily's desires were actions that caused many reactions, so were his. A jilted journalist who threatened to publish a tell-all. A treat of his wife's who wanted things a little too rough. There was the time Augie asked why his second-grade teacher was joining them for breakfast. As they grew older, both of their attractions became limited, honing in on one object of affection. He hasn't thought about the teacher in ages, if ever.

She was a bubbly redhead in awe of the Maine power couple. Teddy made good on his promise and introduced her to directors around town. Of course, she loved children, but the stage was her real passion. They were being used, and it felt good. She got cast in a small part that earned her a spot in the equity union. Drugs and a pregnancy followed. Another broken New Yorker. It says something that Teddy and Trish have been able to survive it all. Sure, Teddy had a leg up with his father, but that also meant he spent his entire life under the bright lights. He doesn't know what normal feels like.

This trip down memory lane is cut short by a squish and a squash. A juicy sound fills his ear. He tracks it to a pile of red mush on the sidewalk. It's a squirrel. A young squirrel. It's amazing that in such a crowded place this isn't a more common sight. High heels stab into the mangled flesh. Sneakers leave treads of blood and guts down the sidewalk. No one is walking around. No one notices the pulverized corpse at their feet. A heavy step and blood splashes up a shapely calf. How did she not feel that? Teddy stands, alarmed. He attempts to yell out, but people are coming too fast. A stroller separates a tiny leg from the body. A man in a hard hat continues on his walk with a good chunk of tail stuck to his boot.

Teddy puts his hand to his mouth. He might be sick. Soon there will be nothing left but a red stain on the sidewalk. Across the street, through the parade of people and buses, he sees another squirrel. This squirrel is still and very much alive. She watches without a twitch as her baby is dismantled with each step. A little bit leaving on the bottom of each shoe. The tourist eating salad laughs loudly. Ranch dressing sprays out of her mouth and dribbles down her chin. All of life's cruelties hit him at once.

Next to the mama squirrel, Augie waves. Teddy smiles, instantly flooded with relief. He waves back, anxious to embrace his son. Augie steps off the sidewalk without looking. A bus flattens him, creating another red pancake. Cars continue to roll over his flesh and bones. Teddy is frozen in shock. A tire drives over Augie's skull, and it pops.

Teddy falls to his knees, not seeing Augie at the hostess stand or him running over.

"Dad!"

Teddy cries and rocks beneath the table. He can't see through his sobs who it is comforting him.

"Dad! Dad! What happened?!" Augie tries to lift his head. Teddy pushes back Augie's hands and grabs his wet face, cradling his chin.

His eyes flutter open, the bedroom ceiling coming into focus. He can hear Philip and Augie talking in the kitchen. A serious conversation. He rolls over and hugs the pillow next to him. He expects it to smell like Trish. It doesn't. He's still here. In today. The same clothes. He remembers crying in Augie's lap. The hostess rushing over. Augie waving help away as he called for a car. No need for an ambulance, he would get his father home. So sorry, everyone, for the disruption. He told the hostess he'd like to buy lunch for everyone on the patio and handed her a pile of money. Not many people carry cash anymore. Teddy and Augie do. Never know when you need to make a quick and quiet exit.

Philip met them at the apartment, and they put Teddy to bed. The day is real. What he saw. Heard. Felt. But it was all manufactured by whiskey on an empty stomach. Days of snacking on Ambien instead of food. A minor self-inflicted crack that can easily be filled. Maybe rehab this time. A retreat to the mountains. That sounds nice. He can finish the play in fresh air. A sharp bolt hits above his left eye. No. He can't leave. He needs her, and she is in the apartment. Emily would never make a trip to the mountains; she won't leave her bedroom. His eyes are swollen from crying. Time to join the worried faces in the kitchen.

Both men stop talking when he enters the room. They exchange a quick glance of "could he hear us?"

Teddy breaks the tension. "I'm okay."

Augie gives him a hug. He's not going to tell him what he saw. He'll never tell anyone about the squirrel. About the mama squirrel and her stillness.

"No one recognized you. Nothing will hit the tabloids." It's kind of Philip to bring it back to business. No one in the room is comfortable with this level of emotion.

"I drank too much. That's all. Popped a few Ambien. Took a few bennies to get back up. I've had a bad few days." If he mentions rehab, all will be forgotten. It always is. "I think, I don't know. Maybe I need to go away for a bit to get straightened out."

Augie doesn't want to let him go. "Why were you upset like that? I've never seen—"

"Just the pills and booze, son." He doesn't often use that word. *Son.*

"I'll have my girl make some calls. See what places have openings. You want to go to Malibu? Stay local? That place in the Catskills stuck for a bit." It's Philip's job to take care of Teddy. He's a connoisseur of fine rehab facilities.

"Whatever. I'll finish the play first—"

Both men jump in.

"The play?" "You need a break." "It can wait." A symphony of pity. His least favorite part of getting clean.

"Ted, when you're at the bottom, you can only focus on getting up. The work can wait."

"You think this is my bottom?"

"The people at that restaurant do." Philip chuckles. It's a welcome sound. "How much cash did you slip the hostess?" he asks Augie.

"Whatever was in my pocket."

"Thank you both." Teddy is genuinely grateful. "I've been a lot lately. The party and now—"

"What'd you do at the party?" Augie asks as Teddy jogs his memory for a conversation gone bad.

"Passing out. That must have worried the hell—"

Augie sounds worried now. "Passed out? At the theater? When?"

"I was talking with your sister—"

"Nora didn't say anything."

"Elizabeth. I was talking to Elizabeth when—what?" He's distracted by their sudden collective inhalation. "What?"

"Dad." Augie's voice is gentle. It's always gentle when they talk about Elizabeth. "I know how much you miss her. We all do."

Teddy thought she cut just him out this time.

Philip is always ready to move on from the topic of Teddy's eldest daughter. "You said it. Let's get you straightened out, then worry about the work."

"Philip, the theater is on the line. I have to finish this play."

"Don't you mean start?"

Philip immediately regrets saying that. He doesn't know what he should be pushing. It feels wrong to focus on anything other than Teddy's health right now. Too many strange things are stacking up. If Teddy completely topples, Philip doesn't think he's strong enough to pick him up this time.

"Jesus Christ, that's right. Dad, do you really think someone stole it? Have you looked again? I'm sure it's in the office." He walks toward Teddy's safe place, followed by Philip.

"No . . . no, it's a mess in there." He has to stop them. He follows them down the hall. They enter the room, paying no attention to his pleas.

No one is there. Thank God. He wouldn't be able to explain it. He can't explain it to himself.

The men are surprised by the mess.

"You weren't kidding," Augie says, walking over to a pile of books. "No wonder you lost it. You can't find anything in here."

Philip is drawn to the rectangle outlined in dust that is becoming more and more pronounced. "It was here."

"Yes!"

Augie joins them huddled around the desk. "Where did you move it?"

"He didn't. Your roommate, what was his name?" Philip asks.

"Who?" Teddy feels a tickle on his shoulder and turns to see Emily and a woman talking passionately in the corner. He's distracted. "Paul."

"How could I forget!" Philip snaps. "Paul. Paul Sharpe. Where's he—"

"He has nothing to do with this."

Teddy's head ping-pongs between the two couples, and he confirms that he is the only one who can see both. He can't hear what the women are saying. He walks closer, but they are behind a veil. A transparent wall of wisps. He's watching one of Emily's memories as a silent movie.

"Dad?"

The women look devastated.

"Dad?"

"Hm?"

Philip has had enough for one afternoon. He wants to leave on a good note, and this might be as good as it gets. "Get to work. You have a week. Then we'll get you booked into someplace nice."

"Thank you."

"Try to stay clean." Philip gestures toward the door. He's not happy, but he knows he can't win an argument with Teddy.

Augie asks Philip as they see themselves out, "Who would take it? You really think it was stolen?"

"I don't know. Seems kinder to agree with him. We need to get him help."

"He does his best work when he's unraveled."

Teddy hears the door shut behind them. He walks toward the veil keeping him from the two women. He takes a step and pushes through the curtain of mist.

Emily turns to him as he approaches. She is proud to introduce the most important person in her life. *"Susie and I were the only poets. Everyone else was prose."*

Sue stands to leave. The space between them is unbelievably sad.

Emily continues, desperate for a different outcome. *"I showed her heights she never saw. 'Would'st climb,' I said? 'With me?' I showed her secrets, morning's nest. The rope the nights were put across, and now, 'Would'st have me for a guest?'"* Emily waits breathlessly in unnecessary anticipation.

"I could not find my yes," Sue says as she evaporates.

Teddy wants to hold Emily. Not for his pleasure, but for her comfort. He's frozen. He doesn't know how to touch someone on their own terms. She comes close and embraces him. After a moment, he finds his hands, and they stroke her hair.

She knows he understands this intense feeling of loss. She whispers,

"I thought of her at sunset, and at sunrise, again; and at noon, and fore-noon, and afternoon, and always, and evermore. When the minister said, 'Our heavenly Father,' I said, 'Oh, Darling Sue,' and when everyone else praised the Lord, I praised Sue. When they sang, I kept singing how I loved her. In thinking of her, all reason was gone from me, and I feared that I must be committed to a hospital for the hopelessly insane, chained up so I wouldn't injure her."

Teddy leans in and kisses her. Intimacy was always confused with touching. Grabbing. Taking. Tasting. Her lips know how to respond to unwanted kisses. Submission lives deep in her muscle memory. He wants more. He steals the need she has for Sue. He soothes himself with her pain. His hands move to her lower back. She flinches and pulls her hands to his chest.

"The big serpent bites the deepest, and we get so accustomed to its bites that we don't mind about them." She pushes him away.

She twists out of his embrace and hands him a stack of papers from his desk. She is quick to switch gears and get back to business, a quality Teddy respects and needs in a partner.

"An ear can break a human heart as quickly as a spear. We wish the ear had not a heart so dangerously near."

It's the first act. She is writing this for him. It's in his handwriting. Another partner who rejects taking any credit. She offers a parting explanation.

"You know, where my hands are cut, her fingers will be found inside."

With a smile, she escapes. With a smile, she is gone. He's been here before. He could destroy these pages. Will his brain to heal. Do this on his own, but no, he always takes the path of least resistance.

Chapter 6

A sober sleep is never welcome. It only comes after a fight: Teddy fighting his vices. He feels much better when he loses. Dreams from sober sleep are stories that can be remembered in the morning, which makes it hard not to drink. Teddy lost tonight's battle on the couch, alone. His body is rigid, fists clenched. His muscles are at their most tense when his eyes are closed. His nose is cold. That slight sensation keeps him from falling into a deep sleep. A meaningful sleep. The sleep that will clean you out. He's stuck in the working sleep of dreams.

He's at the dinner table. No. This is grand. This is a dining table. A dozen noblemen drink in a grand room with a massive ceiling and dark wooden beams. Two small bodies sit uncomfortably in tall chairs. Teddy is eight. His sister just turned thirteen. The adults in the room are up way past their bedtime. Words are slurred. Everything is loud. His mother is at the head of the table. She rests her body in her neighbor's lap. Eyes closed. An unlit cigarette dangling from her hand.

Teddy's father is lunging through the room. His voice is booming and only interrupted by the sound of laughter and applause. He takes on the role of narrator. A British documentarian.

"And there, through the trees, we see a family of bonobos. Man's primate cousins. Do you know how a bonobo says hello?" He thrusts his hips. "Do you know how a bonobo says goodbye?" He thrusts longer and harder. "Do you know how a bonobo says, 'what a fantas-tic report card!'" He's behind Teddy's sister's chair. He grabs the back and shakes it as he thrusts and grinds on the wood. The room is wild with laughter. Teddy looks toward his mother. Who is going to put him to bed?

He turns back as Teddy the grown man. His sister has also been replaced. Emily sits across from him, shaking in the chair from his father's thrusting. He jumps across the table to protect her and falls off the couch.

Awake. Crying. There's an urgency in his bones to rescue her. He can't get to her. Who needs saving? His sister? Emily? He hardly ever thinks about his sister. She made the choice to abandon the family and then had the nerve to come crawling back for cash. Now he imagines a woman in pain. Trapped. Screaming for him. Alone in a dark place.

A light turns on in his office. He stands, wiping away tears and snot. "Emily? Emily, I'm so sorry."

She's sitting at his desk, expecting him when he enters. Her calm detachment is a stark contrast to his emotional state. *"A snakebite is a serious matter, and there can't be too much said or done about it."*

He can't stop crying. Confused but obliging, she strokes his hair and listens to him weep. She wasn't expecting him to be this fragile.

He doesn't know when she left. He fell asleep at her feet. There are more finished pages on his desk. He quickly scans them, but his eyes are too blurry and his brain too foggy to process. There is a "him" and a "he" referenced throughout. He puts it down, caring less and less about the finished product. Is it this slingshot of pressure that's messing with his head? He has to finish the play! He couldn't give two shits about the play! It will be great! It will be a disaster! All with this nagging feeling that someone is out to get him.

Now that she's here with him, can he find a way to stay with her forever? Is the ticket waiting for him in the bottom drawer? Teddy is not a man who questions. He's a man who answers. He doesn't like these new uncertain vulnerabilities creeping in. His phone is vibrating on the floor next to the couch. It's a text. From Elizabeth.

"I have something."

"Something I want?"

Even estranged, they speak a private language. The three pulsing dots let him know she is texting back. He would wait all day for her response, but he can't. Today is Tuesday. On Tuesdays he visits his father. When he told Philip he'd try hard to stay clean, he meant it. He only pops a lorazepam and passes by the multiple makeshift bars on his way out the front door. He needs his mind quiet.

He has a headache from crying. He doesn't know if the sedative will take the edge off that. He chases it with some Extra Strength Excedrin. He's often filling his body with contradictions.

It's a short walk to his father's apartment. They both live on the Upper East Side. Teddy has lived in this four-block radius his entire life. His childhood home was a museum. Three floors of luxury that could have housed a hundred people. Instead, it held just four people and a rotating staff. There were rooms he was not allowed to enter. Rooms he was not allowed to leave. The grand dining hall from his dream was one of his least favorite spots. His mother's large walk-in closet was his favorite.

His father's current setup is designed for function. One level with wide hallways. Ample space for a wheelchair. Simply decorated without clutter to showcase or dust. A bed with rails. Specially made toilets and bathtubs with doors. Small rooms where nurses live. The furniture has all been selected for its stain resistance; old men leak fluids. Teddy leaves there with the smell of cigars and bleach on his clothes.

Like everyone else, Teddy was bound under his father's spell. Loyal in life and now as he marches toward death. Teddy hired the nurses.

Moved his father back to the city from the rotting compound in Florida. He sold the secret hideaway for a loss. A mini mall took its place. Teddy was delighted that something of his father's would be forgotten. Once his mother died, no one oversaw the staff or the upkeep. Palm trees died. Rodents moved in. His father was much sicker than anyone realized. Dementia. Emphysema. Typical diseases for an atypical man.

Teddy glides into the room and takes his seat across from his father. The TV is blasting cable news. A Polish nurse puts out some cheese and crackers. If Teddy had more energy, he would be sleeping with her. She's the right age, height, and weight. Her eyes are narrow and mischievous. She smiles with crooked teeth and asks how he's doing in broken English. He nods, and she exits, patting his father on the head.

"You be good boy for Teddy."

He checks his phone. Elizabeth's response remains three flashing dots.

"Catch the Knicks game?" Teddy asks.

His father doesn't watch sports. Never has. He grunts in return.

"Not a bad team this year."

A part of him wishes death on his father. He would wish death on anybody in this state. A part of him doesn't know what he'll do once he's out from his shadow. Who is he if not Sam Maine's son?

He keeps trying to be a dutiful son. "The kids are good. Elizabeth is talking to me again." He looks down. Still dots. "Nora started a new job. No. She's back in school. A social worker this time. Augie is Augie. We all did something right with that one."

The old man hangs his head low. Teddy isn't sure he'll be able to lift it back up.

"Still working on the Dickinson script."

This causes his father's head to bobble.

"It's different, you know? Writing with a woman—about a woman."

His father laughs and gargles phlegm. Teddy stands and helps him hold his head up. Out of the corner of his eye, he catches a little wren

in a long white dress. She stirs something into his father's tea and holds
her finger to her lips.

"Shhhh."

Teddy is dumbfounded. Is that her? Is his Emily here? He starts
toward the kitchen and is almost knocked over by the Polish nurse.
Liquid splashes from teacups.

"Sorry! So sorry, Teddy, sir. I clean mess . . ."

"My fault. My fault." Teddy takes the tray and sets it down next to
the snacks. He dabs at his shirt while keeping an eye on the kitchen.
"Is someone here?"

"Hmmm?" She is busy tending to his father. She smacks at his back,
loosening up mucus. He coughs violently. Teddy can smell the mud
deep in his lungs.

"A new girl?"

"Girl? No. No. Me and my Sam." She wipes his mouth.

Teddy is happy that his father has this tenderness. He doesn't know
if he deserves it, but it makes his own life easier. When he does die, he
can feel good that he was taken care of.

"You look tired." She motions toward the couch. "Nap?"

"I should get going. Lots of work to do."

The old man erupts in another coughing fit. Teddy watches as the
nurse puts the tea to his lips and helps him drink.

"Bye, Dad."

Last night feels far away. The sunlight can do that. Seeing his father
hunched over helpless can do that. The strong man from his dream demanding the room's attention is gone. If he tries hard enough, maybe
he can convince himself he was never there.

Teddy's relationship with his parents may be more layered than
most, but there is still love. Misguided, suffocating love. His older
brother, Jonah, died at sixteen months old. Their first child. Their first
boy. What could have been an anchor solidifying the new couple's
transition to adulthood and family life became an unraveling instead.
Finding your baby blue in his crib will do that. Teddy and his sister

grew up in competition with a ghost. What might have been is always more appealing than what is. His parents loved their remaining children furiously but at a distance. They had lost one child. They couldn't handle losing another. Teddy and his sister were confused as friends, confidants, accessories, and burdens.

After Jonah's death, both their parents immersed themselves in their art and drowned in their vices. His sister was a happy accident. Five years later, Teddy was another. By the time he arrived, his parents were an award-winning party powerhouse. They were as famous for their plays as they were for the closing night soirées. Teddy's mother didn't act much anymore. It was too hard to remember her lines and follow such an intricate self-medication regimen. She often held glamorous titles like "assistant diction coach" or "costume curator."

Teddy and his sister Abigail had various nannies to watch over them during the day. The hired help had strict orders that the children must be awake when their parents came home from a night of rehearsals or exploration. Sometimes they would return home by 9 p.m., sometimes 1 a.m. Their mother would shower them with kisses, and their father would demand a recital of the day's events. The other adults in the room would be anxious to get home. To get back to a world where children were snug in their beds, not learning choreography and playing dress-up until sunrise. A nanny could lose their job if the kids' eyelids were too heavy. The smart ones filled their bellies with sugar and soda to keep them wired.

There was a picture his mother kept on her bureau. A snapshot from another life. As a boy, he'd hide with it in his room and imagine that the plain-faced girl from South Dakota was on her way home. Her hair was dirty blond. Pale eyes and freckles. He didn't know what kind of magic had morphed her into this current raven-haired goddess with flaming lips and stiff lashes, but he wanted the spell reversed. He'd give up his favorite toy. Swear off his favorite treats. Anything to meet his mother. Sometimes he'd imagine all three of them in the same room. The goddess leaving lipstick kisses on his tired cheeks. Spinning him

around the room, singing a song on repeat. The plain girl would beck-
on him from the doorway. He knew he'd be safe with her. He'd slip out
during a refill and not look back. Once he held her hand, he would
realize that he'd been holding his breath.

Elizabeth still hasn't responded. This will bother him more once
the lorazepam leaves his system. When he's smoothed out like this,
not much ruffles his feathers. He craves smoke from a real cigarette.
Twenty years ago, he could have easily bummed one. Now he'll have
to invest in a whole pack. People are stingy with their bad habits these
days. There's a shop half a block from his building. You'd think he'd be
a regular, but he doesn't often run his own errands.

The air is hot and thick inside the small space. It smells like someone has been cooking beef. He looks at his phone as he waits in line.
He mindlessly steps without looking up.

"'Sup, man?" The kid behind the counter is tall and thin. He has a
snake tattoo wrapped around his forearm. He has a bad purple dye job,
blond roots exposed, and he desperately needs a shower.

"Sorry. Waiting for a text." Teddy holds up his phone.

"That your girl?"

"Not really."

"She ghosting you?"

"What?"

"Ghosting you. Blowing you off."

"She texted me first." Teddy sounds like a teenager.

"Bitches, man."

"It's my daughter."

"Tight. What do you need?"

Teddy points to a pack of Camels behind the register. The ink
snake slithers up under the cashier's shirt as he reaches for the cigarettes. Teddy jumps. In a flash, he sees Emily at his father's, smiling
as she stirs something into his tea. The kid turns around. The snake is
now wrapping itself around his neck.

"You all right?"

Teddy backs away from the counter.

"You want your smokes?"

Teddy runs out the door and steadies himself on a lamppost. He feels his body lifting out of his shoes. He fumbles for his phone to call Philip for help. He doesn't think he can make it home. There are words now where the dots had been flashing. Elizabeth has texted back.

"I see you."

He staggers from a sudden stab to his temple and falls to the ground. The concrete is soft, worn fabric.

Chapter 7

His eyes open. He's not looking up at a hospital ceiling or a street sign. He's looking out at a tennis court. A lit cigarette dangles from his hand. It's a nonsmoking establishment, of course, but when you are rich, rules are only suggestions. Augie is playing doubles. He's eleven. There's a woman sitting next to him who isn't his wife. She rubs her hand on his thigh. The place is familiar. Augie was an all-city tennis player. Teddy has been to every court in Manhattan.

Something is out of place in this memory. This dream. What is this exactly? It's both happening to him now and not at all. He's back in the in-between space. The woman caressing his thigh is real. She knows him well, but he can't place where she's from. They're definitely on some sort of date. She's his type. Long dark hair. Sharp red nails. Why would he bring her here? To his son's tennis match? He doesn't know it yet. This was her idea. She has something to show him.

Teddy is pleased, if confused, with his company. He's settling into the moment. He always enjoyed watching his son play. It was an easy way to parent, watching from the sidelines. He's proud of Augie. He's doing very well. His partner is not. Teddy doesn't recognize this kid. He's fat and slow. He looks ridiculous with Augie running circles around him. Augie is both talented and kind. If he is upset by his partner's performance, he's not letting on. His face is serious, his words encouraging.

"You got this!" He cheers toward his partner as he goes for a serve then lets the ball drop without raising his racket. "Okay. All right." Augie claps. "Try again." He lets the ball drop without raising his racket again. This happens a few more times, Augie's encouragement growing with each failed attempt.

Teddy starts to look around. This can't be legal. He's had like ten tries. The fat kid stares up at the stands and catches his eye. Teddy yells out, "Hey! What are you doing?"

This excites the woman next to him, and she massages his thigh again, pulling at the muscle. He places his hand on hers to make her stop, but she's not having it. There is nobody on the court. Just Augie and his partner. The bleachers are empty. Teddy goes to stand but is stopped by his date. She's holding him down. Pushing so hard on his flesh she could reach bone.

"Stop it." Teddy tries to wiggle free. "Jesus Christ—"

"Watch," she says with a smile.

The fat kid's body starts to ripple and expand. He morphs into something slightly off from human. He starts to walk toward Augie, who is oblivious and shouting at the spot he just left. He doesn't realize he is standing behind him. He can't see him lifting the racket.

Teddy jumps up, and nails dig into his skin. Blood pumps out of his leg. She's now kneading his flesh from the inside out. He can't feel it. He can't feel anything but is still screaming in agony. Augie is being pummeled. This boy creature hits him again and again. Augie drops to the ground and curls into a ball, doing his best to cover his head. With each blow, his grip on his own racket gets weaker, and more of his body becomes exposed. The racket hits his face. His neck. His chest. Ribs crack. Bones snap. Augie rolls limply to one side, blood trickling from his mouth. Strings pop from the force of each blow. Graphite bits fly around the court like little sparks.

He's on his balcony at home. His leg is fine. His shirt is soaked with sweat. He opens the pack of cigarettes. One is missing.

Why is this happening? He's trying. He didn't drink at all today. Beer. But that doesn't count. How is he getting this messed up from a few pills and a Bud Light? He often wonders if people know when they're going crazy. The first time you hear voices, do you believe them? When you snap, is it because you choose to?

Every strange moment is canceling out the next. He wants to see Emily. When he's with her, he's not crazy. When he's with her, he's home.

He walks inside toward his office. He can feel that she is there waiting for him. He stops when he gets to the door. She's not alone. Her father is there. Edward Dickinson is a famously stern and serious man. He was a founder and fixture of the city of Amherst, Massachusetts. The glow that Emily brings with her curiosity is dimmed by his massive presence. Edward places learning and intellect above all else. Wonder is not an asset. Questions are not allowed. One succeeds by doing what they are told, not by doing things differently. There is no space for new ideas, only a total allegiance to what has always been. He is a suffocating force.

She's sitting, shoulders hunched, in the middle of the room. Her father dangles a gold pocket watch in her face. Spit flies as he barks at her. She doesn't have a chance to respond before being struck with a long ruler. He strikes her across her lap. Head down, she stops attempting to answer and accepts the blows. Teddy can hear her thoughts. She speaks silently to him.

"I never spoke, unless addressed, and then, 'twas brief and low. I could not bear to live, aloud, the racket shamed me so."

Teddy bursts through the door. They're gone. He circles the spot where she sat. He's breathless. Stunned. The day has been filled with violence. He is quickly flooded with guilt. He understands that he is not a good man, but has he ever hurt his children? He searches deep into his hidden memories. The ones that aren't buried, but you'd still rather forget. No. He has said plenty that he can never take back. He's missed years of accomplishments and celebrations. He's put himself above all else many times. But he has never put a hand on his kids. He sighs with relief.

There are no new pages waiting. He's been given a clue. He's getting closer to her center. It's his turn to write. The room remains tense from the presence of her father. He hardly notices, as tense is his norm. The words pour out of him as he sits at his desk. After dozens of pages, he stops. It's not working. It's not real. Emily never escapes. She locks herself away. She never stands up to her father and remains his faithful servant. He is dead and gone before anyone can scrutinize how he shaped her words. Teddy balls up each page in heated fists and litters the rug. This serves as a nice distraction. He looks for a stronger one.

He reaches into the top drawer for a bottle. He pulls out the gun. He slams the drawer shut. He didn't move the gun. Has someone been in his office? Someone real? Philip would have taken it. Augie would have confronted him. He's reminded of the bigger mystery at hand. Someone has been in his apartment. Someone real and uninvited. They are messing with his stuff. He can't keep it all straight, the competing risks to his mental and physical well-being. Like most threats, the most dangerous work from the inside out.

The room shifts around him. He's in the dining room at the Dickinson home. The discarded pages from his play scatter the floor, bread crumbs to lead him back to the now. It's a scene similar to his dream. Emily's father stands behind her chair. It shakes with the intensity of each word. Her mother sits at the table, her lips a tight line. She resembles Emily, only she is sitting up tall and straight. Emily is small in her chair, eyes toward the floor.

"A child must be brought under perfect subjection. It is an immutable principle in family government that my word is law!" Her father says.

Her mother responds with a defense that is devoid of emotion. *"She's not to blame. She can't help it, Edward. The physician says it's the poetry at fault."*

Edward gathers the balled-up paper on the floor and throws it toward Emily as he lectures. *"The world is a most dangerous place. Keep the doors all safely locked. If they are secure, then nothing is going to hurt you. Be careful about fire, above all things. Don't go out evenings, on any account, nor too much in the afternoon. It is better for you in cold weather to stay home. School is too dangerous. Emily must not go to school, at all. There is a canker rash which prevails all over the country. And be careful about allowing her feet to get wet, or she will have the croup. Emma, if she is taken from us, I should never forgive you."*

Mr. and Mrs. Dickinson continue to talk over Emily's head. Their mouths move, but Teddy can hear only Emily. She speaks in a low, deep voice.

"They shut me up in prose, as when a little girl they put me in the closet, because they liked me 'still.'"

Teddy takes a seat next to her. He's an intruder that only she can see. Her parents silently debate above them.

She continues. Her detachment is her power. *"When I walk into his room and pluck his heart out and he dies, hang me if you like. But if I stab him while he's sleeping the dagger's to blame. It's no business of mine."*

Teddy grabs her hands. "I tried to rewrite it. Your story."

He grabs one of the paper balls and attempts to smooth it out for her to read. She appreciates this frantic gesture.

She takes a breath and decides to move this scene along. Like Teddy, she cherishes being the one in control. Her voice is lighter and amplified for all to hear. It grabs her parents' attention and stops their arguing.

"I have seen flowers at morning, satisfied with the dew, and those same sweet flowers at noon with their heads bowed in anguish before the mighty sun. Those flowers cry for sunlight, and pine for the burning noon, though it scorches them, scathes them."

Her father nods in approval. She is the flower, and he is the burning noon sun. He beckons for her to stand. She complies, and the three start to exit. Edward turns to Teddy before leaving. Can he see him? Did he know he was there the whole time? He smiles as if welcoming a colleague or peer. A partner in Emily's education. Teddy is disgusted. He will never share familiarity with a man like Edward Dickinson.

He's left alone in his office, which is once again a mess. He thinks about picking up the discarded, defeated pages, but he's done trying for today. His mind is fractured. His muscles ache. His thigh is burning. Why? He fell on the street. Yes. Outside the smoke shop. He must have twisted something. Banged something. Bruised himself on the way down. He feels stupid. A feeble old man who can't be left alone. Can't walk the streets of New York without injuring himself.

Snakes. Elizabeth's text. Augie battered and bleeding on the tennis court. None of it registers. None of the images are clear recollections, but swirling fragments in his head, leaving him with the feeling of forgetting something. A candle left burning. A door unlocked. Danger is close. He doesn't know what it is. He doesn't know how to stop it. But he knows drinking will soften the blow. Push pause on the impending doom. He will never forget watching Emily's father hurt her. He now appreciates the power a parent can wield. A power he himself applies carelessly. He still has time to be better.

Chapter 8

If anyone could make a bad day better, it's Nora. Sweet baby Nora. She spends more time with him when he is sleeping than when he's awake. She is often a welcome flash in a dark dream. She's the fluff from a dandelion that blows away after a wish. To an intense man, she was easy to overlook, her agreeable and shy nature a handicap to someone as determined as Teddy Maine. But when she visits his dreams, he is truly happy.

His head rests on the marble kitchen island next to an empty brown bottle. He will feel this in the morning. A hangover and a pinched neck. He will have to forget both when he sees Philip for their weekly lunch meeting. He knows he's on thin ice. Rehab is a flight away.

They are on a picnic in tall grass. Nora is ten. Her hair is long and has yet to decide on its permanent darker color. Right now it's the same muddy blond as his mother's. They lie on a bright yellow blanket, describing the clouds.

"There's an elephant, Daddy."

"No. Look closer. It's a one-legged pirate being chased by a T. rex."

Nora giggles. "A baby bird and—"

"An eagle flying off with a cat."

"Daddy, cats don't like flying."

There is a rustle in the distance. Teddy doesn't notice. Growing up in high-rises has muted his genetic fear of grass. Ancient foragers burned down continents to reveal the dragons and serpents hiding in a sea of green. Nora is wary of whatever is out there making waves. She snuggles into her father.

She smells like his wife's perfume. Citrus. Fresh air. A vacation. Trish was a serious woman. Her scent never matched. Thoughts of his wife are often a side note. It's not fair. She was a good woman.

They grew up in the same privileged circles. Her parents were both surgeons. She inherited their precision. Nobody could dissect Teddy's work like she could. She worked in the literary department of a hot off-Broadway theater. Her boss had asked Teddy out for drinks. When her boss slipped in the shower, breaking his hip, she showed up in his place.

She was beautiful enough. She was much smarter than he was. She didn't laugh easily. He liked that. He wanted her to be a confident mystery. She played the part. He never appreciated the toll that took on her. She was insecure. She was lonely. She was madly in love with him. She wasn't wired to live hard but did it for him. Once her body accepted the burn of liquor, she never crossed paths with Zinfandel again. She was a Maine by marriage and could not ride the thin line of excess like they could. She became brittle, and aged years in months. The children brought her life. She resented Teddy for making her a worse mother. Teddy showed the least amount of interest in Nora, so Trish kept her all to herself. Sometimes, in dreams of yellow picnic blankets, Teddy has them both. He never remembers how good it feels. A cruel trick. His mind keeps something so lovely just out of reach.

"Daddy?"

"Hmm?"

"Something is out there."

He's awake. His cheek is raw from marinating in drool. He has to throw up. This feels great. This feels normal. He resets in a hot shower. Stepping out of the glass doors, he stumbles, realizing he's not alone.

Elizabeth sits on the toilet. She's sixteen. Her lips are painted dark brown. Her eyeliner is much too heavy. She's in a short schoolgirl uniform. She is skillfully slicing her arm with a razor blade. Trish is yelling from the hallway.

"It's not natural, Ted!"

He hears himself respond from outside the bathroom.

"I'm her father."

"You have three children."

"Don't make this a thing about favorites. We all have our favorites."

"She's too old for you to look at her like that."

"Like what? She's my daughter, and this is my house."

"She needs space."

"You've always been jealous of her." Teddy's go-to comeback anytime he feels challenged. He knows it will snuff out his wife's fire.

Blood is dripping from Elizabeth's forearm. It's thick, like paint. It falls in slow motion, spreading in swirls on the white tile. It's a dark, joyless purple, the way people bleed in black and white. She is careful to cut spaces that can be easily covered. Teddy grabs a towel off the wall and reaches for her. His body moves through her, and he smashes his head on the toilet. His blood is fresh and red. It quickly runs down his limp body and spreads out over the tile.

He jolts awake, barely catching himself before falling out of his chair. He's in the kitchen. Cheek raw from marinating in a pool of drool. This could be another long day. But even the wicked deserve a rest. Teddy doesn't remember the details of his dream. He can smell grass. He has the feeling he lost something nice. He takes a long hot shower without remembering his recent visitors. He heads outside after the chore of getting dressed.

It's too hot and bright for this time of year. The sun is low in the sky, yet radiates midday heat. Philip's lunch meeting was pushed to an early dinner. Miraculously, this was not Teddy's doing. Philip was vague with his reasoning. That doesn't happen often.

Teddy is actually clean-shaven and presentable. Philip joins him in a somewhat private back booth. The table is covered with crisp white linens and spotless silver. He's surprised to see his friend looking so spry.

"You clean up nice. Hot date?"

"Yeah, meeting this prick from Yale."

Teddy has held Philip's accomplishments against him for twenty years. During one of their first meetings, Philip made the mistake of trying to impress him. Teddy loved it. Here was a walking, breathing Ken doll unsure of himself, maybe for the first time ever. He must have mentioned Yale fifty times. Like that would matter to someone like Teddy. On Teddy's planet, you're either born with it, or you're not.

In another life they must have been brothers. That's the only way to explain the connection. To call them yin and yang is a stretch. Teddy is not the dark to Philip's light; he is a universe-ending black hole. Their souls have a centuries-old pact, and their business is unfinished.

"Am I a good father?"

Philip doesn't hesitate to answer. "No."

"I'm serious."

"So am I." Philip is more interested in browsing the appetizers than fanning the flames of Teddy's current existential crisis. This is all a part of Teddy's process. He rips himself to pieces with every new play. "Do you want to be?"

"What?"

"A good father?"

"Of course!"

Philip isn't buying it. "You were good enough. As good as you wanted to be. Look, you have great kids. You must have done something right."

Philip is right. He does have great kids. Elizabeth isn't who he expected, who he wanted, but she is a successful, independent, driven woman. With the softness of Nora and the integrity of Augie, who could ever question the mastery of their upbringing? Teddy is satisfied. Though they both know it was mostly luck.

Philip has justified Teddy's mistakes and triumphs as the result of a man with one singular purpose: to tell stories. The baggage and dark-ness that comes with narrating the mess of humanity is his mistress. Much like the truth is to a judge or righteousness to a preacher. God hasn't created anyone yet who can be both good and perfect. Teddy is the perfect writer, and that is enough for Philip.

"How's sober living?"

"Fine."

When the waitress comes, Philip orders two Jamesons. "You only get one," he says to Teddy.

Teddy bows his head in appreciation. He would never be able to fool his best friend.

This is their dance.

The meeting is a bright spot for both of them. Teddy is functioning. He's excited about the work and appears steady on his feet. He serves a deep purpose for Philip. There is his art. Philip could find easier artists to dedicate his life to. There is the money. Philip could be paid more by better. Hidden behind his kind voice and good looks is a shrewd and vicious negotiator. Teddy needs saving, and he allows Philip to be his savior. Over and over again.

Philip couldn't save his brother. Born twelve years his senior, his big brother lived an entire life without him. When they were both old enough to become friends, Philip would have followed his brother into war. Into hell. He idolized him. His brother could live under a bridge, which he did for a short time, and still steal your girl. He could easily walk into a classroom for the first time and leave with an A-plus on the final. He played every instrument and wrote manifestos. He was the stuff of cult leaders and peacemakers.

Philip never understood his parents' weary detachment. He didn't know about the cars that were stolen and crashed. The checks forged and jewelry pawned. His parents never refused to pay for his college or kicked him out of the house like he claimed. But they could no longer afford him. Hospital bills, legal fees—not to mention he was twenty-six and still a freshman—drained everything they had. Philip was shielded from the realities of loving someone who desperately needed help but denied it. There were all sorts of diagnoses. At one point, electric shock therapy was used. Inpatient and outpatient stays. His parents spent their retirement on any treatment that could keep him out of jail or off the streets.

Philip's college fund? Gone. Inheritance? None. The money wouldn't have mattered to Philip, but maybe it could have helped him understand the hurricane of pain his parents lived through. Instead, he blamed them. He saw a magical spirit abandoned by his family.

When he was old enough, he moved his brother into his studio apartment one Christmas. He didn't have time to grow weary. His brother killed himself on New Year's Day. Philip never forgave his parents. He cut them out of his life. They now had lost both of their sons. When they died in a car accident in Martha's Vineyard, it was a nephew who made the arrangements. A neighbor who gave the eulogy. His aunt sent him the program from the service. Maybe if they had died old and sick, there would have been time for truthful conversations.

Teddy is his family, and Philip will never abandon him.

Two Jamesons turn into four, then six. They are both fuzzy and grateful. The waitress might even go home with Philip.

What a nice surprise. Teddy didn't need to lie his way through supper. The sun is finally setting. This day has had more than sixty minutes in each hour. He decides to take the long way home.

Teddy crosses the street and finds himself back in time at the Dickinson homestead in Amherst. It doesn't bother him that one step off the curb has carried him from New York City to Massachusetts. He's with Elizabeth. This is one of his life's best days.

It had been a few months since Elizabeth started wearing her hair in a long braid down her back over a white dress. She was still madly infatuated with Emily Dickinson and had graduated from reading her sweet poems depicting the natural world to doing scholarly deep dives.

No one could have scripted a more precocious scene. The mouthy rich girl hiding under the covers, devouring textbooks by flashlight.

Trish had wanted to celebrate Elizabeth's birthday with a sleepover. She'd invited some "normal" girls over and hoped they'd talk about boys and nail polish. Teddy had already made his own plans: a private tour of the Emily Dickinson Museum just for Elizabeth. Trish had scolded him for encouraging her. They drove off in his vintage Porsche convertible, the reason he'd gotten his driver's license as an adult. They didn't talk much on the three-hour drive. The wind carved out smiles, and the sun tanned their cheeks.

Would he be driving her back there in five years? This might be the only place he could let her go.

The weather was perfect. Bright. Crisp. Elizabeth's long dress billowed around her ankles. They were in a postcard. Teddy felt like more than her father. What kept them tethered was bigger than that. Augie was his son, Nora his daughter. Elizabeth was something different. A relationship evolved past anything currently labeled.

She was not the first girl to arrive at the museum in a white dress and training bra. Not even the first to have the place to herself. But she would leave a lasting impression. The woman greeting them at the gates would recognize her immediately years later on Page Six.

The tour started in the garden. Elizabeth didn't hide her impatience. The woman leading them kept tugging at her cardigan. Each tug tilted her gold name tag, *Ms. Jennifer Moore*. She looked like a goose in flats and a sweater. Her nervous flutters were a sharp contrast to Elizabeth's graceful glides.

"Is that Sue's window?" Elizabeth asked, looking up to the second floor of the stately yellow Dickinson house.

"Sue and Austin lived at Evergreen."

"Is that where Emily stood looking for Sue?"

"Emily looked at all sorts of things from her windows. She could see all of Amherst." Ms. Jennifer was quick to steer the conversation away from Sue. "Do you like gingerbread?"

Elizabeth didn't answer. She was studying a bloom like Emily might have.

"Emily would lower treats in a basket from that window there. She loved children. Baking, too. She built herself quite the life here. Leaving home is overrated." Ms. Jennifer's attempts at camaraderie missed the mark.

"Why did she wear white?"

The goose fluttered. "Her fashion choices were rather quirky."

Elizabeth frowned at the response.

Ms. Jennifer tried to appease her by answering her question with a question. "Why do you think she wore white?"

Elizabeth quickly responded. "Out of protest."

"Protest!" Their host laughed uncomfortably. "Emily was inquisitive. Never forceful. Women were quieter back then."

Teddy wondered if they were at the right house. Was Jenny holding back for his sake? Elizabeth was going to eat her alive.

Sensing she left a trail of blood in the water, Ms. Jennifer lowered her tone from condescending schoolteacher and continued. "I suppose many of Emily's quirks were in response to being a woman of her time. Shall we go inside?"

Elizabeth nodded enthusiastically, finally showing the excitement of a newly minted teenager. Once inside, she asked questions without waiting for answers. "Is this what the house really smelled like? Did they keep it this cold? Could any DNA still be here? Would the drapes be kept open like this? Why was she so scared of going blind?"

The last question caught the expert's attention.

"Emily had a painful eye condition that was difficult to diagnose even by the best—"

"I've read that it was a somatic symptom disorder. Typically referred to as hysteria in Victorian times."

Lips puckered, and an eyebrow rose. This woman did not appreciate being schooled by an eighth grader.

"Do you think it was her father's constant fear of consumption that

freaked her out? I mean, he was clearly OCD—" Elizabeth was talking
a mile a minute.

"Her father was stern. That's for certain."

"Obviously, the whole family was mental. The thought of being
trapped in this place without her books or being able to write . . . was
too much—and, oh! Having seizures must have been—"

"At the museum, we like to think of our Emily as a happy Emily.
It's easy to read too much into things."

"But—"

"Why don't we end the tour upstairs? I trust I can leave you two to
experience her space alone?"

When they got to the room, Elizabeth mimed turning a key.

"We're free, Daddy."

Chapter 9

He's home. He doesn't care how he got there. Life can always be just like this. He's ready to work. There's a light on in his office. Emily is there. Alone, thankfully. He watches her from the doorway.

She's writing. Women in Emily's world were given few choices, and being a writer wasn't one of them. Wife, teacher, spinster. Many women became professional children. Women worked hard at being vulnerable and pure. Naive and innocent. When Emily grew in fame, her male contemporaries were reported to have fallen in love with the dead girl from Amherst. She was fifty-five when she died. In her life and death, she was often celebrated for her smallness, not her greatness.

She was both the virgin and the whore. A coin with two enticing options. Some see her words as simple gifts delighting in nature and wonder. Others see her as a pioneer exploring her sexuality and refusing to be bound by titles or norms. She can be both to the same person. This is what lured in Teddy. But she is so much more.

He steps into the room and watches her work. She is copying hundreds of lines. Editing as she goes. Her hands move swiftly. Her posture suggests that she could conquer the world. Everything she does is with meticulously placed intent. Teddy is embarrassed. He's been in love with the wrong woman. He had a simple mind and accepted simple explanations. He stands behind her, placing his hands on her shoulders. She welcomes his touch. He promises to never be wrong about her again.

Copying is just the start of her final draft. Next, she makes a collection. She wraps her poems into little booklets as a parting gift. To make a book, she stacks folded sheets of copied poems on top of one another. She pokes holes through the edges and binds them together with a string. The paper is embossed with blue lines. It smells fresh like citrus and a vacation.

She's not a sister or daughter or even poet. She is something not yet labeled. An undiscovered species painfully alive in the wrong place at the wrong time. She's making her escape sheet by sheet. An SOS back to her mothership. These secret artifacts reveal the truths she keeps most private. Her in-depth knowledge of death, pain, and desire. She repeats this ritual over a thousand times.

She turns toward Teddy, and without apology or a smile, explains, *"I took my power in my hand and went against the world."*

He watches her for hours. Maybe days. The words fly from the pages, entangling him. They take him inside her mind. He's rocked in the wake of millions of firing neurons and twists deep into her synapses. He's living her memories. Some true. Some imagined. Some exaggerated. Some forbidden.

Two young girls run behind a pack of friends. Long skirts skim the dirt paths of summer. Heeled boots kick up dust as they hold hands and tug in different directions. The birds chirp along to their laughter.

Emily is in the kitchen baking with her mother and sister. The air is warm and smells like bread. The little girls laugh as their mother hums and kneads moist dough. She puts a dab of white flour on each of their noses, and the girls squeal.

A young and studious pupil is called on multiple times. She keeps watch over her best friend and soaks in her smile with every correct answer.

A stolen kiss in the library. A bold peck on the cheek.

Emily, still a girl, is packing up her things in her small room in the girls' dormitory. She protests to her older brother, Austin, who has been sent to take her home.

"We never know we go when we are going—"

Austin is kind but losing his patience. He did not volunteer for this errand. "Please, Emily. The carriage is waiting."

"We jest and shut the door. Fate following behind us bolts it. And we accost no more." She tosses more books into her bag than clothes. Her cheeks glow with anger.

They leave Teddy standing alone in the room. He's not sure where to go. He steps outside into a gorgeous fall day. He finds Emily and Sue together again, reading on a blanket. They are older now. Both have relaxed and loosened the tops of their dresses. The untied knots and flashes of flesh are welcome surprises. Teddy hurries to join them.

He steps into a different atmosphere. The air around them is stifling, and the sun is a blinding halo framing Sue's face. Teddy winces from the brightness. Emily can't look away.

"To own a Susan of my own is of itself a bliss. Whatever realm I forfeit, Lord, continue me in this!" The whites of her eyes sizzle.

Men's heavy boots are approaching, crunching the dry leaves. The two make a hurried promise. Emily is being taken away again. The outline of a formidable presence stands in the periphery, blocking out the sun.

Emily whispers frantically, *"If you sh'd get there first, save just a little space for me—"*

Sue grabs her face and responds forcefully. Where Emily wants to go is dark and final. She knows Emily is willing to make this last trip. Sue is not so sure.

"No. No, Emily, there is another way."

She smiles through tears. *"The smallest robe will fit me and just a bit of 'crown.' For you know we do not mind our dress when we are going home."*

There has to be another way.

"Come with me." Sue takes her hand, and they flee. Teddy can hardly keep up with them as they run through the dark woods.

They come across a small, abandoned cottage. Sue strokes Emily's hair in an attempt to calm both of their racing hearts. "This will be our home."

This is most certainly a fantasy. He's happy to be out of the dark and needs to think about what just happened. With all her writings on death, he never thought of her as suicidal. That was the home she's speaking of, right? He likes this home much better. The cottage is quaint. There is a fire and a pitcher of ale. A rocking chair, lantern, and a bed made from straw and piled blankets. They don't notice him. He pours himself a drink and waits for this Wild Night to unfold. The women drink and dance. They sing and talk loudly about goblin feasts and dripping fruits. Their long hair is matted back with sweat. Skin flushed and tingling. Teddy is bursting.

Emily presses her forehead to Sue's. Her hands travel down her bodice. She is breathless. *"Oh, Susie, I do love to run fast and hide away from them all. Here in dear Susie's bosom, I know is love and rest, and I never would go away."*

He is a guest so inconsequential that they don't notice when he starts to undress. He is making a fool of himself. He realizes this quickly and slinks back to his drink. Years of experience that would make a professional blush can't help him here. Here he is, a clumsy fifteen-year-old boy sticky with anticipation and destined to disappoint.

Even though he hasn't been invited to do anything else, he's still happy to watch. He's eager to see a familiar scene play out in a new setting. But he is wrong to think this is anything he knows or has experienced. There is no taking. Only giving. No convincing or compromise. Tenderness. Softness. A complete lack of threat. It's not sensual. It's honest. This is how bodies are meant to express love.

Teddy absorbs their joy and holds this warmth with a terrible sadness. He now understands all he's missed. Everything he's never had. He takes comfort in knowing he is not alone. To most, sex is fitting a key into a lock and hoping it opens a door. He thinks of his wife. He genuinely hopes she has experienced this moment with someone else. If this were another life, he could share this with Elizabeth. He hates God for making him her father. There are lines that even he won't cross. If he ever dreamed of sharing this type of love with his one true love, he'd kill himself. Like Emily, he has to live with something he can't have.

The last time he was this shaken by a woman's naked body was his first time. He was seventeen. A shamefully hostile late bloomer. He grew into a man eclipsed by his father's charisma. He had to find something to set him apart. Being a virgin at seventeen was the most taboo thing he could have done sexually. He'd been so overexposed that sex was already boring. Besides, it was too much of a base instinct for someone with his huge intellect. That's what he told himself. He was above the chasing-tail hormonal-boy bullshit. He would never play some stupid game to get into a girl's pants. He was a rare plant that could survive on sunlight alone. His mind changed once he got a taste of fresh water.

Amelia was nineteen. She was flat-chested and dangerously thin. It was the result of either cancer or an eating disorder, he couldn't remember. Cancer would have been kinder. She succeeded at starving herself two years later.

Amelia was the daughter of world-class dancers. She was better than both of them. Better than almost everybody. Repeated stress fractures ended her ballet career before it could start. They attended the same elite arts high school. It wasn't unusual for a senior to be nineteen or even twenty, returning to school after they'd toured Europe with a dance company or opened a show on Broadway. Many had only tutors their whole life. Now, abruptly retired, they had nowhere to go except high school.

Amelia was serious with sharp edges. Teddy became a project for her. She liked that he didn't fit into his body, either. She liked that he didn't smile easily. His awkwardness was unavoidable. She wouldn't live to see him outgrow it, deny it. He would always be her timid, brooding, misplaced boy from Algebra II.

She snuck him a note asking if he had any smokes. They met by the dumpsters and smoked Marlboro Reds. They didn't talk much except to say their parents were awful and everyone at school was the worst.

A few months and cartons later, they were naked in her bedroom. Her parents were heavy sleepers, and she was an adult. Under layers of sweatshirts and leggings hung bones on a child's frame. It was shocking. Teddy thought it was beautiful. His own muscles were stretched and long. It would be years before he filled out. Next to her, he was Hercules.

She smelled like medicine and cotton. Her skin was soft with down. A duckling abandoned by its mother. Until then, he thought of bodies as prickly and damp. Heavy, uncontrolled limbs that couldn't be trusted. He didn't know a body could be so fragile or that he could have that much power. He was at a crossroads. Holding this girl in his hands, he could have interpreted that power as responsibility. A feeling of duty to shield and protect. Instead, he took her vulnerability as a prize. Something he could do with what he pleased. He didn't hurt her. Never hurt her. But he could have. And that felt amazing.

He needs to pay attention to the woman he's with, or he'll be left behind again. Sue leaves with a wave and a smile. Emily is still and quiet. When Teddy goes to approach her, she exits the small cottage without acknowledging him. He follows her out the door into new surroundings.

They are outside. It's a lovely afternoon. A quaint area has been set up for a ceremony. A wedding ceremony. Emily walks down the aisle and takes her seat. Austin is waiting at the altar for his blushing bride, Sue. Emily keeps her eyes cast down as Sue makes her entrance. It's too painful to watch. Sue smiles triumphantly as she walks past her to her older brother. Their plan worked! With Austin's help, they can be together for always! Emily knows it will never be that way. It will never be enough. She finally recognizes Teddy and speaks softly to her wedding date.

"Had I known that the first was the last, I should have kept it longer."

After the short and religious ceremony, they stand apart from the crowd to take in the celebration. Petals are thrown to celebrate the newlyweds as they leave the small circle of guests. The petals land on Emily like snowflakes. They continue to pour down on her after the happy couple has gone. They turn to plaster on her skin, wrapping her limbs.

"Emily!" Teddy calls out. He tries in vain to catch the petals and push them from her skin.

She spreads her arms and raises her face to the falling flowers. She wishes this embalming process would move quicker. Her body is turning to stone. A white, living stone climbing up her legs and torso, reaching for her neck and face, entombing her. Teddy is furiously scratching at her skin. She keeps her head toward the sky. She has to yell over Teddy's panic.

"'Tis sweet to know that stocks will stand when we with daisies lie. That commerce will continue, and trades as briskly fly. It makes the parting tranquil."

"No. No. No. No. Don't let this happen."

He is pulling at the plaster anywhere he can get a grip. It's not working. Emily slowly closes her eyes and allows her face to be sealed. Teddy pounds on the hollow shape. His fists break through, and he is in a cloud of dust. He coughs and shields his face and eyes from the swirling, burning air.

Once it clears, he finds himself in her bedroom. Is this his office or Amherst? Emily is older and dressed in white. She stares out the window toward her brother's house. Time has taken something from her; it's clear by the way she holds herself and the hollowness of her voice.

"I wonder if it hurts to live and if they have to try."

Teddy doesn't know what to say. How to comfort her. He says the most general thing he can think of. "It will be okay." He immediately regrets opening his mouth.

She turns to him and leads him to a door. Her maturity has become so fierce it snuffs out the sparkle of her youth.

"After great pain, a formal feeling comes. This is the hour of lead. Remembered if outlived. As freezing persons recollect the snow. First chill, then stupor, then the letting go."

She pushes open a door.

They are on an edge, the room behind them gone. Teddy reaches aimlessly for something to hold on to. There's nothing. They are teetering on the top of a long, terrible, dark staircase. It is made of stone and smells like cold earth. Teddy hopes she doesn't begin to descend the bottomless steps. He isn't manly enough to follow.

"What's at the bottom?"

She answers without looking at him. Her voice is steady and almost cruel. *"I cling to nowhere till I fall. The crash of nothing, yet of all."*

She pushes him, and they descend. He squeezes his eyes shut and screams inside his brain. "This isn't real . . . this isn't real . . . this isn't real."

He quickly realizes that they are fine. They are not falling but rather floating down a silent dark tube. This chute feels organic, alive. The ground comes up to meet them, and they land softly.

They stand in a barren field. The sky is a dark gray. It's so thick it can't be real. Not an ounce of light or shadow.

Emily takes his hand. It's the first time she's attempted to comfort or even include him on this terrifying and disorienting field trip. She has a right to be angry. Resentful. She's lived through this all before. Hundreds of times. She's doing this now for him. But if her plan is to bring them closer, she needs to be careful. There's an order to these things, and he has to keep it together until the end. This next bit won't be easy. They'll need each other to get through.

"When I was younger, a friend I loved so dearly came and asked me to ride in the woods, the sweet-still woods, and I wanted to exceedingly. I told

him I could not go. I could not cross my father's land, lest if I once go out, I shall grow so happy that I shall never come home." A tear escapes her eye.

The earth opens into six-foot plots all around them. Teddy grabs her protectively. They move quickly as the landscape changes around them. It settles, leaving them on an island in the middle of holes. A slow-moving parade weaves its way around the field. A whole town of everyone who has ever mattered. Teddy and Emily have their backs to each other as they survey the crowd.

"What is this?" Teddy is dizzy and sick to his stomach.

She's scared, too. *"For each ecstatic instant, we must an anguish pay."*

Faces are coming into focus. One by one, friends, lovers, and family fling themselves into the open graves. They are silent except for the thump of hitting the dirt bottom. Thump. Thump. A sad rhythm beating all around them. Thump.

"Make them stop!"

She can't. She can only wait and cry. *"To die takes just a little while. They say it doesn't hurt."*

Teddy's muscles twitch, getting ready to run. She grabs his arm. The fierce grip reminds him of something unpleasant. He doesn't fight it. Walking toward him is a familiar face. His sister. Thump. Mother. Thump. Nora. Thump. Trish. Thump. Amelia blows him an expressionless kiss. Thump.

Emily squeezes his arm and takes a step back. *"Each that we lose takes part of us."*

He doesn't see Elizabeth coming. She walks toward him with blood dripping from her arms. She pushes him hard down into a hole. Thump.

He's left Emily's mind and is back in his own. He thinks. It's the early '70s. Everyone there sees him as a ten-year-old boy. He doesn't recognize this place. He's in a green plastic chair in a hallway next to his sister. It's a school, but no school he's ever been to. It's dreary and dated. Toddlers are crying. If the air were a color, it'd be a sick shade of mustard.

His teenage sister hisses at him, "I will never forgive you for this."

He wants to respond but can't. His mouth is dry and stuck. His lips are dry and chapped. He's desperate for a glass of water. He has no idea what's going on. He has no memory of this. By the looks of it, this might be one of the last times he was with his sister. She took off at seventeen. He tries again to speak, but his rough tongue keeps getting caught on the roof of his mouth.

His mother walks hurriedly toward them. Her shoes don't make their familiar fashionable click on the linoleum floors. Her flats squish and squeak. She is missing layers of glamour. The only thing that looks like it came from her closet is the fox jacket covering a T-shirt and ill-fitting jeans. She walks past them to speak to a woman behind a counter.

"Where do I take them?"

"Home." The employee responds without looking up from her paper.

Fresh dirt is falling on his face. From the bottom of the hole, he can see a bright, bleak sky. It's as if the air has been bleached. Dirt continues to fall from above. He's being buried alive. He struggles to escape. Emily gives him her hand and pulls him out in one easy motion, like he's a discarded sweater.

She is buoyant and fresh as dew. He coughs and shakes earth from his hair. She is eager for him to take in their new surroundings. The land has become an indescribable kaleidoscope. Teddy doesn't have time to process what is happening. Like everything he's been through, he's forced to just feel it. He is swept into a tide of color and is completely overwhelmed with joy. This is the best drug he's ever been on. The whiplash of going from extreme panic to extreme bliss is causing his sense of reality to crack. He is going to have a hard time finding his way back.

They wash ashore, dry and euphoric. They skip and dance in a field of flowers. Emily yells enthusiastically. He's never seen her this loud or happy.

"Could I but ride indefinite, as doth the meadow bee, and visit only where I liked, and no one visit me, and flirt all day with buttercups and marry whom I may, and dwell a little everywhere, or better, run away!"

Teddy kisses her as they twirl. He'll do all of this a hundred more times if this is where he lands.

She playfully pushes him away. *"I said, but just to be a bee upon a raft of air, and row in nowhere all day long, and anchor off the bar."*

They lie back on pillowy blooms. The sky is now an artificial blue with fantastic pops and sparkles. He holds her hand, and they drift to sleep.

He awakes, refreshed, in a chair across from her in the office. It's morning or maybe afternoon. She's been watching him.

"Thank you," he says, groggy and happy from the back end of their high.

She walks around their room, resigned but satisfied. She's relieved to be back and grateful for the updated comforts.

"Home is a holy thing. Nothing of doubt or distrust can enter its blessed portals. Here seems indeed to be a bit of Eden, which not the sin of any can utterly destroy." She looks out the window, wishing her brother's house, Evergreen, would come into view. *"We grow accustomed to the dark when light is put away. Either the darkness alters, or something in the sight adjusts itself to midnight, and life steps almost straight."*

She could grow too accustomed to Teddy. They both possess a sad charm, and his is definitely creeping its way into her plans. He's noticed her gaze lingering longer. She makes a point to get back to business. She stands at attention and smooths out her dress. She walks across the room like a teacher leaving her troubled pupil. Next to one of her neatly made booklets are pages for him. The play is almost complete. She hands him the heavy stack.

"I once thought that words were cheap and weak. Now I don't know of anything so mighty. There are those to which I lift my hat when I see them sitting prince-like among their peers on the page. Sometimes I write one and look at his outlines till he glows as no sapphire. A word is dead when it is said, some say. I say it just begins to live that day."

He shakes his head. He can't keep taking from her. From everyone around him.

"No. This is yours."

She could sell this a few different ways. She decides that her work needs no convincing. This is a transaction, and she's not interested in changing the terms now. *"Publication is the auction of the mind of man."*

Teddy's pocket vibrates. He has thirty-six missed calls.

"Yeah?"

"Where the hell have you been?" It's Philip. He's panicked.

"I'm at home. I've been home."

"You haven't answered your phone in three days."

Three days! They've been gone that long? His knees wobble. Emily might be able to sustain herself on magic, but he can't.

"Teddy? Teddy? You still there?"

"Yes."

"Are you okay?"

"Never better."

Philip is about to smash his phone. "Jesus Christ, Ted—"

"It's finished." Teddy takes the pages from Emily, and they both smile broadly.

"What's finished?"

"The play."

They proceed to Act Two. Philip is no longer pissed or concerned. He's intrigued and relieved. This makes sense. Teddy went off the grid to work. Isn't that what Philip has been nagging him to do?

"The play? I have to read it. You're killing us all with this one."

"It will be worth it." Teddy winks at Emily. She steps closer and leans into the phone.

"It better." Philip pauses. "I have some news. Can you come into the office?"

"When?"

"Now."

Chapter 10

Teddy rests on the short subway ride to the theater. He likes the smell of public transportation and tries to avoid car services. If he's going to write about the real world, he has to live in it sometimes. He's still a bit buzzy from his trip with Emily. The woman next to him has the same Coach bag that he bought Elizabeth for her law school graduation. They weren't speaking then. He learned the news from Augie. Top of her class. He wasn't surprised. His assistant picked it out. She described it as the perfect gift for a young working girl.

The perfect gift for his working girl would have been a life of creating. Experimenting. Pissing people off. This token sticks with him, as it was one of the most defeated moments of his life. They had fallen to such a basic place. A predictable olive branch for a high-achieving estranged daughter. She sent him a thank-you note. It was typed. That hurt.

He thinks about her all the time. He tries to imagine her daily routine. He's sure it's ordinary, which makes it difficult. He never had "ordinary" planned for either of them. She drinks sweet lattes with skim milk. She doesn't notice the barista checking her out each morning. She walks briskly and fills her day with other peoples' business. Her apartment is sparse and trendy. She occasionally puts on a strapless dress and makes an appearance at a benefit or two. She doesn't sleep or eat much. Her life is a cable show, minus the romance.

He wonders if she ever laughs at lunch with Nora or goes shopping with her mother. If Trish did have a relationship with her, she would keep it from him. He's sure she's loving every moment of this break that is proving to be permanent. All three of her chickens have come home at last.

He's always done this. Taken one detail and turned it into Elizabeth's whole story. She grew out of her white-dress phase in a matter of months, not years. They had a handful of inside jokes, not a lifetime's worth. As she got older, she became less and less interested in being his special girl. She cared more about One Direction than Shakespeare. He held on tighter, and she pulled away harder: boys, drugs, trouble.

It doesn't have to be all or nothing. She can have a serious haircut and a serious job with a life brighter and fuller than Teddy could ever imagine. She did not share her father's desire for unhappiness. Her natural state wasn't the same as his—sitting high above people in judgment and disgust. She wanted to make mistakes and be bored. She wanted to wear the same sweater as the other girls in her class. She would have preferred a Barbie for her seventh birthday over an aquarium complete with a miniature shark. She craved ordinary since her first birthday. The magic Teddy admired so much was merely a coping mechanism. It was not easy being Daddy's favorite.

Her apartment is crowded with overstuffed pillows and redundant plush carpet. She's into millennial pink and is obsessed with *House Hunters*. She's covered the scars on her arms with daisy tattoos. She donates to tiger conservation and only walks briskly when she's around him. She writes. She's been writing a lot lately.

Without Teddy, she has room for others. She calls her mom every day on the ride home from work. She has always wanted to be close to her. They are more alike than Teddy could see. A side effect of his tunnel vision. She runs 5Ks with Augie and goes to movies in sweatpants with Nora. She has the family she needs. The people she loves. All made possible by Teddy's absence. One day she'll invite him in just enough for him to feel all that he's lost.

Nora. Sweet Nora is her favorite thing about this life. She did everything to make sure she grew up to be exactly the person she was supposed to be. Of all her accomplishments, she's most proud of that. She's rewarded for all that worry with every text. Every secret. Every daydream shared. They have sleepovers. They do each other's makeup and name their future babies. Nora will be a marvelous mother to her two girls: Cookie and Bunny. To the outside it might seem like an odd relationship for two grown women. To them it isn't odd, only delayed.

Nora will always be a little bird. A thing with feathers that gives the world hope. Her big sister will always be there to protect her. Shield her. Elizabeth thinks of herself as a bird, too. A different type of bird. A tiny bird with a dangerous beak.

A shared love of nature initially attracted Elizabeth to Emily Dickinson's keen observations. She thought she was the only one who could see the flowers as they grew little by little and feel their pain when the sun was too high in the sky. As a sly girl herself, she appreciated that Emily Dickinson played the type of weird the world embraced. Like most overly bright children, Elizabeth's brain learned things it couldn't yet understand. It wasn't until later that she realized the truths and pain she was shouting to the world in disguise. Coming back to Emily's poems as a woman didn't bring her much comfort even though she was now closer to her than ever. She was beyond comfort by then.

Attempting to be a weird girl herself, Elizabeth used a few of Emily's most famous words when presenting about a bird, the shrike, in seventh grade. Teddy was beyond pleased that she managed to make a science experiment about poetry. She turned the assignment on birds into a full-blown performance art piece. It started off with Dickinson's most beloved piece:

"Hope" is the thing with feathers—
That perches in the soul—

And sings the tune without the words—
And never stops—at all—

Elizabeth read it earnestly and sweetly. Her classmates were confused. Her teacher was annoyed. The room gasped when she ripped up the paper and smeared her white dress with red paint. She held up a poster with "Butcher Bird" written in heavy black letters. The shrike is small and carnivorous. It received its nickname for the bloody mess it makes of its larger prey. It is a successful and diabolical hunter. Accepting its limitations, it plans ahead. The little bird lures its dinner to a sharp branch. Elizabeth had the class on the edge of their seats as she acted out how the little bird might deceive an unsuspecting rabbit.

"So tiny. So cute. Play with me! I'm just a dumb bird. The bunny follows the Butcher Bird to her lair, where a sharp stick is waiting. She backs the bunny into a corner and goes after it with her pointy beak. The bunny fights to escape. It could easily overpower the bird but has no way out and backs up right into the stick! It squeals as the branch rips through its fur and guts. It's alive and dangling from the tree, screaming to no one as the Butcher shreds its warm flesh and savors every bite!"

The teacher called home. She was going to fail the assignment. Poetry has no place in a science presentation, and she only answered one of the four required questions in an absurd, dramatic fashion. Why did they let her carry on in that silly white dress? They needed to help Elizabeth fit in better. Her eccentricities were going to get her teased. Creativity was a liability for middle schoolers.

Teddy was appalled. Why was he paying a fortune to these narrowminded private-school teachers? Trish was delighted. Any ammunition to cut the cord between the two of them.

But it wasn't failing a class or her mother that got Elizabeth out of that white dress. It was a cute boy. She knew she could easily slide into the group of cool kids he ran with if she normal-ed up a bit. She was self-aware enough to make it a choice. Teddy took it as a betrayal. Just like now.

Elizabeth knows the barista is checking her out. She reapplies her lipstick every morning while waiting for the walk sign on her way to get her latte. If he doesn't ask her out soon, she's going to reach over the counter and kiss him. This is Elizabeth. This is Elizabeth, standing in the sun, out of her father's dark shadow. This is an Elizabeth Teddy would never recognize. She could be sitting right next to him, and he wouldn't know it.

He arrives at his stop. Teddy nods and lets the woman across from him exit first. He walks up the subway steps and almost trips over a rough-looking homeless guy. He was going to cuss him out when he sees what he stumbled on. The man's legs are stretched out in front of him. His ankle is turned at an unnatural angle. His bare foot is purple and black. He's missing large chunks of skin, revealing a web of dark and coiled ligaments and muscle. A piece of bone shines like it's under a spotlight. Teddy stumbles backward. The man laughs and claps his weathered hands.

Teddy is rattled. Even a lifelong New Yorker can't be prepared for that. He watches other people pass by. Nobody notices this man or what's left of his foot.

Philip's office is two flights above the theater's posh lobby. It might as well be in a different building. Its walls are yellow from the days when you could smoke inside. The floors are scuffed. The chairs are stained. Random clothes racks and dress forms create a maze. Philip's corner is light and new, straight out of a Swedish furniture catalog. An island of productivity in a sea of who-cares and dump-it-there. Teddy doesn't often grace his cluttered desk with his presence. Philip recently placed a nice fake potted plant there. He does his best to make the place homey.

Teddy takes his seat in a modern beige chair.

Philip is nervous. "You stink. Take the subway?"

"You know it."

"What are you on?"

Teddy mimics his tone. "What do you mean?"

Philip is mildly amused. "What drugs did you take today?"

"None. Why?"

"Wondering if I should tie you up so you don't disappear again. Head to the woods on some bad mushrooms."

Teddy laughs. "No mushrooms today."

Philip is serious. "Please don't ghost me again. Nora taught me that. When you don't, uh . . ."

"Respond to a text."

"Yes. Or, in your case, thirty-seven missed calls."

"I thought it was thirty-six—"

"Ted. You can't do shit like that. Not now. You're too old. We thought you were dead or wandering around the city after a stroke."

Teddy lays it on thick. "I'm insulted. I'm way too young for a stroke."

"Fine. OD'd somewhere." Philip interrupts himself. "I'm sorry. I can't believe I said that."

Teddy shrugs. "What? Seems likely." He smirks and grabs a half-eaten bag of chips from his friend's desk.

Philip shakes off the odd exchange. "I got a strange message."

"That's why you called me down here?"

"Where's the play? The version you just finished."

"At my house. I told you it's pretty much finished—"

Philip isn't interested in word count right now. "Has anyone seen it?"

"No."

"You're sure it's there?"

"Yes. Right in the middle of my desk—"

"Like the last time?" Philip is getting a bit panicked.

"Trust me, this is nothing like last time."

Philip hands him his phone. "Read it."

Teddy recites the text from a blocked number. "'I have something.'" He looks up. "Who sent this?"

"No clue."

"Wait." Teddy trades phones and scrolls through his messages. He swears he's read that before. He mutters, "I got—"

Philip leans over. "Did you get the same message?"

"I can't find it."

"Who sent it?"

"I don't remember. Elizabeth, maybe?"

"Who? We should call that cop."

"You think this is about the play?"

"What else would it be? Paul?" Philip hates saying that name out loud. He cringes in anticipation of Teddy's reaction.

"Who?"

He sighs at needing to repeat himself. "Paul. Paul Sharpe."

"What?" Teddy shrugs it off. "There is no Paul."

Philip isn't finished digging down this hole.

Teddy stammers. "I mean—yes, he exists, but he has nothing to do with this. Nothing to do with me."

"When was the last time you talked to him? Do you have his number?"

"Why the hell would I have his number? He could be dead for all I know. Raising goats somewhere. I don't give a shit about Paul Sharpe."

Philip is careful. "If we have to, we can fix this. If it's him—"

"It's not! Jesus Christ. The one time in my life I was actually nice to someone—"

"Okay. Okay. You're right." Philip, always a man of action, plows through his doubt. "I want you to go home and bring me your new draft. Let me make some copies before this mystery asshat can get their hands on it."

Teddy keeps scrolling.

Philip stands and grabs his coat. "Go. Bring it to my apartment. I'll order us dinner."

Teddy wasn't inside that long. Standing outside the theater now, it feels like a different day. The sun is burning orange. Now it's surrounded by a film of clouds. Or is that smoke? He wonders why he is the only one looking up. He heads to the subway station but makes a detour toward the park. In the fresh air, he feels a lingering buzz from his recent days with Emily. He wants to use it before it's gone. Philip was right to assume that he was off on a bender. He wants to lie in moist grass and check out this orange sun.

There's a clearing in the park he hasn't noticed before. Central Park has been both his front yard and backyard his entire life. He knows every dip and puddle. He must investigate. Something big is in the middle of a circle of grass. He squints. He thought he had put in his contacts, but he can't seem to make out anything more than fuzzy shapes. His ears are clogged and humming. He smells something raw. He takes a step and his foot sinks deep into the soil. His senses are dulled, and he's stuck in the earth.

The circle zooms into focus. A large buck is staked in the center. The tan body is upside down with a pointed spear through its middle. Strong muscles twitch reflexively. It has no strength left to struggle. Dozens of small birds feast on its smooth flesh. Efficient beaks rip and tear down to the bone. Blood pumps from small holes, soaking the grass around him. He tugs at his ankle. More and more birds land. First one, then three and four, now ten birds hop toward him. They seem curious, not vicious, about this panting scarecrow.

A feathered head bobs at his exposed shoe, fraying the laces. He swats it away as he keeps tugging at his other leg. Dainty feet land on his shoulder, pecking behind his ear. Should he freeze? Should he scream? He flails his arms and yells sternly at the pests. This attracts more inquisitive birds. They swarm around him like he's covered in sesame seeds. He yells louder. The winged army's screeches are muffled by the humming in his ears. Yelling turns to panicked screams, which pop the corks in his eardrums. Terrible sounds flood in. A snip of skin is stolen from his face. A mole is bitten off his left forearm. Death by a thousand papercuts. Beaks fight to expand fresh wounds. It starts with a peck, and then the skin is peeled away, layer by layer. They slow down to savor the meat.

He falls to the ground. His ankle twists in the hole, and his arms sprawl out in front of him. Before all goes dark, he remembers what these little birds are called.

He's sprawled on his living room floor. Someone is pounding at the door. He stumbles toward the entry, running his hand along the wall, searching for a switch. He's sure he's bleeding. He makes it to the door and feels his limbs for wetness. Dry. No sticky, bitter blood to tend to. He opens the door. The banging isn't for him. A cop and a paramedic crew stand at his neighbor's, Mr. Poole's.

Teddy doesn't know him. They've shared a wall for over a decade, and he's only responded to his gentle hello's with a wave a time or two. He's a retired professor who looks the part with his shaggy white hair and wire-rimmed glasses. He locked himself in his apartment fifty years ago, and the board has tried for years to boot him out so they can finish converting the building to million-dollar condos.

Teddy was annoyed by the fuss he caused, but he admired Mr. Poole for not giving a shit. To sit in your little box and know that everyone around you in their slightly bigger boxes wishes you dead. That takes guts. The commotion in the hall suggests the neighbors may have finally gotten their wish.

A uniformed officer barks in Teddy's direction, "Do you know who lives here?"

Teddy shakes his head.

"You see him lately?"

Teddy shrugs.

"Let's knock it down."

Teddy flinches as they kick in the door. They rush in. The lights are on. A commercial is blasting from the TV. From the hall, Teddy can see Mr. Poole's feet. They look full and the wrong color. He's in pajamas. A cup of milk is shattered on the floor close by. It doesn't take long to load him up. It's not a crime scene, just another old man who died alone.

In the midst of this, Teddy is surprised to see a familiar face. Philip is walking down the hall. He picks up his pace when he sees the commotion.

Philip grabs him by the shoulders. "You all right?"

"Yeah. Neighbor."

"Jesus. You know him?"

"Nope."

You don't live in a sixteen-million-dollar apartment because you want to know your neighbors. They are interrupted by screaming. A woman in her forties is running down the hall toward them. She collapses when she sees the covered body. Philip instinctively goes to her. He kneels, putting a hand on her shoulder. Teddy's first instinct is to go inside.

"Did you call in the welfare check, ma'am?"

She speaks between sobs. "That's my father. It's been three days. We talk almost every night."

Philip and the officer help her stand.

"I shouldn't have waited. I should have come sooner!"

Philip holds her and murmurs words of comfort. He's obviously lying. He's a stranger who just happened to be in the same hallway on one of the worst days of her life. That's it. He has no idea if her father died two days ago or two minutes ago. He tells her it was fast and painless. That there was no way she could have known, and there was nothing that she could have done. Why is she listening to him? How could this be soothing her? For all she knows, he just strangled her father to death. Teddy is immensely jealous of the two of them and their ability to trust each other. The woman leaves with the stretcher. A cop hands Philip his card. He thanks them like a good neighbor would.

Back inside the apartment, a fire is going in the living room and the lights are on. Teddy is surprised. He couldn't even turn the lights on, let alone start a fire. Both men exhale.

"I came here ready to kick your ass. That took the wind out of my sails. You good?" Philip is visibly shaken, like they both just escaped a near-death experience.

"Why did you do that?" Teddy is still disoriented.

"Do what?"

"Tell her it was fast. You don't know what happened."

"It was a nice thing to say."

"But why would she believe you?"

"Because she wants to. Comfort doesn't always have to be compli-cated." Philip is able to move on quickly. "Where's the play? You were supposed to be at my place hours ago."

"Shit. Sorry."

Should he tell him why he never made it? Because he was too busy being picked apart by tiny birds in Central Park?

Philip pours himself a drink as Teddy heads to his office. He passes Trish sleeping in the master bedroom. He goes into the room enough to watch her back rise and fall. He thinks about waking her to tell her about Mr. Poole or to let her know that Philip is drinking in the kitch-en. He leaves the room feeling happy that she's there.

For a moment, Teddy panics, reliving the last time he went to his office to collect this play. What he thought would be the play. No. This is all working out exactly the way it's supposed to. The menacing texts, the threat of controversy, his worrisome episodes—they are all distrac-tions. Temporary roadblocks.

Philip has made himself comfortable by the fire. A picturesque scene in stark contrast to the bleak drama that played out moments earlier in the hallway.

"Look at that! Have you ever seen a more gorgeous stack of paper!" Philip claps. He takes it from Teddy and plops back down in a leather chair, then hands him a tumbler. The good stuff. No ice. "Have a seat."

"You're going to read it now?"

"I'm not leaving this room without putting it to memory." Philip drinks. "Don't be shy." He hunches over and flips to page one.

Teddy is strung out and vulnerable. Now isn't the time to read his work, even if it's not his. He wants to drink with his best friend. Not best friend-slash-manager. He wants to ask his friend if anyone will wail for him when he's rolled out on a stretcher.

Has he broken everything with everyone who matters? Does he have enough time to fix it? He wants to be comforted like the sobbing stranger. He doesn't care if it's a lie. He just wants to hear that he's a good man. That he will be missed when he's gone.

He should have woken Trish. Told her about Mr. Poole. She would say the right thing now. What about when he's gone? Will she weep over his body? He only knows about half of the dozens of times she has wept over him. She's tapped dry. Nora? No. She could never break open like that, and she'll still have her mother. That's all that matters to her. Augie is too strong. He'd spring into action with a plan to capitalize on his legacy. Good. The family will be taken care of. What would Philip do? Teddy often suspects Philip is waiting in the wings. An understudy ready to be the head of his household. Trish would be well served by him.

Elizabeth would crumble. Yes, he has someone, one person who would be broken by the loss. Despite the last few years, Elizabeth would be destroyed by his death. He has to believe that. He knows he couldn't function without her. The connection they have, even when stretched, is so strong, so otherworldly, there's no way it's one-sided.

What about Emily? Will she be there? Will she help him? Will they be together on the other side? He gets a sinking feeling and gulps the contents of his glass. Without looking up from his page, Philip leans over with a refill. Teddy takes one more gulp to soothe him to sleep.

He drifts off by the fire as Philip makes his way through Act One.

His dreams are becoming more and more lucid, or perhaps it's that they are happening more and more when he is awake. He is definitely sleeping now. His mother is with him.

He's a little boy. Maybe four. This could be one of his first memories. He's surrounded by flowers and lying on the lawn at their summer home. The grass is like a carpet. His father was at the top of his game by the time he married his much younger mother. He was too old to have babies, even by today's Upper West Side standards.

They had spent the morning picking flowers and playing

hide-and-seek in the gardens. His mother sang him Sondheim songs while tickling his feet with petals. She painted his legs and arms with white and pink blooms. He laughed and snuggled close. He wants to stay there forever.

His mother bolts up, sitting in a rigid posture, when his father's large sedan pulls into the circle drive. He honks and waves; she waves enthusiastically back. Teddy likes it better when his father is away. She's quick to rush them inside.

It's late at night. The flowers they picked earlier are wilted in a vase. No one thought to add water. Teddy is a little boy in fitted pajamas. He sits on a chaise lounge in the formal living room. His sister is on the love seat next to her father. He is keeping her awake with tickles. Teddy's eyelids are boulders that he can't hold up much longer. His mother sings to him and begs him to stay awake. She keeps looking over at the love seat. It's clear his parents are playing some sort of game, but his mother isn't having any fun.

"Sing with Mommy!" She coos and ruffles his hair. "*She'll be coming 'round the mountain when she comes! She'll be coming 'round the mountain when she comes—*"

"Mama, I'm sleepy."

"Come on, baby. Sing with me. *She'll be coming 'round the mountain, she'll be coming 'round the mountain . . .*"

Her voice is distorted like an old record. She pinches his arm.

"Ouch!"

She leans in close, pleading. "Teddy Bear, I need you to stay awake. Stay with Mommy."

"I want to go to bed."

She rubs his arm where it's pink from her fingers. "Just a little bit longer. Please, baby."

Teddy does his best to make her happy. He doesn't know why she's crying.

"Are you hurt, Mommy?"

"No, honey. Mommy's fine. I just love you so, so much."

They play patty-cake and sing nursery rhymes. Her eyes are sharks constantly circling the love seat. During their second round of "I spy with my little eye" his father announces that he's going to bed. His mother has won the game.

"Good night, dear," she says, stroking Teddy's hair.

His sister slumps over without a shoulder to rest on. His mother sits for a moment, catching her breath. Young Teddy is glad she won but doesn't understand why she would play a game she clearly doesn't like. Teddy doesn't do anything he doesn't like.

"Let's go, my darlings." Her voice is centered and soft. She sounds different when she is alone with her children.

She scoops up the little girl on the love seat, kissing her forehead for an extended beat. Teddy drags his blanket and follows behind. He is so tired. It's a miracle when the three of them finally get to rest in his sister's bed.

This game happens often. His favorite nights are when they win, and they get to celebrate their victory in that soft pink bed.

As he stretches awake, Philip is still sitting in the seat across from him. The fire is low. Philip is staring at him.

"How long did I sleep? Christ, what time is it?"

Philip doesn't answer. He looks at his friend, seeing parts of him for the first time.

"Were you watching me sleep?" Teddy is slightly amused and mildly annoyed.

"You have some catching up to do." Philip hands him a half-emptied bottle. "This is your best work."

Teddy takes a swig, blinking away his catnap. "Nah."

"Who hurt you?"

This catches Teddy off guard. "What?"

"This . . . this play, or poem, or letter . . . I don't know what I'd call it. It's so painful, and you made it all lovely."

It's not *his* loveliness.

"It's not about me." Teddy wants to end this endless night.

For as close as they are, Philip doesn't often dig deep. He knows he won't like what he'll find. He continues to push it. "You can't write something like this without feeling it yourself."

"A good writer can. I think you told me that . . . was that in . . . in . . . 2007—"

"No. Not like this." Philip pauses. "I'm proud of you."

Teddy has never been comfortable with praise. "I didn't write it."

"Who did?"

"Emily."

Philip smiles and thinks carefully about what to say next. "It could help you. You know, to say it out loud. It could help a lot of people."

"I think you're drunk."

Philip backs off. He's getting too close to the fire. "I think you're right." He walks over and kisses Teddy for an extended beat on the forehead. "You prick. You keep me on my toes."

"Now what?"

"We put on a show."

Teddy wishes he read the script first. If this is Philip's reaction, what is the press going to say? What about Augie? He'll be next to read it. Teddy doesn't want Augie to handle him the way Philip is now. Cautious and paternal. He never wants Augie to feel like the parent.

"It's not finished."

Philip isn't listening. "Let's not lose this one." He stumbles a bit getting up from his chair. His legs are stiff from sitting. "We're getting old. Hey—don't call me until noon." He says this while making his way to the door. "You better call me, though. No more of this . . . what do the kids say . . ."

"Ghosting." Teddy hands him his jacket.

"Ghosting! You really are a prick." Philip was just hit with an avalanche of hard liquor. He struggles with his coat. He stops fighting with the zipper and kisses Teddy's head again. He gasps when they open the door.

"Oh, my God. A guy died tonight. You know, I've never seen that. A body bag. You?"

Teddy thinks for a minute. Has he? No. He's surprised. It didn't feel new. It should have been more shocking. That's what decades of bad TV will do to you.

Philip hugs him hard. Teddy feels sorry for him. How scary life must be to believe it's all so precious.

"Call me."

"I will." Teddy means it this time.

The sky is getting brighter. The sun will rise in less than an hour. Teddy stands in the kitchen, contemplating sleep. He doesn't want any more dreams. He's had more than enough for one day. He can still smell his mother's breath. Stale and sweet.

"Sing with me, baby."

Maybe he'll crawl into bed next to Trish, or he could finish the bottle by the fire. He turns down the hall toward his bedroom. His mother is there. Her hair is pinned up. She must have worn a wig at rehearsal. Her stage makeup is still on. She has a silver letter opener in her hand. She cuts it deep into her opposite palm. The blade is dull and rounded. She needs to press hard to break the skin. She exhales gratefully when the skin releases. She continues pushing to stretch the cut. Deeper. Deeper until she yelps and drops the blade. Blood pours from her clenched fist.

This isn't a dream. This happened. Teddy remembers it well. He squeezes his eyes shut and pushes his way down the hall to the bedroom.

He sits on the edge of the bed fully dressed. He wonders if his bleeding mother is still on the other side of the door. He's frozen and breathing heavily. When he can, he moves carefully so that he doesn't wake Trish. He wants to be near somebody. He very gingerly slips off his shoes. He doesn't bother taking off anything else. He pops a pill from a bottle on the nightstand. He won't have more dreams now. He's crashed. Exhausted. Feels burnt from the inside out. He needs nothing for a little while.

When he wakes up, Trish is gone. The bed next to him looks perfectly made. He looks toward the door, the image of his bleeding mother still fresh. It's so bright. His stomach flips, thinking he's slept through another day or two. He doesn't want to put Philip through that again. He finds his watch. It's only 9 a.m. He opens the door.

"Dumbass," he mumbles to his hungover self.

Trish must have gone shopping. There's finally creamer in the fridge. There's a fly buzzing around the light when he opens the stainless-steel door. He doesn't notice and continues to make his coffee on autopilot. He doesn't want to be alone. He heads to the office, hoping to find Emily.

She isn't there. That's okay. He can wait. He's sure of her now. He doesn't know what to do with himself now that the play is done. He really needs to read it. What was Philip getting at anyway? He should talk about what? There's nothing Teddy could say out loud that would make anyone feel better. In three hours, he'll wake him up and hope he remembers his drunken ramblings. His desk faces a window. He turns the chair around so that his back isn't to the door. He hears footsteps in the hall.

"Trish? Is that you?"

There's no answer. He can sense someone breathing on the other side of the door.

"Is somebody there?"

A voice playfully calls out from the corner of the room. *"I'm nobody! Who are you?"*

It's Emily. He stands hesitantly.

"Are you nobody, too?" She's a welcome sight. *"Then there's a pair of us."*

He's relieved. "Philip read your play. He says it's the best thing I've ever written."

She straightens up proudly.

Teddy slumps. "I'm a fraud."

She places a hand on his chest. *"I hide myself within my flower, that wearing on your breast. You, unsuspecting, wear me, too, and angels know the rest."*

"Thank you." He shrugs sheepishly. "I . . . umm . . . I haven't read it."

She motions to a stack of papers on his desk. *"I've nothing else to bring, you know, so I keep bringing these."*

He's embarrassed. He should have read it. It's the least he could do. She saved him. She understands. She knows more than anyone how devastating a verse can be. He's not ready yet.

"Just as the night keeps fetching stars to our familiar eyes. Maybe we shouldn't mind them, unless they didn't come. Then maybe it would puzzle us to find our way home."

She kisses him on the forehead. He wants more and reaches for her hand. She walks away, allowing for her arm to be pulled gently back. He doesn't fight it and lets her fingers slip away from his. This is for the best. He needs to get showered and off to his father's. Tonight, he'll give her work the attention it deserves. He opens the bottom drawer of his desk. It's the only drawer big enough to fit all the loose pages. He places the gun on top, a deadly paperweight, and leaves their shared space to start another day.

Chapter 11

Teddy takes the short walk to his father's house. It's colder out than he expected. The wind is sharp. He pauses when he passes by the coffee shop at the end of his block. There's police tape blocking the door. He's ordered a black coffee from the owner, Mr. Chang, thousands of times. He appreciated that he could be a regular without the need for conversation. They had a routine. Chang would nod and have his coffee ready as he walked in the door. He'd leave five dollars on the counter. There could be a line ten deep, and he would still be in and out in thirty seconds.

He looks around the police tape. "What's going on?"

A detective answers dismissively, "No coffee today, sir."

A woman surrounded by officers recognizes him as a friendly face. She races to the door and hugs him over the yellow tape. He hesitates before giving in. The embrace feels good.

"They shot him. Seventy-two dollars in the register. Dead for less than a hundred." She sobs into his collar.

The detective is now interested. "Did you know the deceased?"

"No." He quickly corrects himself when he catches a glimpse of the crying woman's face. "Not really." He untangles himself from her. Must be Chang's daughter. "I'm so sorry."

She reaches out for him.

"I'm so sorry. I have to go."

The detective hands him a card. He snatches it and takes long, quick steps down the sidewalk. He needs to get away from there. Death keeps finding him. What are the chances he comes across two dead bodies in the same week?

He rounds the corner and exhales. Shit. Chang seemed all right. No one should be dead over seventy-two dollars. That thought is fleeting, and he quickly reverts back to himself. Who is he going to hug when his father dies? Will he fling himself at the first familiar face?

There is no one left but him. He never planned on being this good of a son. He was too slow to figure out new flight coordinates. To escape into his own orbit. Or maybe he never wanted to stop circulating the family patriarch, lying in wait to be anointed the next sun. His mother and sister didn't give him a choice. They left the first chance they could. He won't forgive them for that.

His mother should still be here. She died twenty years ago. She didn't kill herself. She decided not to live anymore. Apparently, that's different from suicide. Apparently being brainwashed to not live anymore doesn't hold up in court.

A few years before being diagnosed with breast cancer, his mother had a radical transformation. She became a devout Evangelical. Or Baptist. Teddy was never sure. Whichever it was, she found the most extreme branch of the coconut tree.

After praying with church leaders, it was decided that this was her path to Jesus. She was meant to get this sickness, and Jesus would provide all the healing she needed. If the Lord required her service here on earth, she would live. If not, she was to be called home. There would be no pain. Slowly dying from cancer would cleanse her spirit and rid her wretched soul of all its earthly sins. She welcomed it. Felt she deserved it. Was grateful her heavy sins would soon be washed away.

Teddy was furious. Religion preys on the stupid. How could she have fallen for it? His mother was a lot of things, but she was not dumb. She was beautiful. Reckless and selfish. Soft and often far away. As he grew older, she spent more and more time wrapped in a cozy blanket of pills and booze. She never got sober. Not even Jesus could fix that.

She would have beaten cancer. She could have spent more time with her granddaughters. She should be taking care of her husband. Teddy's sister could be dead. He wouldn't care. He should have helped her years ago. Would. Should. Could. Useless words to go along with useless feelings.

His arm explodes in tiny bumps. He shivers and hustles the last block.

He enters the same building he has for the last two hundred Tuesdays. He's confused. There's something different. Strange. He doesn't like it. He feels like he's slipping again. Losing his grip on something. The lobby is empty and bright white. He doesn't recall it being this devoid of everything. The elevator door is open and waiting. When it alerts him to his stop, the chime echoes. The hall is too long. Stretched down to a point. He's afraid the farther he gets from the elevator, the bigger he'll be. *Alice in Wonderland* with the walls closing in. He turns back, and the elevator is gone. Not to a different floor—there is no elevator where an elevator should be, just a solid white wall.

He picks up his pace, trotting. He ducks but doesn't need to. Nothing is shrinking, and he's certainly not getting bigger. Is this what vertigo feels like? He'll call Philip.

His father's door is as unwelcoming as ever. No wreath or decorative door knocker. Thank God. He hasn't completely lost it. He turns his key in the lock. A chain stops the door from opening. Is it even Tuesday? He pushes on the door.

"Hello?"

Hurried feet squeak on the entryway tile.

"Mr. Teddy?" The Polish nurse fumbles with the door.

"It's Tuesday." He has to work hard to make that come out as a statement.

"Yes. Yes. So sorry." She opens the door while rubbing down her scrubs.

"It's fine."

"Sit. Sit. Sammy, you have visitor."

She has jelly around her mouth. Chunky purple jelly. Teddy's not the type to save anyone from embarrassment. He has no intention of telling her, but he can't hide his disgust.

"Something wrong?"

"You have, you have something on your face."

"Oh!" She dabs at her chin.

Teddy points to the crusted corner of her mouth.

She sheepishly wipes at it. Once her back is turned, she licks her fingers.

"I'll bring snacks."

"I'm good."

Teddy turns off the TV in front of his father. He can't deal with background noise right now. He'll miss the distraction. With his heightened senses, he takes in his surroundings as if for the first time. The furniture looks like it came from a strip mall waiting room. The chair his father spends his day in is hard. There are no armrests, and the back is too low to serve any purpose. The walls are bare except for three small, framed pictures. The photos are black and white. The frames are thin and cheap. Teddy squints to see portraits of himself, his mother, and his sister. He's freezing. It's colder in this living room than outside. There are no blankets or pillows. Nothing of comfort. He makes a note to tell Trish. She can order something.

The nurse comes back with the cheese and crackers that he didn't want, and no one will eat. She smiles. Her crooked tooth catches her bottom lip. That hasn't happened before. It's sharper. She winks and leaves them.

"I was thinking of Mom today. On the walk over." Teddy was not expecting to say that. His father has no reaction.

She was a cat and his father a muscular dog. Her tailed puffed anytime he came close. He blames his mother for leaving him alone. He blames his father for not caring enough that she left. Under the spite, he aches for her like a little boy whose mom works two shifts. He wants his mommy to come home. He wishes she was there to see his father like this, weak and small. He wishes she was there to cover him up with something soft.

"My neighbor died."

This makes the old man grin.

"All alone. Dead on the floor. And Chang . . . shot for seventy bucks."

Like his mother, Teddy grew up as a cat, slinking around, avoiding his father's bark. He spends more time with him now than at any other time in his life. He talks to him now. Now that he can't talk back. Unlike his mother, he lived to see this dog lose its bite. He's been around this version of him long enough that he has a hard time remembering what made them all so skittish. Sometimes he remembers. Sometimes the light will stream through a window in the exact same way it did in his childhood kitchen. Sometimes he'll look down in his glass, and the ice will be shrinking exactly like the ice in a highball his mother left on his nightstand when he was eleven. The semicircle of cheese and crackers in front of him takes him back to being six or seven, hiding next to a buffet table.

His parents were hosting a reading for an out-of-town playwright. It was brunch with a lot of vodka and a little bit of food.

His father didn't notice him. He was barely taller than the table and his crisp, fancy shirt blended in perfectly with the linens. He spied on the grown-up conversation while shoving crackers into his mouth. Cubes of cheese. Juicy green grapes. His sweaty little hands touched the whole bowl before plucking only one.

The conversation was getting heated. The younger man talking clearly needed more eggs and fewer screwdrivers. An actor was trying to convince his father no one could play a killer. Not even he, who had done it multiple times. Sure, he fooled an audience, but there was no way he was in the moment. Unless you've crossed that line, you couldn't know what it feels like to take a man's life. He couldn't have really tapped into those wants and desires unless he was capable of doing it himself, and since he's pretty sure Sam Maine has never murdered anybody, the best he could have pulled off was acting, a sin for actors, and not being.

Teddy had never heard anyone talk to his father like that. He was giddy that it was someone who didn't matter. He couldn't bear to watch what would happen if it was someone he loved.

His father put a hand on the table and leaned in close. He had had twice as many breakfast cocktails but was a man and not some puff boy who'd just gotten promoted from intern. "You don't have to do something to know that you can."

At first, the actor laughed. Snorted, really. *Here's just another middle-aged blowhard.* Then the way Teddy's father held his gaze drained the blood from the young guest's face.

"I could kill anyone in this room and wake up tomorrow exactly the same."

"You're joking."

"Why would I tell *you* a joke?" He emphasized the "you".

"So, you're a murderer? Is that what you're telling me? That's how you got the Tony for *Othello*?"

Teddy's father laughed. "I'm an animal. You're an animal. We're all beasts sharing the top of the food chain who sometimes agree on the same God. We're apes with dictionaries. Snakes with hands. What difference does it make if I kill someone, or I'm the one killed? Either way we both end up dirt."

"Why haven't you done it then?"

"I haven't needed to."

The young actor became successful and a regular at their parties. Teddy often watched him watching his father. He never spoke to him directly again but laughed along with the crowd and hung on his every word.

"It's weird. Don't think I've ever seen a body bag." Teddy takes a cracker. The salty crumbs are familiar and cover his shirt.

His father mumbles, "We all end up dirt."

Teddy is stunned. His father hasn't said a word in months. Maybe years. He feels incredibly exposed, like his recent memory has been laid out next to the cheese and crackers for all to see.

"Nurse!" Teddy stands, brushing off cracker crumbs. By the looks of it, he's had more than one. He yells again, and the Polish nurse runs in.

"What's wrong with my Sammy?"

"He talked. I . . . I could understand him."

She drags a chipped fingernail across his father's neck. "What did my Sammy say?" Teddy is taken aback by her tone. It's almost seductive. She squeezes the old man's cheeks. "Sammy has lots to say if you come to listen."

No one in ninety-six years has ever called him Sammy.

"He talks to you?"

"We talk to each other. Don't we?" She tickles behind his neck with her ragged nails. His father doesn't dislike or like the attention. He's a stone in a chair.

"Where's the other nurse?"

"Sheila? That cow is long gone."

Teddy's head is starting to pulse. He hasn't had a migraine all week. The skin around his temple is tight and clammy.

"You want soup? You don't look so good?"

"Soup? No. Tell the agency I want to be notified before any staffing changes."

"You're the boss, Mr. Teddy."

"When is a new girl starting?"

"No new girl. Just me. Isn't that right, Sammy? Just you and me."

Teddy is overstaying his welcome. He doesn't know if he should be concerned or happy that someone cares for his father so much. Either way, he can't deal with this now. Maybe this is the push he finally needs to just move him into a home and be done with it. He needs to go before his head gets worse.

"Can I get a bottle of water?"

"Yes. Yes."

The nurse goes to the kitchen. Teddy can see a mess when she slips through the door. Piles of purple- and red-stained towels. He'll definitely be making a change.

"Thanks." He takes a swig from the water and goes to leave. He gags. It's filled with salt. "What is this?"

"Water, Mr. Teddy. Like you asked."

"There's something wrong with it."

She takes it from him and drinks. "Is it not cold enough for you? I'll get you another—"

"No. No. It's fine." He stumbles backward toward the door. He watches her pour the salty water down his father's throat.

He spits on the sidewalk outside. He wipes his face and practically plows over an attractive woman walking toward him.

"Excuse me." He mumbles.

"Ted? Teddy, is that you?"

Her voice is familiar and lovely. New York really is a small town. It's Katherine Cline. Dr. Katherine Cline, a blast from his past. Eighteen years ago, he almost ran away with her. She was more than an extraneous lover—she could have become his second wife. Maybe she should have. The years have been kind to her. Her hair is long and blond, her outfit impeccable. She's tall and sturdy and never needed anything from him or anybody else.

He was a grown-up with her. He ate better when he was with her. Drank less when he was with her. Wrote very little. They read books and went to museums. She was a vacation from himself. She had no interest in his children but wouldn't have minded being a weekend stepmother. She felt sorry for his wife and tried to help him be a kinder husband. She was too intellectual to be concerned with the idea of adultery. She understood their arrangement and felt no guilt taking him away from his family. Adults don't do things they don't want to do. It wasn't up to her to save or destroy his other relationships.

Before falling into the trap of self-help guru, she was a well-respected psychologist. She had faculty positions at Columbia and Brown. They were introduced when he was researching the Church's misdeeds toward boys. Her specialty was uncovering buried trauma. She was helpful without being terribly empathetic. He admired and trusted her detachment. Elizabeth could do worse than being a serious woman. Only Teddy would take comfort in the thought of his daughter turning out like his mistress.

"It's Katherine."

"Of course. Kate." He leans in and pecks her cheek. "You look well."

"Visiting your father?" She looks toward the building.

"Yes."

She always had a keen interest in Teddy's father. She'd had dinner with the two of them multiple times. Teddy couldn't help but feel like a subject in one of her experiments.

"How is he?"

"Old."

She smiles.

"I heard you moved." Small talk is painful for him.

"Philadelphia. With my husband."

"Congratulations."

"Well. You never called me back."

That's true. He ended things without ending them. He knew she would get the hint without any fanfare or fighting. She could have always done much better than him. He rationalized his cruelty as doing her a favor. Given her line of work, she must have expected it, knowing she was always on borrowed time being with someone as broken as Teddy Maine.

She smiles graciously and keeps her tone light. "It works. His daughter is touring Juilliard this weekend."

"Must be a talented girl."

"Or rich." She gets an idea. "Maybe you two can connect? She wants to be a writer."

This is what it has come to, polite favors. All relationships follow the same arc, after all. She hands him her card, complete with her million-dollar catchphrase. She can read his body language, even though he is desperately trying to be nice.

"I know you don't approve. It helps people. You should read my new book. Maybe it will help you."

"I'm beyond help."

"You've always been an astute student of yourself." She hugs him, first gingerly and then hard. She really loved him once.

She pauses to take in the new lines on his face. "Get some sleep."

She continues on her way. Neither say goodbye.

He makes it home without incident. Chang's death leaves him feeling melancholy and sorry for himself. He hasn't thought about Kate in years, and now he's holding on to the space she's left. He's always been good at feeling sorry for himself even though it's something he despises in others. He digs in a kitchen drawer and pulls out a joint. There are more efficient ways to get high these days, but he prefers the ash and smell of burning paper. He likes to see how tiny he can get it before burning his fingers.

Trish has left grocery bags on the counter. He unpacks a sack of peaches. He takes a bite, and thick juice streams down his chin. He spits it in the sink. It's rotten.

"Trish!" There's no answer. He walks through the apartment and sees that all the rooms are empty. It should be concerning, but he's relieved. Back in the kitchen, he throws all the recently purchased fruit in the garbage. He opens his laptop and types in Katherine's website.

He's surprised the font is so trendy. She's a long way from the serious scholar he used to admire. He settles in and clicks through the links.

She has over thirteen million YouTube followers. Her husband is a lucky man. He settles in to watch a recent TED Talk. Her tone is slick. He's impressed. He never thought of her as a performer, or a salesperson. It's a packed auditorium. Her voice is confident and loud over the wireless mic.

"Often, when we hear the word *incest*, our minds go to made-for-TV movies and V.C. Andrews novels. Or maybe we stop listening altogether. It's too much to think about, children being violated by those they love and trust the most. Society goes through cycles of sensationalism. Underground satanic cults, large-scale human trafficking organized by opposing political parties. It's so taboo that we can only relate to it as this monstrous, cinematic thing that happens in the shadows. But the truth is, all of us as a collective unconscious are incest survivors. Are you uncomfortable yet?" She pauses, and the crowd laughs. Teddy shifts uneasily in his chair and rolls his eyes.

"The medical community, the mental health establishment, doesn't yet fully recognize incest as a disease that is given and passed down in a family's DNA. We look at each case as this horrifying one-off. Of course, like the majority of sexual assaults, we only know the tip of the iceberg in terms of occurrence. Furthermore, what might be perceived as a family's norm could be incredibly damaging to all its participants. The long-lasting effects make victims unreliable patients and witnesses, even to themselves. We are left treating symptoms of the wrong problem."

"Patients are medicated for anxiety, depression, and bipolar. We give them labels under the anti-social umbrella and look to medical causes for sleep, attention, and pain disorders. People spend years in CBT and DBT therapies and whatever other trendy initials we come up with. The best-case scenario is, to me, the worst outcome for the individual. They find ways to cope with maladaptive behaviors that are still socially acceptable. So now this is just their personality. Just who they are. 'Oh, so-and-so . . . he never sleeps.' 'Jane, isn't she so fun and quirky? Too bad she has the worst taste in men!' 'There's the friend who wears a sweatshirt year-round or only dresses in purple.' 'That suffocating neighbor who can't take a hint . . . we had one barbecue, I'm not interested in a couples' vacation, okay?'"

The crowd laughs again. What a talent, to put strangers at ease while talking about such uncomfortable things. She's going to sell a lot of snake oil.

"They don't leave their house after dark, have to sleep in a certain pair of socks. There can be long periods of almost frenetic creative output and then nothing ever again. A journal filled with a hundred songs no one will ever hear. Survivors can be most comfortable thinking of themselves in the third person. There is a detachment from themselves that can manifest in both positive and negative ways. When we see a person who appears so sure of themselves, so content in going against the grain or forging a unique path, we often look to them as an example of self-actualization and confidence. But what looks like quirkiness is actually very painful. The negative attributes are easier to spot. Risk-taking behaviors, substance abuse, layers of self-sabotage. You have that cousin who thrives in drama, can't manage money, hops from job to job. We tell ourselves . . . well, that's just who they are. No. They were made that way."

"Now, we all have our quirks and bad habits. I, myself, could be considered a total weirdo—"

No, she couldn't. She is the least weird person Teddy has ever known. Why is he still watching this garbage? He's missing her less and less.

"This is not about manufacturing trauma that isn't there or assigning each of us the role of victim. But the number of times we overlook the consequences of incest far outweighs any chance of over-categorizing its impacts. So, what do I mean when I say we are all incest survivors? Well, you'll have to buy my book."

Big smile and pause for laughs. She's a pro.

"As a student of Carl Jung—"

Done. Teddy shuts the laptop. He scowls at the outdated tech like it had something to do with what he just watched. He has never suffered fools well, and he feels this time the fool is him.

He's not sure what to do with himself. He wants to avoid Emily until he's read the play. He's afraid she'll be in his office, and he won't be able to resist falling into another string of lost days with her. He should rest. Get some real sleep in a bed while it's still dark out. He calls Philip instead.

"Meet me at a bar."

Chapter 12

It's black outside. No moon. No stars. The streetlamps can't make a dent in the dense night. The air and pavement are wet. He doesn't recall any rain today. It's like the city is dripping. He walks past a group of college girls. They stop their chatter to check him out. He's an older man most girls would go after. The type of girls who go after such things. It gives him a boost.

He hasn't been to this bar in ages, but his legs still know how to get him there. He's on autopilot, dodging the drips. The light above the door is red. This place isn't members only, but it only appeals to a specific type of person. He beats Philip there, of course.

Inside it's sticky and ragged. The walls are stone with dangerous corners. If Satan had a son, he would celebrate his birthday here. It's a funhouse with mirrors reflecting back the darkest and most basic human desires. Sex. Dominance. Violence. It's not loud. There's a grating buzz of conversation and the occasional outburst of laughter or screams. It's hard to see in the ambient light cast by dirty red bulbs. Guests feel as though they are packed in a box away from the real world.

The way some men are holding court reminds him of his father at one of his famous parties. There is definitely a division between the haves and have-nots. The kings and their subjects.

The variety of people is disorienting. Brains use patterns to make sense of their surroundings. There's no rhyme or reason in here. A woman in a floor-length fur coat walks a senator in overalls on a leash. The bartender's earlobes are stretched nearly to his shoulders. Some are in desperate need of a bath, others in Prada. A tall, slender, topless man walks by with a girl in pigtails. He's covered in tattoos from his skull to his toes. The whites of his eyes have been colored black.

Teddy slides behind a thick wooden table. The booths are high and red. Metal claws adorn the wall next to black-and-white drawings of horrible things. He's missed this place. A waitress with short bangs and a lip piercing stops to wipe his table. She clears empty glasses littered with ash and cigar butts.

Teddy orders. "Whiskey."

"Drinking alone?"

"For now."

The waitress raises her eyebrow.

A group of Asian businessmen hurry by, ushering a young girl to the back. Tangled hair covers her face. The waitress motions to the bartender, who buzzes open a private door. Teddy watches as they disappear behind the metal door. Flirting with the waitress seems less cute now. This might not be a place for him. Not anymore.

An enormous man with stringy hair and no top teeth drops off a dirty glass of whiskey. Teddy drinks it quickly. As he sets it down, a sudden rage goes off in his head. His brain feels like it's being cleaved in half. The deafening sound of scratching steel fills the space between his ears. He puts his palms to his head, desperately trying to keep things in place. His eyes can't focus.

The noise stops. The pain subsides. There's something wrong. His eyes adjust to his new surroundings. He's in a cage. He is two people inside one mind. His body is reacting to someone else's thoughts. He's watching things unfold from the inside out.

There's a man beaten to a pulp on the ground. Teddy's fists are cracked from punching. His bare chest and face are speckled with blood. His body paces and his voice yells. He pounds his chest, sending blood and sweat into the air. He is the victor. On the other side of the cage, his family sits dressed in black. Nora. Elizabeth. Augie. Trish. Philip holds Trish's hand. They are stoic and silent. Trish locks eyes with him and then turns her head away. He wants to ask her what's going on. He wants to look at the face of the man on the ground covered in blood. Who is he? Is he okay? But Teddy's the one watching, not the one in control.

Another screech of metal. He falls to his knees as one body and one mind. He's in excruciating pain. He can feel parts of his brain popping and boiling. He reaches out to his family, but they are gone. He blacks out from the pain.

He wakes up in a chair at his mother's bedside. His knuckles are bloody. That's the only evidence of past violence. A machine tracking her heart rate is rhythmically beeping. A nurse joins them to replace a bag that's dripping into her arm.

"Nurse."

The woman turns sharply.

"Is she going to be okay?"

She answers flatly. "She's dying."

The time between each beep is getting longer.

"Is she in any pain?"

"Why don't you ask her?"

The nurse leaves without looking back. Teddy pulls his chair up to the bed. He grabs his mother's hand and pulls it up to his face.

"I'm here. I'm with you."

She doesn't respond, her eyes fixed on the ceiling.

"Mom. Mommy . . . it's okay." His tears dampen her fingers.

"You rest. Rest as long as you need to. I'll be here when you wake up."

The beeping stretches together in a green line. Teddy stands, jerking her arm up with him, still gripping her hand with all his might.

"Nurse! Nurse!"

His mother's head turns. She's beautiful. Glowing. Her peaceful smile calms him immediately.

She opens her mouth, and thousands of flies fill the room. He falls backward in the swarm, disappearing into the buzzing blackness.

He lands on the pavement. There are footsteps coming fast behind him. Sirens are waiting at the corner. He limps down an unfamiliar city street, trying to keep his pace steady. He's holding a bloody knife. He attempts to hide it up his shirtsleeve. He ducks behind a dumpster before passing the squad car.

Behind the dumpster, he finds himself in a foggy field of short grass and mud. The city is gone. Surrounding him are vicious dogs on chains. They lunge at him. His flesh is just out of reach. They snarl and bark, testing the chains' strength. He cowers, covering his face. Once he realizes he is safe, he breaks down in cackling laughter.

His eyelids move up and down slowly. He is back in the red booth. His insides are warm. He feels good. His body is relaxed, his thoughts dulled. He could happily sit here for hours. His eyelids drop down for an extended beat. As they open, he spies a new group of businessmen entering the bar. They head toward the back. They have a young girl with them. Older than before, but still much too young. A teenager in too much makeup. Her parents probably think she's at a sleepover or school dance. They hold her up by her arms, dragging her feet as they go. Her head bobs; she's hardly conscious. Dark lipstick is smeared on her face, and there are handprints on her collarbone. Her short skirt covers shredded tights.

Teddy looks closer. He recognizes the shoes scraping the floorboards. It's Elizabeth. She's seventeen. This must be one of the times she ran away from home. His thoughts are moving in slow motion. His muscles are jelly. He struggles to get out from behind the heavy wooden table. The bartender buzzes the back private door. He must hurry.

Teddy jumps into the crowd of men as they pass, knocking

Elizabeth to the floor. She props herself up and smiles before slumping backward. Her eyes roll to the back of her head, and her body seizes and contorts. Teddy screams for help. A few patrons look casually at the commotion. Nobody moves from their chair.

He swings wildly at the men trying to get to her. They don't swing back. They are incredibly strong. They push him like a rag doll, passing him from one man to the next, preventing him from helping Elizabeth. He can't make out their faces. They're shiny and blank like store mannequins.

The enormous man with stringy hair grabs Teddy by the throat. He holds him up with one hand and launches him through the stone wall. He falls into a tunnel. It's dark and smells like earth. He struggles to get to his feet. He hears a rumbling. He turns to see a flood of red rapids heading toward him. He doesn't bother running or trying to escape. Instead, he tilts his head back and stretches his arms wide, making a cross.

The sound of trains colliding ravages his eardrums. He puts his head down on the heavy wooden table and cries. He does his best to wrap himself in his arms, shielding himself from whatever comes next.

Philip has arrived. He has a hard time spotting his friend in the dim space with his head covered. He spots him and rushes to the table.

"Teddy! Hey . . . hey." He shakes his shoulders. "Ted!"

Teddy jerks his body upright. He's laughing silently with tears streaming down his pale face. Philip slowly slides into the booth across from him. Teddy's laughter becomes audible. Philip yells toward the bar for some water.

"I thought it was real," Teddy says, trying to catch his breath.

"What? What's real?" Philip is more concerned than usual. This is an extreme moment, even for Teddy.

"She was right there." He wipes snot from his face. "On the floor. I couldn't get to her."

"Are you all right?" Philip won't ask who *she* is.

"No!" Teddy laughs loudly, causing a large woman overflowing out of her tube top and sporting hair in a messy beehive to *shhh* him.

"No! I've gone fucking nuts!" He's making a scene. Two identical-looking men in leather face masks stand at their tables, holding baseball bats.

Philip leans in close. "I hate this place. Let's get out of here."

Teddy's laughter grows. The enormous man with stringy hair approaches and stands close behind him. "Good idea!" he shouts.

Philip helps Teddy up, and they quickly leave the bar. They walk a few blocks down and regroup under a busted streetlamp. They pass a joint without speaking. After a moment, Philip breaks the ice.

"Maybe coffee would be a better idea." Philip would rather not be smoking weed in the dark.

Teddy takes a long drag and exhales. "Nah. This will mellow me out."

Philip needs to take it down a few notches himself. "We need to talk."

"Obviously."

"Can you talk now? I don't . . . I don't know what's going on with you. Why don't we wait 'til morning?"

Teddy bends over and spits out a wad of snot and dust. "This might be as good as I get. What's on your mind?"

"The play."

"Obviously." Teddy pats his pockets, looking for smokes.

"It's great. Really. Really great. But it's not finished." It's unusual for Philip to stumble on his words.

"I told you it needed a little more work."

"It's missing something."

"The ending." Teddy finally finds a cigarette.

"No."

No? How did Emily finish it? What does Philip know that he doesn't? He should have read it the second she handed it over.

"The next day I read it . . . sober . . . and, really, it's so good, but . . ." Stumble. Stumble. Stumble.

"But what?" The cigarette falls out of his mouth when he yells.

"I shouldn't have brought it up now. Let's talk tomorrow."

Teddy starts to protest but then sways and falls into his friend's arms. Philip holds him for a minute then leans him against the lamppost. "You all right? Can you walk?"

"Whoopsie."

"Come on. Time for bed." Philip tosses the joint and wraps Teddy's arms around his shoulders.

The walk is long and wet. Teddy's condition worsens with each block. He can barely hold his head up by the time they get to the apartment. Philip tucks him in.

"What's wrong with the play?"

"Get some rest, bud."

"Thanks for meeting me." Teddy is barely conscious.

"My pick next time." Philip props another pillow behind his head, treating him like a child. His phone lights up in his hand. Augie is calling again. Philip made the mistake of texting him earlier in the night, concerned. He heads to the living room, shutting the door behind him. Teddy can faintly hear their conversation.

"Should I leave? I feel like he can't be alone. Yeah. Yeah. No, I know. Yeah. I know, but you didn't see him tonight. It's . . . it's next level. He said it himself he's gone fucking nuts." He pauses for a moment, listening. "Sort of. I brought it up, but we didn't get into it. He's . . . he's . . . I don't know. This is more than booze and stress. Maybe we should bring in a doctor."

Get into what? Teddy wants to get up. Get up and drink with his friend. Get up and write with Emily. He's asleep enough to not be able to move but still alert enough to hear Philip.

"No. I didn't tell him about the texts. Did you get another one? It's got to be the same guy, right? He sleep with somebody's wife recently? It's not cute anymore. Don't delete anything. I'll call that cop friend again." Philip spends some time listening, with the occasional "Hmm."

Teddy imagines him nodding his head. "I'm going to stay here tonight. No. No. It's fine. I don't mind."

Teddy is glad Philip is staying. Bad things are happening when he's alone. Knowing his friend is in the next room, he gives in to dreaming deeper. Something cracked tonight. Something feels inevitable. That brings a sense of relief but also resignation and doom. In that tunnel in the bar, being baptized by blood, he started to let it all go.

His dream brings him to his mother's closet. He watches her wrap his younger self in scarves. Little Teddy is delighted. Older Teddy is filled to the brim with sweet nostalgia. His mother brings over a box of jewels. Teddy loved it when they played King and Queen with her costume jewelry.

"Grab the moonstone!" No one can hear him.

The smooth moonstone cocktail ring was his favorite. It was cold and milky-white. He loved to rub it on his mother's cheek and have her purr back at him.

His mother layers the young boy's neck with pearls. He lays his head on her lap, resting as she sings. Teddy leans, relaxed against the closet door. There is good in him. No matter what is coming for him, he was once somebody's little boy.

Chapter 13

He wakes refreshed, like he's slept for days. His body feels stretched in a good way. He can move without a joint cracking and sit without clenching his jaw. The sunlight seems natural for the first time in a long time. The air is dry and smells like a basket of clean laundry. It's early afternoon. Philip has left a note.

If you're reading this, you didn't die in your sleep. Good job. At the office. Call me.

He stands in front of the fridge and chugs orange juice from the bottle. Trish must have gone shopping again. There's a beautiful ham glazed and covered with pineapple chilling on the middle shelf. He'll have to check in with his wife. Looks like they're having company for dinner.

Philip left his copy of Emily's play on the coffee table. It's marked up with notes. For a second Teddy hesitates, like he's about to read someone's diary, but his contemplation doesn't last long. He's read lots of diaries.

Red notes on top of his chicken scratch make it hard to read. How did she do that? Write in his hand? Luckily, he doesn't need to read closely. What's on the paper is nearly a word-for-word reporting of the things he's seen in his office. The things he's felt when he's been with her. He feels it differently reading it. He's not distracted by his need to touch and please her. Philip is right. This work is incredibly painful and beautiful. He squints and tracks the words with his fingers when he gets to an unfamiliar section. Emily's voice is in his ear as he imagines her words unfolding in a black box theater on a scuffed stage. There's little scenery. A wooden chair and table. The actors move stiffly and deliver their lines like a Greek chorus from an ancient script.

"'*Twas here my summer paused. What ripeness after then the other scene or other soul. My sentence had begun.*" The actress is talking to the character of "Scribe", her companion in the play.

"*My life closed twice before its close. It yet remains to see if immortality unveil a third event to me. So huge, so hopeless to conceive as these that twice befell. Parting is all we know of heaven and all we need of hell.*"

The Scribe and Emily turn their attention to the door. The imposing figure of "Master" enters the scene. These characters haven't been assigned genders, but Teddy can't help but imagine himself in the role of Scribe. The Scribe puts down their pen and shields Emily, proclaiming:

"*A face devoid of love or grace. A hateful, hard, successful face.*" The character is instructed to investigate further and crosses the stage. Teddy is rooting for him.

Emily stops him. "*A face with which a stone would feel as thoroughly at ease.*"

The Master confronts her, pushing the Scribe out of the way. They stand center stage. The Master's face is covered. "*As were they old acquaintances first time together thrown.*"

Emily stands firm. "*I know thee better for the act that made thee first unknown.*"

The scene ends abruptly. Philip has made notes in red.

Expand. Who is Master? Is the mask cliché? Lots of static talking. Should 'Emily' pull off mask or become physical? A punch . . . should there be choreography? How episodic are we taking this?

The next scene is a painful callback to the parade in the dark gray fields. Emily and the Scribe stand back-to-back. Teddy's heart beats fast reading the sound cue calling for hollow thumps.

As actors silently cross the stage in time with the rhythmic drumming, Emily announces, *"Father, I observed to Heaven. You are punctual."*

Emily speaks calmy as the Scribe grows more and more panicked.

"I don't like this place. Please, Emily, take me back."

Emily scolds him, turning over her shoulder. *"'Tis easier to pity those when dead that which pity previous would have saved."*

The other actors circle them as Emily speaks even louder over the menacing sound cues.

"Those dying then knew where they went. They went to God's right hand. That hand is amputated now, and God cannot be found."

The Scribe falls to the floor. The circle of actors stops moving. The stage is silent. Emily leaves him on the floor and steps center stage.

"He ate and drank the precious words. His spirit grew robust. He knew no more that he was poor, nor that his frame was dust."

Is she talking about him? Teddy doesn't want to read anymore. He tosses the pages on the table and eyes them to see if they have more hidden messages. Someone is at the door. He feels caught with his hand in the cookie jar and quickly slides the play into a basket of remotes and magazines. Trish enters with shopping bags.

"A little help, please?"

He meets her at the door. She has cloth shopping bags filled with wine and olives. Stiff breads and cheese. He catches a glimpse of Elizabeth's favorite fig spread. Trish looks amazing in her coordinated yoga gear. She is equally refreshed and renewed. He doesn't remember the last time they had a simple interaction like this, but suddenly can't remember a time that was ever different.

"The kids are coming for dinner."

"I saw the ham."

She begins emptying the bags on the marble kitchen island.

"Aren't those pineapples fantastic? I felt like something different." She holds up each bottle of wine as she talks. "White for Nora, Merlot for Elizabeth—the fig spread, of course, and I figured you and Aug would have something brown from the bar."

Teddy feels like he's stepped into the second half of a movie. This is nice. He doesn't want to question it.

"Looks great."

Trish pauses from unpacking. "Augie told her about Jon."

"Who?"

"Elizabeth. Don't gloat. You two are finally friends again."

He has no idea what she is talking about. He doesn't want to ask and risk breaking the spell.

She continues. "Obviously you were right—but, Ted, listen to me, it's not what she needs to hear right now."

"Sure." Hear what?

"I hope Augie doesn't bring it up. There's plenty else to talk about."

Teddy hopes he does.

"Did you shower?" Trish asks.

He smiles. Trish hasn't been around to direct him lately. He likes it.

She smiles back. "What?"

"Nothing. Tonight will be fun," Teddy replies.

Jon. Jon. Jon. His brain chants as he stands in a hot shower. Who the hell is Jon? The bathroom is wet and filled with steam by the time he's finished. He wipes off the mirror just enough to see his reflection while shaving. Jon. Jon. Jon! He's got it! He's solved the puzzle, picked the lock in his memories. He slices his chin from the excitement.

"Shit."

Blood drips into the sink, decorating minty-smelling blobs of shaving cream.

"Shit. Shit. Shit." He grabs a towel and presses it to his face.

He's delighted. He remembers Jon. How could he forget that asshole?

Elizabeth was eighteen when she met him. She was taking a gap year. Since she refused to apply to colleges, it was actually just a gap. She'd barely finished high school. She'd left twice junior year for rehab.

Philip brought Jon on to expand their licensing. Teddy didn't think it was necessary, but Philip thought it was essential. Eventually Teddy would be done writing. His bad habits had to catch up with him sooner or later, and he wouldn't be able to produce new work. Important to get a tight infrastructure in place now so they could all keep getting rich off him.

Jon was a month out of law school. Knowing he would never be the smartest, he made sure to fine-tune his mouth. He was slick and slippery. He made *no* sound like *yes*. He tricked you into listening, waiting for a big revelation that never came. There was always a secret on the tip of his tongue, and maybe, just maybe, you would be the lucky one to hear it. People swarmed around him like they did around Teddy's father. Teddy could smell his bullshit from a mile away.

Philip was in love with this brunette version of himself. To be fair, Jon was a good worker. He knew how to do things in ten minutes that would take Philip two days. Teddy and Philip enjoyed many long lunches those days, and a weekend or two in Atlantic City. Passing the torch looked good on Philip. He was relaxed and willing to indulge his indulgent friend.

There were perks, so Teddy let Jon stick around. Augie was a year from graduating law school, and the two became fast friends. That mildly irked Teddy. He didn't think it was a good idea. Philip was family, but it didn't have to be in every employee's contract that they, too, became family. When Elizabeth started hanging around the office, Teddy's mild irritation grew into an all-consuming rash.

Trish was pleased. Each day Elizabeth spent with Jon she'd shed a layer of gloom. She wore less and less makeup. Stopped prancing around like a goth sex doll and biting her nails down to the nubs. Trish praised him for keeping her sober. Teddy should have been pleased. Jon was doing the heavy lifting.

Elizabeth was no longer troubled-but-interesting. This time she had no interests to share with her dad, and that hurt him. He wasn't naive or hypercritical enough to be bothered by the sex. He knew she wasn't a virgin. He just couldn't handle that it was someone else who fixed her. Who was changing her. Shaping her into their preferred image.

She started applying to colleges. She was going to be a lawyer, too! Elizabeth, a lawyer? No way. Augie defended Jon. Trish adored Jon. Philip scolded Teddy for being jealous and overbearing. They ganged up on him. Accused him of driving a wedge between Elizabeth and the rest of her family just when they got her back. Like he didn't know that? Like he wasn't desperate to have her back?

She started to spend the weekends at Jon's apartment. Teddy complained she was too young for sleepovers. When she stopped coming home altogether no one else was bothered. They knew where she was, at least. After eight months they were engaged. That was the end for Teddy. This wasn't 1776. His daughter, his Elizabeth, would not be married before she could drink.

He was the bad guy. No one else thought it strange that she was hell-bent on becoming a child bride. He was being unreasonable. Rich girls in New York grow up fast. This will be so good for her! A chance to start fresh and settle down. It was a miracle, really. And let's not forget, he was the love of her life. She genuinely loved him and who she was when she was with him.

Teddy did the thing all overbearing fathers with means do—he sent Jon away. Without telling Philip, he went ahead, taking great initiative, and opened up a West Coast office. They were going to branch into film, and Jon was just the go-getter they needed. Elizabeth called his bluff. She moved across the country without saying goodbye.

He refused to pay for a wedding. Trish told him they would just elope. He knew she was right. Besides, he was paying Jon a fortune. They could pay for their own damn party. He proceeded to throw a middle-aged temper tantrum. Elizabeth was the grown-up who finally put an end to the drama. He'd insisted she choose, so she did. She chose Jon.

By that Christmas she was back home. Jon had been sleeping his way through the Valley, and a jilted blonde with a tramp stamp decided to break the news to lovely Elizabeth. Teddy welcomed her home with open arms and a big fat "I told you so." It was precisely the wrong thing to do at exactly the wrong time to do it. Elizabeth vowed to never speak to him again.

Jon was fired. The West Coast office closed before it opened. Augie graduated and took over as Philip's go-to. Jon sued, claiming he was owed a buyout of his contract and moving expenses. It's very boring watching lawyers fight each other. Philip and Trish worked out a deal behind Teddy's back for Elizabeth's sake. Jon needed to be out of their lives. He was. And so was Elizabeth.

She wasn't home for long. She got into college. She talked to her mother just enough to keep getting checks. She finished early and had her pick of top law schools. This was all easy for her, having two men driving her spiteful ambition.

Elizabeth blamed Teddy for Jon's wandering eye. He drove him into the arms of other women. Easy women with easy fathers. He was never going to let her go. He was a miserable and awful man determined to keep his prize daughter trapped. He didn't take offense. He was miserable and slightly awful. Never pretended to be otherwise. He was happy to keep Elizabeth trapped if it meant keeping her away from jerks like Jon.

He didn't take their rift seriously. She was a dramatic teenager who'd gotten her heart broken before it was fully formed. But months turned into years, and nothing he did could bring her back.

All of this rushes to Teddy's frontal cortex in the time it takes a drop of blood to splash in the sink. He sits on the edge of the bathtub in total relief. Yes. Of course, this was the break in their chain. This is simple. This only takes time to fix. Trish said they were friends again. He must have served his sentence. He holds his breath, hoping that flood of memories comes next. He wants to remember hugging Elizabeth after all that time. The first time after the last time. It must have felt like coming home.

No. He won't bring up Jon tonight. He will not celebrate his spot-on assessment, his accurate prediction. All those years ago, he was absolutely justified in being the lone dissenter. Jon was not a good guy.

Moving across the country only to sleep around wasn't proof enough to convince anyone. Recently being arrested for selling child porn on the dark web did the trick. Teddy won't make his past mistake and throw it in Elizabeth's face. He is looking forward to beating it over Philip's head.

He puts on a shirt he doesn't remember ironing and smooths his hair. Trish is surprised when she sees him.

"You dressed up."

"You made a delicious dinner. What's the occasion?"

"It's Wednesday."

Dinner is long and loud. The ham is a hit. The kids make fun of their mom for being a closet 1950s housewife. Nora is getting a paper published. Teddy is a beat behind but enjoying every minute.

Trish breaks through the chitchat with an announcement. "Did you hear your father sold the boat?"

Nora and Augie gasp. Underneath their sarcasm is genuine disappointment. The family made nice memories on that boat. Mom and Dad were much happier on water than on land. More relaxed. Trish laughed more. Teddy spent days shirtless with a beer in his hand. They had epic Monopoly tournaments. Having nothing to do suited them. Left with no alternative, Teddy could be a fun dad.

His fantasies of life on the open seas were passed down from his father. Sam Maine was obsessed with boats and maritime history. Teddy wouldn't go as far as leaving the city for an island compound like his parents, but he bought the *Teddy Bear* with his first big payday.

It was the top-of-the-line 1980s dreamboat. It would be better suited for a drug cartel than a family. The interior was all white leather. It had two generous staterooms, a kitchen, and a bathroom. Teddy sacrificed looks for size. There were three different sundecks on two levels and a totally tubular sound system. He loved that boat. They all did. Except Elizabeth.

"Good riddance," Elizabeth says with more bitterness than sarcasm.

"Oh, Bitsy," her mother teases. "Sharks were never going to eat your toes."

Elizabeth was a nervous sailor. She didn't appreciate the sun and saltwater like the rest of her family. Her big brother, like big brothers do, pounced on her apprehension and convinced her of all sorts of hydra-horrors. Water snakes would crawl up her butt when she used the toilet. Sharks would bite off her toes if she hung her feet over the railings. On the brightest, most perfect days, he convinced her every cloud was a hurricane forming. You would think she'd outgrow it, but she grew more and more reluctant to hit the water as she got older.

The boat has been in storage for years. Teddy got his money's worth, though he was rich enough that it didn't matter.

"I can't believe you've held on to it this long. When's the last time you took her out?" Augie, always the practical one.

Teddy can't answer. He has no idea. He can't remember much about his boating days right now. He does remember one weekend.

"You liked it sometimes." He responds to Elizabeth.

In eighth grade, Elizabeth fell behind in her advanced geography class. She was embarrassed and didn't tell her parents. The teacher was mean and didn't appreciate needing to spoon-feed knowledge to rich brats. Trish was able to stop Teddy from becoming "one of those parents." No, he wouldn't demand her grade be changed, nor would he demand this overly qualified educator's resignation. They met as a unified team to make a plan to raise her grade. The teacher's idea to chart a new sailing route was a tall order but easy to do with a yacht and time at one's disposal.

The whole family was going to go on a weekend adventure, but Nora came down with an ear infection. Teddy was thrilled to step in as Super Dad. He and Elizabeth made it out a mile from shore. It felt like they were a hundred miles from anywhere. As much as Teddy tried to deny it, he knew the teen years were around the corner, and these weekends would be hard to come by. They pored over incomprehensible charts and maps and imagined discovering a new land complete with a flag and theme song. Elizabeth was President Princess Chief Operations Officer. Teddy was her humble First Mate. She made them macaroni and cheese for dinner, and they drank sparkling grape juice under the stars. Without her brother, Elizabeth certainly found her sea legs. Teddy had hoped for a repeat, but this was one of the last times she tolerated her father before becoming obsessed with her phone and Korean boy bands.

He searches her face to see if she is walking down the same memory lane as he is right now. She catches his gaze but remains expressionless.

"That's right, you two did a little pirate extra credit project," Trish says, pouring herself a glass of red.

"It was cartography," Elizabeth mumbles.

Teddy smiles from the inside out. She does remember!

"Ah, yes! Christopher Columbus over here!" Augie laughs at his sister's expense.

"He's canceled, Augie," Nora teases back on her sister's behalf.

"Really? No more Columbus? Fine. Magellan then."

"I'm sure he raped and murdered people, too. Hey, how come you never took me out cartographing?" Nora's cheeks are rosy from the wine. "Aug got to go on all those fishing trips."

Trish interrupts. "Which was really just an excuse to drink beer with his fifteen-year-old son—"

Teddy winks in his son's direction. "I let you drink beer?"

Trish laughs out loud.

The noise. The teasing. The laughing. This is all Teddy's. Sitting at the head of his family table, he feels like he's sitting on top of the world. Elizabeth isn't participating, but she's there. That's enough.

Teddy keeps his eye on her. He feels bad. She clearly doesn't feel connected enough to her siblings to join in with their jabs. He always wanted to keep her apart, even if it's hard to watch now. He's too old and selfish to take any responsibility.

The bottles are empty. Pineapple pieces are all that's left in the grease and ham trimmings. Teddy is sleepy and stuffed. He steps outside onto the balcony to smoke with his son.

"Those things will kill you," Augie scolds as his dad lights up.

"Something has to."

"I'm glad you didn't bring up Jon."

"I don't always have to ruin things. How did she take the news?" Teddy wishes he were having this conversation with her.

"You know. She's impossible to read. I wanted her to hear it from family. Not read it on Facebook. You were right."

"Say that again?" Teddy chuckles and blows out smoke.

Augie remains serious. "She really loved him. Me, too."

Teddy never thought about how the news would impact his son. It would be a terrible blow to find out someone you picked as a best friend was someone you didn't know at all.

Teddy attempts to comfort him. "Most people are awful."

Augie changes the subject. "Philip says the new draft is great. Interesting."

Interesting? That's a terrible compliment.

"It's not finished." Teddy is defensive.

Augie backpedals. "I know."

"Almost." Teddy flicks his cigarette over the iron railing.

Back inside, the spell of the evening has worn off. Teddy is ready for his nest to be empty. The kids leave after dessert. Elizabeth gives him an awkward hug.

"I'm so glad you came," he says in almost a whisper. "It's been a long time."

"Longer than you think." She gives him a peck on the cheek and leaves with her sister.

He wants to go to sleep with a full belly and a full heart. He needs to figure out what is so interesting in Emily's play. As Trish handwashes the stemware, he makes himself comfortable by the fire. Too comfortable. He makes the effort to grab the play, but his eyes blur and close before he gets through a page.

His neck is stiff and sore from spending the night in the living room chair. Pages from the play are spread out on his lap. The house is quiet. The kitchen is spotless. He wonders if Trish is pissed that he passed out without helping. He walks slowly to the bathroom. His reflection catches him off guard. He could have sworn he shaved yesterday. Yes, he even cut himself. He gets close to the mirror. Nothing but stubble. He is missing the pep in his step he had yesterday. That's a big ask after a night of ham and booze. Whatever possessed Trish to buy that ham?

Emily meets him at the office door. *"He is alive this morning. He is alive—and awake."*

Is she pissed? Could she be jealous that he spent time with his family? That he enjoyed spending time with someone else?

She hands him a cup of tea from her mother's fine china collection. *"The world that thou hast opened shuts for thee."* She's hurt. She was left out.

He's quick to make amends. You *can* teach an old dog new tricks.

"Absolutely. I'm sorry." He takes a sip of tea. "I don't say that often. You missed me?"

"I do not care. Why should I care? And yet I fear I'm caring."

"I missed you, too."

She's getting too close. *"No friend have I that so persists as this eternity."*

He puts his cup down and squeezes her hand. He starts to ramble.

"I'll be better. So much has happened. My neighbor died. I didn't know him. Chang died. He sold me coffee. I don't know where to get coffee now. My kids came over for dinner. Even Elizabeth. She gave me a hug. I forgot how good it feels to be around her."

Emily's so tired of being sad. *"One thing of thee I covet. The power to forget."*

"Elizabeth loves you. I think you would love her, too. She's . . . she's everything you wrote about. It's like the two of us created her."

Emily takes her hand back and walks to the window.

"I'm kidding."

She doesn't find it funny. *"One thing of thee I borrow and promise to return,"* she snaps at him.

Teddy doesn't understand her mood swing. Should he apologize again? He decides to change the subject.

"I read the play. Most of it. I'll finish it today. I really—"

She interrupts him firmly. *"There are two mays and then a must and after that a shall. How infinite the compromise that indicates I will."*

Teddy stands, embarrassed for being scolded. "I'll read it right now. It's in the living room."

She hands him a copy. She takes her tea and sits down next to him. He's confused and not sure what to do next. She motions for him to read. He struggles to find his place. She impatiently points to where he left off.

The lights dim. The two are alone in the audience, watching a Greek tragedy unfold on a sparse set. Teddy doesn't know what to look at. Watching Emily watch herself is every bit as interesting as what's happening onstage. He wants to ask her if he's the Scribe. If he's made it into her play. But he'd rather just assume than be disappointed.

He has stopped trying to follow the script in his hand. He has no idea if this is the beginning, the middle, or the end. He sees a lot of red notes on the page. Clearly Philip has similar concerns. Emily mouths the words while watching the action unfold onstage.

"Behind the hill is sorcery. And everything unknown. But will the secret compensate for climbing it alone?"

Austin and Sue enter the scene. Emily steps aside and watches the newly married couple eat dinner as she would have from her window, alone in her room. The two exchange brief pleasantries and freeze. The actress playing Emily weaves around them like they are statues.

"To see her is a picture. To hear her is a tune. To know her, a disparagement of every other boon. To know her not, affliction. To own her for a friend. A warmth as near as if the sun were shining in your hand."

Sue stands, while Austin remains frozen in his chair. She and Emily meet center stage and face each other. Sue smooths a strand of hair dangling in Emily's eyes. She kisses her soft and long. Austin stands. He looks down at his watch, not paying any attention to the two women.

"Sue, my dear, we're expected at Father's." He takes her hand. Sue reaches out and clutches Emily with the other.

Sue stands in the middle of the two siblings and speaks directly to Emily. *"Parting with thee reluctantly, that we have never met. A heart sometimes a foreigner, remembers it forgot."*

Austin pulls her slightly, and she exits, keeping her eyes locked on Emily.

In the audience, Emily is crying. Her emotion is a mix of loss and joy. She leans in close and whispers to Teddy, *"I was regarded then. Raised from oblivion. A single time."*

Onstage, the actress continues. *"That she forgot me was the least, I felt it second pain. That I was worthy to forget was most I thought upon."*

The more Teddy experiences her relationship with Sue, the more his heart breaks. It's a feeling he has never felt firsthand. Emily is making him a better version of himself. A complete version. She is working purposefully and skillfully.

Teddy is a terrible audience member, and today is no exception. His attention fades in and out like he's skimming paragraphs in a familiar book. The Scribe and Emily share a few connecting scenes. He is drilling her about something. She responds forcefully.

"Not murmur—not endearment. But simply we obeyed. Obeyed—a lure—a longing? Oh, nature—none of this."

The actress exits. Emily stiffens next to him. Teddy leans over to ask a question, but Emily silences him before he can start. She directs his attention back to the stage.

Emily and her mother are having a heated argument at the table. The set includes a small bed and blanket, and a table and two chairs. Emily stands, knocking one of the simple chairs over. Both audience members are caught off guard and straighten to attention in their seats.

"Lives he in any other world my faith cannot reply . . . Though by his awful residence has human nature been."

The older actress crawls into the small bed to faintly deliver her line. *"Some arrows slay but whom they strike, but this slew all but him."*

The scene continues in pantomime. Emily props her mother up in the bed and brushes her hair gently. Her mother is not long for this world. Teddy recognizes this immediately and chokes up, seeing images of his own mother during their final visits.

The Scribe enters and takes notes at the foot of the bed. Teddy wants him out of the scene. He's intrusive and extraneous. He scans the pages to see if Philip has made a similar note. Emily leans in close to narrate what's happening onstage.

"I watched her face to see which way she took the awful news. Whether she died before she heard or in protracted bruise remained a few slow years with us. Each heavier than the last. A further afternoon to fail as flower at fall of frost."

She's surprised to see Teddy wipe away tears. He stops watching. He wants to talk about their mothers.

"My mother was sick. It was quick." He sniffs loudly, putting a tight lid on any further emotion. He looks down at his feet.

A smooth, cool hand holds his. Emily's hands are warm and weathered. He looks to his side to see his wife, Trish, dressed in a beautiful silver dress. He's in a black suit. They are in the front row. Nora stands above them in white. Her face is covered by the same lace veil Trish wore decades ago. Yards of fabric made special by who wears it now, and who has worn it before.

Elizabeth is holding a bunch of daisies tied with a pink ribbon. She nods and smiles in his direction. She's a 3D object popping up from a page. Like him, they are both there but also somewhere else. He's relieved they are together.

A handsome man he's never met stomps on a glass wrapped in a napkin. Just like that, his youngest is married. The room erupts in cheers. He has no choice but to be swept up in the excitement and love. Trish squeezes his hand and kisses his cheek with tears in her eyes. They did it!

A whirlwind ensues. A limo ride to the reception hall that is decked out in pink and crystal. Hundreds of pictures. He's too bewildered to smile, which is expected when giving your baby away. His wife asks if he's eaten anything and snags a glass of champagne and a scallop from a passing waiter.

"Here. You look a little off."

The champagne bubbles go through his sinus cavity like an electrical current. The scallop is salty and tender. He grabs another while he can. He is escorted by his wife to shake hands and say nice things to strangers who must be his friends. A little boy with shaggy hair almost knocks him over.

"Grandpa!" The boy weaves in and out of his legs.

Grandpa?

"Sorry, Dad." Augie collects his son.

Elizabeth stays close by, observing him. Her gaze grounds him. With all the duties of hosting a spectacular party, he doesn't have time to ask questions. He doesn't need to. It's very clear where he is and what he's doing. It feels so good being happy amongst all these other happy people that he isn't spending too much time worrying about how he got there, or why so much of this is new. If he's losing his mind, this is a pleasant way to do it.

Philip brings him a drink. It's clear he's spent much of cocktail hour at the bar.

"Great party."

They clink glasses.

"Your speech better be on point. *The Times* is here."

"Speech?"

"Don't play dumb, Father of the Bride." Philip takes a long drink. "You did good. Real good."

His tone has an edge. Some days it's hard to be the guest. Philip is special, but a guest nonetheless.

Trish is radiant. She floats and dances from table to table. She and Nora share a private embrace between celebratory hugs from distant cousins. She's not holding her back. She's setting her free. Teddy is surprised and impressed. He doesn't have a feeling to compare this to. He doesn't think he's ever loved his wife this much. It helps, watching Philip out of the corner of his eye. We always like what we have much more when we know someone else wants it.

Nora's husband appears kind and strong. Teddy is glad she ended up with someone like her brother and not himself. Nora waves and blows him a kiss from across the room. She mouths the words "thank you." Teddy's eyes moisten. In that instant, he finally feels like he has two daughters. Nora should hate him for neglecting her all these years, but clearly he has done something right.

His father is parked in his chair next to a tall plant twinkling with string lights. His head is down, and he looks exceptionally small in his wrinkled suit. He's alone. Teddy should expect to see him there, but it's still surprising. He's concerned that he's alone and heads over.

"Hi, Dad." He stands close to his chair. "Can you believe this? I'm not convinced it's real—"

The Polish nurse interrupts him. She joins them with a plate overflowing with food. Her formal wear looks like a costume: a mismatch of flapper and '50s pinup. It doesn't work. Her mouth seems stretched, exaggerated. Her crooked, pointed tooth is more pronounced than ever.

"What a night, Mr. Teddy."

He's not sure what to say and is a little embarrassed to be chatting with her.

"Thanks for being here with Dad."

"My Sammy loves parties."

Teddy was being harsh. He decides to lighten up. "That's the truth."

She awkwardly feeds the old man artichoke hearts wrapped in bacon. Grease drips down his pocked chin.

A group of kids runs by. Teddy recognizes one of them as Augie's son and wonders if any more of them are his grandchildren. Both the younger and older man smile as they pass.

"You're a lucky man, Mr. Teddy. Look, Sammy, at all those yummy babies."

The old man grunts.

Teddy is beyond uncomfortable, and whatever this is—a dream, a vision, a jump in time—he wants it to feel good.

"Well, enjoy the night."

As Teddy walks away, the nurse nuzzles into his father's neck, whispering over the loud music.

He is headed to the bar. Or the bathroom. Anywhere to put some space between himself and his father and that increasingly disturbing nurse. He's ashamed that once, years ago, he assumed they would have sex, and he would need to fire her. She was oddly alluring, and there was a time he enjoyed hearing "Mr. Teddy" in her thick accent. Is this part of becoming a better man? He's not looking at every woman as an object up for grabs. He is actually seeing the person in front of him. Looking at them. Listening to them. The more he is around the nurse, the more he wants to stay away.

He doesn't get far. The DJ is calling him to the dance floor. "Let's all take our seats and kick off dinner with a welcome and toast from none other than Teddy Maine!"

A sea of clapping bodies parts, making a path for him to the mic. Their cheers are muffled as they propel him forward. Philip stands in the back. He's not clapping but slowly sipping on one drink too many. Teddy takes the microphone and is silent. He knows hundreds of eyes are on him, but he can't see them under a harsh spotlight.

"Hello," he says, lacking all charm.

A few smart-asses yell out "Hi!" from the dark crowd.

"Ummmm." His breathing carries over the cheap sound system. A few more whoops and whistles from the crowd as the moment grows more uncomfortable.

"Ah, I don't know how I got here." He finds his voice. "I hope I never have to leave. Being here with my family, with all of you, I don't deserve it. I'm the luckiest man in the room. Okay . . . the second-luckiest man in the room." He looks toward his nameless son-in-law as the crowd laughs. "Nora." He chokes up. "Sweet Nora. You are so beautiful today. Every day, you're beautiful and kind. Goodness walking around for all of us to steal from. I needed to be better for you, but you loved me in spite of myself. Whatever this magic is that I'm living right now, I won't take it for granted. I won't take any of it for granted ever again."

He can't get another word out and is completely overwhelmed with emotion. An adulthood's worth of gratitude. Nora rushes to his side, and the room explodes with cheers as they hug and share the perfect wedding day moment. She grabs the mic from his hand.

"I love you so much, Daddy."

He attempts to make a graceful exit. Random hands pat him on the back as he stumbles toward the door, wiping at his face. Nora's fresh husband joins her, and they continue thanking their guests.

He makes it through a blurry maze to the outside. He steps onto the expansive stone balcony. He takes a few breaths of cold air and pats his legs, searching for a pack of smokes. That will calm his nerves. He looks around and spies Elizabeth smoking alone.

"You know those will kill you," he jokes as he cautiously approaches.

"Something has to."

She offers him one. He takes it rather than digging into his own pockets. Does he even have cigarettes? He has no recollection of getting dressed for this big night.

He's still collecting himself as she lights his cigarette.

"I liked your speech." There's no hostility in her voice. There's plenty of indifference.

It doesn't matter. Just hearing her voice makes him well up all over again. He takes a long drag and waves her compliment off.

"I'm a mess."

They both chuckle.

He gathers his composure. "You look beautiful. Truly."

"Thanks. I'm glad we're here. You're wrong. You do deserve this. All of this."

Teddy's eyes close as he attempts to keep his bursting heart together. They are a "we" again. He breathes deeply and counts backward to ground himself before he floats away.

He's smiling as his eyes open. He's in the living room. Trish is at the sink scrubbing crusted pineapple and ham grease out of a pan. The kids just left. There are still dishes to clear on the table. He's too busy riding an emotional high to be concerned with which now he's in.

He joins his wife in the kitchen. "Sorry. Dozed off."

She smiles, keeping her attention on the dirty pan.

"Can I help?" He yawns.

"Go to bed. I'll be there soon."

He kisses her on the neck and heads down the hallway toward the bedroom.

A woman waits for him in the dark. Emily's mother stands in the same spot his mother did a few nights ago. He catches himself before he can fall backward when he sees her. He mumbles frantically, trying to get his brain to register what or who is in front of him. She holds something shiny in her hand. It catches the little bit of light coming down the hall from the living room.

It's a letter opener. Even in the near darkness, he can see it's the same letter opener his mother used to slice open her hand. Emily's mother's body rocks ever so slightly. Without warning, she holds the dull blade to her neck. It glides through her throat. Dark, thick blood sputters and pumps from the opening. Teddy yells, and falls trying to get to her. He scratches at the wood floor, trying to get back on his feet.

He snaps awake in his office. The chair next to him is empty. The office is bright with sunlight. The afternoon rays highlight the dust. He must have fallen asleep while watching the play with Emily. He's filled with melancholy, realizing Nora's wedding was just a dream. There's also a hint of determination. He can make that a reality. Elizabeth is back. They all had a wonderful dinner. This play will be finished. That bitch will never publish her book. He'll stitch back together his busted mind and relationships. He'll find a space for Emily. They need each other.

The pages of the play are scattered on the floor. They must have slid off his lap when he dozed off. He collects them, trying to put them back in order. A note on the last page catches his eye. In red Philip has written:

Emily? What's the point?

It's underlined for emphasis.

What's the point? What's the point!? Teddy has never been good at accepting criticism, but Philip is usually an exception. Not this time. He snatches up the pages and runs out the door.

He's too focused on the four words written in red to notice life around him on the subway.

What's the point?

Who the hell does he think he is? He's profited off Teddy for decades, and this is what he has to say about the work that is killing him slowly from the inside out? What's the point? What's the point of having a no-talent ass around to cash his checks and pick up after him?

Anger burns through his body. The rage is intense. Is this part of getting old? Losing his mind? There's no longer a range of emotions. It's all-consuming or nothing. A fire close to spreading out of control rages under his skin. He doesn't notice the woman sitting across from him stroking a dead cat on her lap. He doesn't see the blood dripping onto the floor every time the businessman next to him opens his mouth. There's a baby crying in a stroller. If he looked closer, he would see there are holes where the eyes should be. He's always been too self-centered to collect the breadcrumbs life leaves for him.

He gets off the train, oblivious to the crowd around him all dressed in the same black suits. He bumps into a homeless man at the top of the stairs. He doesn't stop to notice his mangled, bloodied feet poking out from his soiled suit. His singular focus is to get to Philip and fire him.

He makes it to the theater doors in record time, not stopping for traffic. He takes the steps two at a time to the office.

Philip isn't alone. He's with a woman Teddy would recognize if he looked. She's bending over his desk. Their closeness is strange in an office setting.

"Teddy!" Philip looks up as he bursts through the door. "Meet our new—"

"What's the point?" He throws the pages at Philip.

Philip and the woman exchange a glance, and she quickly exits.

Philip struggles to understand what is going on. "Buddy—"

"You've been out to get me from the start. You never wanted this project finished. You—"

"What are you talking about?"

"I read your notes. You're a real piece of shit."

Philip scrambles to collect the pages. "You weren't supposed to see that. Where did you get this—"

"Do you hate everything I do, or just this?"

Philip shifts his tone from peacekeeper to parent. Teddy hates it, but it always works.

"Would you calm down? Sit down. I love the play."

Teddy isn't buying what he's selling.

"I like it. Very much. You know better than to read my notes. Shit. I don't even remember what I wrote."

Teddy sits down hard. He hangs his head in his hands. It's amazing how fast Philip can put his fire out. Perhaps that's why he lets it rage. He knows where to go to get back in control.

Philip continues. "You said yourself that it isn't finished."

"I don't know." Teddy is now letting pity take up all the space his anger formerly occupied.

"Is it finished?"

He doesn't answer but shrugs his shoulders, defeated.

Philip joins him on the other side of his desk. He puts his hand on his rounded shoulders.

"There's great stuff here. You know that. The family dinner? Really strong. In fact, that's where the heart is. And then the—"

"What are you talking about?" He is so exhausted from being confused. If the last stop in going crazy is giving in, he's ready.

Philip changes course. "Why Emily?"

"Because." He winces and rubs his head. Constantly playing a game of mental chess with yourself takes its toll.

"You all right?"

"A headache. It's nothing."

Philip holds up the page with his red note underlined for emphasis. "What's the point? Why is she there?"

"She's everything." Teddy is focused on rubbing his head.

"To you."

The words stew in a heavy pause.

Philip presses on. "Why? Why her? Why not Sylvia Plath?"

Elizabeth didn't love Sylvia Plath.

"We've had this conversation."

"You've never been able to answer—"

"She needs me."

"Who, Emily Dickinson?" Philip chuckles.

"She deserves a better ending." If he weren't so exhausted, if his head wasn't pounding, he'd tell Philip about their recent excursions. They'd be imaginary research breakthroughs, of course.

Philip doesn't skip a beat, stopping Teddy's momentum before it can start. "You've got to cut it."

Teddy is stunned. "Cut it? She's the whole damn play!"

"What? No, no, no. You've been working so hard you can't see the forest for the trees. She's really not that big of a through line. She's a distraction, really—"

Teddy opens his mouth to protest but can't. He doesn't trust any-thing he's read or seen. He has no idea what's really in those pages.

"Ted, you're no Dickinson scholar. Leave that to the gals at Dartmouth. Look, I don't want to push this, but the rumors are out there. The book is dead, but the rumors will hang around. It's bullshit, but you know how this town works. Let this be so absolutely *you* that no one believes that ghostwriter shit. You. Teddy Maine. There is no-body else who can tell your stories. Not now. Not ever. Make us believe that. It's not that big of a rewrite, really."

Philip has been anxiously waiting to have this conversation, and now he lets it all spill out. He doesn't know if this is the right time, but Teddy has seen his hand, so he has to play it.

Teddy's tone is soft and resigned. "You hated this idea from the start."

Philip's laugh is quick and genuine. He seems to have gotten through to him. "Hate's a strong word." He leaves Teddy's side and starts to gather his things. "You look like shit. Let's finish talking in the car and get you home."

"No. I'll take the train."

"You sure?" He waits for his reaction, a small nod. "You got something?"

"For what?"

"For your head? I've got . . ." Philip's voice trails off as he looks for bottles in his top drawer.

"I'm good."

While Philip's attention is still in the drawer Teddy grabs an orange bottle from his pocket and pops two pills in his mouth. He swallows hard, without water. He doesn't know what he just took, but anything should help the pounding.

Philip zips his bag and focuses back on his friend. "I get it. You fell down a rabbit hole. Fell in love with a dead girl. Isn't that her shtick?"

He walks to the door. Teddy remains dejected in his chair.

"Keep the Emily stuff," Philip says. "It's good. Maybe even great.

Once we have a hit, and the dust settles, get back to your passion project. She'll still be there."

"What about the board? The marketing?"

"If it works, no one will give a shit. They want butts in the seats. You need a win. The PR girls will love this."

Philip opens his arms in a grand gesture and barks in an overly dramatic voice, like a master of ceremonies in a strip-mall circus, "*The story he was born to tell. Groundbreaking playwright Teddy Maine shocks the world, abandoning his highly anticipated literary-historical-poetic thingy, which will be very fine someday, to finally sharing all the family secrets!*" He poses. "See, it sells itself. Let's get out of here."

Philip flips the light switch, and Teddy exits in the dark.

Chapter 14

He hustles down the block. He needs to get home before the pills kick in. The subway is full. He should have gotten a ride with Philip. He's cold. He left the house in nothing but a short-sleeved T-shirt. All his missed opportunities, little mistakes, are starting to add up, even the mundane. He sits shoulder-to-shoulder with strangers. As much as he hates being this close, actually touching, he's not going to stand for anyone. He's tired and the oldest around. He's earned this seat. Every sway and bump pushes him into a stranger. Each time the doors open, more people get on. Nobody leaves.

He looks out the window, only to see reflections of the bodies around him. He needs to escape. He can feel every emotion on the train. He hears every whispered prayer. He wants to feel nothing. He breathes in hot air. It carries a hint of incense and hair product with a dash of body odor. It's thick and weighs him down. He fumbles in his pocket for the orange bottle. Does it have a label? Will it offer any clues to what he's feeling? It's not all bad, but he feels more unpredictable than you would want to while riding a full subway old and alone.

Even when blackout drunk, he is propped up by bravado. A confidence that is only sometimes earned. Right now, he feels fragile. Exposed. He's missing more than a sweater but a layer of skin. He's a foot shorter. He's a little boy lost in a department store, and with all the bodies surrounding him, there isn't a security guard in sight.

His heart rate is rising. Is this fear or a side effect? He distracts himself by rubbing the soft fabric of his shirt between his fingers. His pupils are dilated. The light hurts. Burning halos flash with each blink. He shuts his eyes and waits for the fire rings to subside without a new light source. His only focus is keeping the blazing light out. He falls into a bleak sleep.

It's late. He's in children's pajamas. His sister flips through magazines on the floor at his feet. She's older. He must be, too. Keys in the door alert them to their parents' return. Both of their small backs sit up straight.

His parents are arguing. His mother's voice is slurred, his father's steady. His shoes echo on the marble tile as he walks to the living room.

"Abigail." His voice precedes him. "Abigail. It's time for bed."

She hesitates before stacking up her reading materials.

"Sam!" The urgency of his mother's voice stops everything. His father sighs and continues toward his daughter.

Teddy is the only one listening to his mother's cries. He slips off the sofa and goes to her. She's pacing in the entryway. Her heavy stage makeup is streaked with sweat and tears. She must have worn a wig during rehearsal; her hair is pinned in little circles close to her scalp. She doesn't notice her young son. Nobody does.

In a moment of clarity, she grabs a silver letter opener from a credenza. Without hesitation she squeezes her eyes shut and drags the rounded blade over the skin of her hand. It's too dull. She winces as just a drop of red wells on her pink palm. Eyes wide, she forces the metal into her flesh and pulls and scoops her way from thumb to little finger. A waterfall of dark purple rushes down her forearm as she holds her hand close to her heart.

"Sam! Help! Help!"

His father reluctantly returns to tend to his wife.

"I'm hurt."

"What did you do!" Once the severity of her injury comes into focus, he runs to her. His shoes skid on the blood pooling around her pumps.

"Goddamn it." He is equal parts alarmed and annoyed.

He seizes his keys from a decorative bowl on the credenza and ushers his wounded wife to the car.

"Abigail!" she screams as she's pushed out the door. "Look after your brother!"

His head bobs as he wakes. The train is empty. His eyes dart across the empty seats. Where is he? He instructs his arms to pat his pockets for his phone and wallet. They don't move. Half of his brain remains in a deep sleep. His eyes close and open to a crowded car. Only a few moments have passed. He relaxes. The next time he blinks, his lids stay down.

Trish calls him to the door. It's his sister. The two women have only met through photographs.

"What are you doing here?" Teddy doesn't give her a chance to answer. "How long have you been in town?"

She starts to cry. Teddy does not invite her in.

The person next to him hits his legs with shopping bags as they exit the train. His eyes flutter open, taking in shredded fluorescent light.

His mother is on the floor, curled up on a tasseled Persian pillow. She's in a silk robe and long nightgown. Lipstick stains her wineglass. Red wine stains the skin around her mouth.

"It's your turn, son."

He's playing cards with his father. A half dozen bottles of Coke litter the table next to him. His teenage sister sneaks in the front door. It's a very heavy door that doesn't lend itself well to sneaking. His father sets down his cards.

"Abigail?" His father's questions always sound like accusations.

She doesn't respond and runs to her room. Her feet are fast and loud as she rushes up the carpeted stairs. His father stands when she slams her door. Without looking back at Teddy, he heads to the second floor.

"Get out!" Teddy can hear his sister scream.

His father's voice is too low to make out what he's saying. Their footsteps pound above him. He goes to his mother. Luckily, she passed out near the record player. He thumbs through a box of albums, careful not to disturb her. He starts the machine and plugs in headphones too big for his ears. He lies on the floor by his mother, stretching the cord attached to the record player above. He falls asleep in his clothes listening to The Monkees.

The train sparks as it turns underground. Without a neighbor's shoulder to bounce off, his limp body sways in his seat. His head bobs from side to side. He snaps awake just before falling during a tight turn. He's alone. He massages his face vigorously. This isn't real. The train was just packed. Another turn, and he tips over.

His sister cries at his front door. "Teddy, please."

Trish stands behind him and motions to him to let her in. He shakes his head.

"I'm sorry. I'm not doing this."

He's not sorry. He shuts the door.

He opens his eyes wide and sees nothing but his reflection on the dirty window across from him. The train is empty. He's never been alone on the subway before. It's terrifying. He stands quickly to search for other passengers and a way out. He pushes through the double doors into the next car. There are two women sitting close to each other. His heart slows a bit. He can only see the backs of their heads. He doesn't hesitate to rush to them for help. He needs to find out where he is.

"Excuse me." He's not one to talk to strangers, but he's got to get home to ride out this high.

He stops at their seat. He opens his mouth, but no words come out. It's his sister and Emily. Both are dressed the same as the last time he saw them. They hold hands without looking up at him. Neither have a mouth.

He stumbles backward. The train stops, and he leaps out the doors, sprinting through the empty tiled tunnel.

Out on the street, he takes a minute to catch his breath. Luckily, he's only a few blocks from his usual stop. He walks the rest of the way home. It doesn't strike him as odd that he is the only person on the sidewalk in the middle of Manhattan.

He makes it home. The brisk walk has sobered him up a bit. That's disappointing.

There's a light on over the kitchen sink.

He yells for his wife. "Trish?"

He flips switches on in the kitchen and digs through a row of junk drawers.

"Trish? Where's the address book?"

He lifts his head, expecting to see her. No one is there.

"Trish?"

He explores the apartment, turning on every light he passes. Every room is empty. In fact, it doesn't seem like anyone has been home for a long time. Digital clocks are all flashing a different wrong time. The grandfather clock hasn't ticked or tocked in some time. Confused, he heads back to the kitchen. He pulls out his phone and changes the blinking light on the microwave to 8:05.

He has one drawer left to check. From underneath random

envelopes and rolls of Scotch tape, he pulls out his address book and flips to find his sister's phone number.

"We're sorry. You have reached a number that is disconnected or no longer in service."

He stands alone in his chef's kitchen and misses his older sister for the first time.

He has no idea if she's alive or dead. Sick or healthy. She looked much older than her age the last time he saw her crying on his door-step. Was she living in Texas? She has no next of kin aside from him. Wouldn't he be listed on a form somewhere? A stranger would call him if she were dead or in the hospital. Right? Probably not. He's made it crystal clear over the years that he should not be used as anyone's emergency contact.

He talks to her as if she's a ghost. He's not as sober as he thinks.

"I should have listened. I should have let you in."

He wonders if he can summon any ghost like he summons Emily. Wait. Is Emily a ghost? He's never asked or thought about it much. Obviously, she died, but she isn't dead to him. She's flesh and blood.

"I'm listening now."

He waits impatiently. He's acting silly and emotional. Two things he will not tolerate from anyone, especially himself. He grabs a bottle of liquor from a cabinet that houses bowls and colanders. It's amazing where things end up these days.

He pours a glass and drinks it in one gulp. He pours another for the road. He collapses as he passes the marble kitchen island.

He's on the floor. His face burns like it's been hit by shrapnel. He must have banged the corner of the island on his way down. His chest rises and falls with shallow breaths. His drink pools by his face, and broken glass has scattered on the floor. Is this how they will find him? The space underneath him is warm. He is in pain but also incredibly comfortable. He doesn't know if his arms can't move or won't move. The tile under his exposed skin itches. As he drifts away, he attempts to focus on its surface, trying to stay alert. He realizes it's not expensive tile but stained, matted carpet.

His mother and father are shouting. Teddy and his sister sit dutifully in their pajamas, waiting in the formal living room. Teddy is there, watching himself as a child. He is visiting this memory, not reliving it. Being a guest in his own mind leaves him unsteady. He holds on to the back of a velvet couch.

His parents' voices are muffled. He can't make out much of what they're saying. Can they see him? He has made these travels before. He doesn't remember if he's an active participant or a trapped observer.

"Hello?"

No one responds. Knowing he's safe, he gets into the action. He circles his parents, watching their faces closely. They are stuck. Both have yelled their demands, and there is no peace. Just a surrender.

His mother ends the standoff. "Fine!"

She swallows two pills and sits on one of the smooth love seats. She may be done arguing, but she is not done being angry. She looks like she will never not be angry again. Her eyes are narrowed and focused on Teddy's father. She takes out a cigarette and has a hard time sparking the lighter. A moment later, her head slumps, and she falls to her side on the love seat, dropping the unlit cigarette in the shag carpeting. Teddy kneels next to her face to catch her warm breath on his cheek. This can't be happening in real time. No pills work that fast. He smooths her hair from her face and stands to survey the scene still unfolding.

His father is sitting very close to Abigail. She's humoring him as he talks about the breakthrough that happened during rehearsal. In another year, she'll get up and run away. Slam the door. Like Elizabeth, Abigail slammed the door a hundred times or more before she slammed it for the last time. At one point, his father threatened to take it off the hinges. He could never go through with it. Growing girls need their privacy.

The young boy stares at his horizontal mother. His fingers move secretly, tugging at a string on the throw pillow covering his lap. He's using all his energy trying to camouflage in plain sight.

"Hey." Teddy snaps toward the boy's fresh face. Nothing.

He remembers being an angry child. A bored child. Moody and entitled. He doesn't remember ever being so still. A frozen deer surrounded by hunters.

His father's hand lingers high on Abigail's thigh. Her nightgown is short, bordering on inappropriate. A sparkly purple unicorn relic from her tween past. Her body rests in the same desperate rigidness as her brother sitting across the room.

Teddy looks around, alarmed. These kids aren't safe.

"Mother." He calls loudly. He knows he's invisible, but he has to try. "Wake up."

"What's going to happen?" He sits close to himself. "I don't remember any of this. What's happening?"

Abigail speaks. Teddy hasn't heard the voice of either child yet. "I'm not tired."

"Of course you are. It's late." His father's voice is loud but warmed by many post-rehearsal drinks.

"I think I'll read. Just for a little bit."

"Well, I'm going to bed."

Abigail's face softens with relief. Her father stands, and she quickly grabs a book from the side table. She has no intention of opening it. Young Teddy holds his breath as his father walks by. He stops before leaving the room.

"Let's go, then," he calls to his daughter.

She snaps into high alert and fumbles with the book. "I'm reading."

"Who's going to put you to bed?"

What? No one needs to put either child to bed. Abigail babysits. She can certainly tuck herself in.

"Mom." She's panicked.

"Your mother is taking care of your brother."

No, she's not. What the hell is going on?

"Mom. Mommy!" Abigail calls out desperately.

"She can't hear you." Teddy's father delights in this little drama.

"Do something." Teddy scolds the little boy. "Help her."

Abigail continues to yell for her mother to wake up. "Mommy, put me to bed!" She cries more like a four-year-old than a fourteen-year-old.

Teddy stands between her and their father. "Don't." He's not sure what he's trying to stop. "Leave her alone!"

"Abigail! Get up right now!" Teddy's father has sobered up enough to lose his patience.

She stands immediately.

"Wait. Abby." Teddy doesn't know what else to do. "You don't have to go with him."

But she does. He's starting to get it. It's a lifetime too late. Katherine said it in her ridiculous TED Talk. Survivors of this type make unsympathetic victims. Unreliable witnesses. Terribly broken people who often keep themselves together in only the most toxic or destructive ways. It's not entirely Teddy's fault for turning his back on his sister. She made it impossible not to. Stealing. Lying. Leaving every grown-up problem or decision that had to do with the family to him. Now he understands. Now it doesn't matter.

Abigail is the only one who moves. She walks, crying, to their father. Teddy watches as her tears turn into a dark, thick substance. As her lashes flutter, mud and flies pour out from the inner corners. Her father comes close and wipes her tears, smearing the wet dirt on her face.

"Good girl."

He takes her hand and leads her to bed. "Children must obey their fathers."

Something is crawling on his face. A dozen tiny black legs trek down his jawline. He instinctually swats the air as he comes to. There's blood on the floor from where he cracked his head. There are flies everywhere. He gets to his feet as fast as his pounding head will allow. As he races to move out of the swarm, he cuts his heel on a shard of glass. He yells and hops down the hall.

In the guest bathroom, he pulls down a Turkish hand towel and ruins it by wrapping it around his bleeding foot. He soaks another one in cold water and holds it to the hole on his face. He banged himself up good. Oh, God. Does he need to call for help? Who would he call? What would they say? Would he ever be left alone again? How long did his father live like this? Falling. Forgetting. Losing time. Teddy feels like he is running out of time.

Footsteps walk by the bathroom.

"Trish?"

Thank God.

"Trish? I'm hurt."

He opens the door, holding the wet towel to his head. A woman is walking away from him. It's not his wife.

"Hello?"

He takes off after her, limping on his injured foot.

"Who's there?"

The woman stops and turns. It's Katherine.

"Hi, Teddy."

He drops the towel. "What are you doing here?"

"You're hurt." She comes close to him and inspects his face. "I'm with a client."

"Client? My wife?"

The doctor's laugh is condescending. "Now that would be a conflict of interest." She takes a few steps and opens his office door. "Join us."

They step into a large auditorium. It's red. Empty, plush, red seats. Red carpet. Light wood paneling on the walls and the floors. Wide stairs lead to a brightly lit stage. Someone is reclining in what looks like a dentist's chair. It's Emily. Katherine helps Teddy to the stage.

"What is this?" His voice is laced with pain.

Katherine ignores the question and tends to a tray of sharp, shiny tools on a shiny steel table next to her patient. Emily's eyes are covered with a dark wrap.

She talks to her doctor, describing her symptoms. Her voice is also laced with pain. *"Drowning is not so pitiful as the attempt to rise."*

"I see. And is this when the pain in your eyes started?" Katherine shifts her attention to Teddy and whispers, "The act of 'rising' is a metaphor, of course." She lowers Emily's chair. "Tell me more about your father."

Emily is talking fast. She's nervous. Teddy can't recall if he's ever seen her nervous. She's using her hands to communicate as a substitute for her eyes.

"He was my host. He was my guest. I never to this day if I invited him could tell, or he invited me. Though by his awful residence has human nature been."

Katherine hums a confirmation. "Relax. Take some nice, cleansing breaths."

They breathe together as she holds up a silver drill. Its spinning edge shines under the stage lights. The shiny bit is much too large to fill a cavity.

Emily continues gesturing. *"I held it so tight that I lost it."*

Katherine attempts to unwrap Emily's eyes. Emily pushes her hands away in protest.

"Shame is the shawl of pink in which we wrap the soul to keep from infesting eyes the elemental veil—"

Katherine calms her. "You don't need this anymore. Deep breaths..."

She takes the covering from her eyes. Emily squeezes them shut tight and balls her fists at her sides.

Teddy pushes through his confusion. He's still bleeding from head to toe. "Wait."

Katherine pushes a button, and the drill squeals and rotates.

"Emily, what is going on? She's not that type of doctor." He's frantic.

Emily talks through clenched teeth. *"When pushed upon a scene repugnant to her probity, shame is the tint divine."*

"Just relax." Katherine pries open Emily's left eye. In her other hand, the drill.

"No!" Teddy stumbles as he attempts to rush the stage. He is totally useless.

"Relax," Katherine sings as she inserts the spinning instrument into Emily's eye.

He's on the floor in the bathroom. He's holding a blood-soaked towel. His body is stiff from resting on another tiled floor. How long has he been out? There's a black-and-blue crater on the side of his face. The center is fleshy pink.

"Jesus Christ."

He sits on the toilet and pulls a piece of glass from his heel. He needs to clean himself up. He has to get to Emily, make sure that she's okay. There is no way Katherine was just drilling her eyes in an auditorium attached to Teddy's living room. He knows that. But he also knows what he feels, and he's starting to trust that more. He rummages through the medicine cabinet and vanity drawers. There's nothing to help his head. Adrenaline pumps through his body and pushes him out the door to find help, or, better yet, to find a way to help himself.

It's late. He stumbles down the building steps and looks around. What does he do now? He should search on his phone. Yes. Find a nearby clinic or emergency room. He reaches in his pockets. Damn. It's upstairs in the apartment. He can't climb the stairs again. He limps down the sidewalk, hoping for the best.

He's in luck. There's a big-box pharmacy in sight. He can stock up there and hurry home. The lights in the pharmacy are brutal. He's tried to cover his wound with a hat, but he can feel it cooking under the harsh lights. He's wearing rain boots big enough to fit a towel under his pierced heel. He doesn't know how many days he's been in these clothes. They are matted to his body with sweat and blood.

He shuffles through the aisles, foraging for first-aid supplies. He fills his basket and waits at the counter. As his wait extends, he wonders if he's the only one in the store. Is he really still on the bathroom floor bleeding to death? A young pharmacist calls out from the back.

"Be right there!"

Thank God.

She enters in a white coat. She's pretty, with an unfortunate mole on her chin.

"Sorry, short-staffed—oh, my gosh. Are you okay?"

She doesn't seem to know whether to jump over the counter or run away from him.

"I think you need a doctor," she says, straining to get a good look from a safe distance.

Teddy puts his basket on the counter. "I fell." He unloads small boxes of bandages.

"Have a seat over there." She points to an area at the end of the counter in a small nook for consultations.

He's grateful to be off his feet. After a moment, she joins him, wearing gloves and with an armful of more appropriate supplies. She smiles and gets to work, cleaning the area gingerly.

"I was an EMT." Her voice is soft and reassuring. "If you go to the ER, they might give you something for the pain. Without a script, the best I can do is ibuprofen."

She flushes out the center with a water bottle, pats the area dry, and covers what she can with antiseptic ointment. Teddy can feel the warmth of her touch through the latex. He leans into her hands.

"Is there someone I can call for you?"

"You've done more than enough already. Thank you."

She knows better than to ask too many questions. "Let me bandage this for you, and I can get an Uber."

"I'm fine. I live down the block."

She's skeptical. The only things close are multimillion-dollar apartments. She applies thick, clean gauze and secures it with tape. It stands out as the only clean thing on his person.

"You'll want to change the dressing every few hours. Sooner, if pus leaks through. If anything looks green or discolored, be sure to get it checked out."

She packs up the boxes of supplies. Teddy goes to his pocket for his wallet.

"No. No." She waves off his attempt to pay.

He smiles a grateful smile and works hard to walk out with a normal gait. He couldn't stand any more kindness and would break down if she spent more time caring for him, fixing up his foot. He makes a note to come back when he's better and presentable to thank her properly.

The walk home is quick. Practically instant. That changes when he gets inside. The elevator to his apartment is moving in slow motion. Did he push the button? He reaches his hand out, and the car jumps and sputters up. He braces himself. The commotion puts pressure on his bloodied foot. He needs better protection than a rain boot.

He feels ten years older than he did this morning, and this morning he didn't feel that great. He doesn't want to see Emily. The urge to be with her, confirm her safety, has been replaced by his need to rest. He unlocks the door and doesn't call for his wife. He limps through the dark without pausing at his office. Right now, he needs to fall into bed. If he doesn't wake up, that would be all right. If he sees the morning, he'll try to put himself back together.

His recent injuries aren't the only things causing him this immense pain. This impossible exhaustion. It's the guilt of abandoning his sister. The years of watching her suffer are causing a collapse from the inside out. A stranger, the young girl at the pharmacy who should have been afraid of him, just showed him more kindness than he ever gave Abigail. He wishes he had lost his mind before putting those dark puzzle pieces together.

He sits on the bed and winces as he takes off his boot. The towel is soaked through with blood. He falls onto his pillow, expecting a short journey with a soft ending. Instead, his head bounces after hitting a hard surface. He cries out and disappears into sleep.

It's a gorgeous night in the city. His senses are heightened. He's taking it all in even as he struts at a fast pace. There's a hum in the air from millions of people turning on millions of light bulbs. The sky is navy. The smell of fried food mixes with the stench from overflowing dumpsters. He's alive in the city he loves.

He saunters into his favorite bar. It's a secret place where people do secret things. He loves it here. He feels like he's drinking alone at the bottom of a well. Tonight is a special night. Tonight he's going to drink in a special room in his secret place.

A waitress with dark red lips and short bangs nods as he passes the thick wooden tables. The bartender's earlobes are adorned with hollow circles that stretch down to his neck. Teddy points toward a steel door on the back wall, and the decorated man buzzes him in.

He takes a seat in a metal chair behind a metal desk. He's alone in a dank interrogation room. A sparse space built for dark deals. He's happy waiting. The anticipation is a drug. His favorite drug.

The door buzzes open. Two men with dark hair dressed in boxy business suits hold a young girl up by her armpits. From the looks of her uniform, she hasn't made it home from school. Middle school, maybe, or ninth grade. Teddy communicates to the men by saying nothing. The deal is done.

Thank God, he's in his bed. For a moment, before he's fully awake, he's a blank slate. He needs to hold on to that feeling in order to make it through the day. The girl at the pharmacy did a good job. His head is already healing. He can feel his flesh merging like icebergs joining distant continents. His foot is throbbing and tender. He remembers hearing that feet can be the hardest things to heal. He hates walking with a limp. Each hobble reminds him he is brittle. Broken.

In spite of all this, he is happy to see the morning. Emily once told him, *"the longest day that God appoints will finish with the sun."* She's right. He's ready to talk to her. She's the only one who can carry some of his heavy burden. It's selfish, really, but he's never claimed to be anything else.

He hobbles across the hall to his office. Emily greets him at the door. She softly gasps at his appearance. She gently surveys the area around the bandage with her fingers.

She's curious and concerned. *"Somehow myself survived the night and entered with the day."*

"I'm okay."

She raises an eyebrow. *"Pain has an element of blank it cannot recollect when it begun or if there were a time when it was not."*

He rushes past her and drinks what's left of her tea sitting on his desk. He doesn't know the last time he put anything into his body. The little bit of hydration reminds him of his urgent need to see her.

"Are you okay?" He gets close and takes her face in his hands. "Your eyes?"

She doesn't know what he's talking about. She blinks playfully. He smiles and releases her.

"Philip wants to cut you out of the play."

This doesn't bother her. *"The absence of the witch does not invalidate the spell."*

Teddy never hears what she's saying. "It's about money. It always is."

"Someone prepared this mighty show to which without a ticket go."

He's not surprised at her indifference. He's starting to get that this project was never about her. "I stole your work. Why did you let me?"

She busies herself picking up the room. *"My wars are laid away in books. I have one battle more."*

"I don't know what he's talking about. I mean, I read it . . . I lived it . . . with you. These other scenes, I don't know what they are . . ." His voice trails off. He rarely doesn't put a fine point on his statements.

"Wonder is not precisely knowing and not precisely knowing not. A beautiful but bleak condition." She's assertive. Confident. Maybe it's because he's physically weak, but she has no problem taking charge.

"Something bad happened to my sister." He sits. "I let it happen and blocked it out all these years like a coward. A failure."

She shakes her head and soothes him. *"No. To flee from memory, had we the wings, many would fly."*

"You know what he did to her, my father." He takes a moment. "It happened to you, too."

Emily is quiet. After a beat she shakes it off with a smile. Her body language is loud and clear; she's shutting down the conversation.

"Are you going to tell me nothing happened? I've been there. I've seen him. I knew I recognized it right away. Something about him was just like my father. Bastards."

She's trying to keep a smile, blow off the conversation, but tears spring to her eyes. *"Nothing is the force that renovates the world."*

"I'm so sorry." He takes her hands. "I didn't help my sister. I can help you."

"Unto a broken heart no other one may go without the high prerogative itself hath suffered, too." She strokes his hand and appreciates his offer.

"It's the reason we're together. I'm sure of it."

She remains warm and kind but is readier than ever to end the conversation. *"God made no act without a cause."*

He starts to pace the room. "He should be punished. Your father. Should I call someone? There's a lady . . . at the museum." He's not making much sense. "People study you. Should I tell them?" He frantically finds a pen and paper. "Tell them yourself. Tell everyone." He hands her the writing tools. She smiles and puts them down.

"Mine enemy is growing old. I have at last revenge." She reaches up to brush hair away from his bandage. *"Anger as soon as fed is dead. 'Tis starving makes it fat."*

Teddy's voice sounds like it belongs to a little boy. "Did it happen a lot? I think—I know it happened a lot to my sister."

She leaves him sitting and walks to the window. He's not taking a hint. She firmly attempts to put the subject to rest. *"She died. This was the way she died. And when her breath was done, took up her simple wardrobe and started for the sun. Her little figure at the gate the angels must have spied, since I could never find her upon the mortal side."*

"I want to hurt them. Both of them. They deserve to suffer."

She keeps her gaze fixed out the window. *"The harm they did was short and since myself who bore it do forgive them, even as myself, or else forgive not me."*

Teddy wishes his father were well so he could hurt him. He *will* hurt him for this. He winces from a rumbling under his bandage. This draws Emily's attention back to him. She crosses the room quickly. She reaches toward his head but stops short from touching his open skin or leaking dressing.

She finds his body fascinating. *"Such are the inlets of the mind. His outlets would you see."*

"Shit." He touches the sticky spot.

He's embarrassed and worried. Emily is still as she watches him fall to the ground.

Chapter 15

He's in the back seat of a car. He doesn't know how he got there or where he's going. His hands fly to his face, and he feels fresh bandages. He looks down and sees he's wearing nice clean slacks. He's clean-shaven. His hair is still damp from the shower. Emily must have taken care of him. It feels like he's had a good night's sleep.

"You good, Mr. Maine?"

The driver glances in the rearview mirror and sees Teddy using his arms to brace himself against the doors.

"Yeah. Yes."

"Need me to pull over?"

The driver looks over his shoulder. His face is covered with bumps and boils. Teddy takes comfort in this hideous, familiar face. You don't forget a face like that.

"Charlie, right?"

He's delighted. "You remember."

"Guess so. Where are we going?"

Charlie's deep laugh shakes the sedan.

"Your theater. You forget about your own party?"

"Party?"

"Closing night."

"Of course." Teddy forces a chuckle. "Mind is playing tricks on me."

"You said that last time. Said you were going crazy. Feeling better?"

"Worse."

Charlie laughs. Teddy wasn't being funny. He smiles. Anything else would take too much effort. They drive in silence. Teddy uses the time to think of normal things to say to normal people. He won't be a crazy person. Not tonight. He has to find more opportunities to drop anchor, or he'll soon let himself be washed out with the tide.

The driver can't keep quiet long. He catches Teddy's reflection in the rearview. "Wow. Looks like you got banged up good."

Teddy grunts. "I fell."

They drive a bit more.

Charlie's voice is subdued. He's almost talking to himself. "I know what that's like."

"What?"

"Walking around hurt."

They arrive at the theater. Teddy gets out of the car and turns back to wave. Charlie lifts his hand to reciprocate. His right hand is a meaty, mangled mess. Skin hangs down in rotten flaps. There are remnants of some sort of medical covering, but it's soiled and torn. What's left seems to be grafted to raw skin. Teddy's jaw drops. He doesn't have time to ask any questions. People are shouting his name. So it's opening night, not closing night. Paparazzi push and shove for the best shot. Though, since it's not a movie premiere but opening night at a theater, there's actually only a handful of bulbs flashing. The small crowd parts. They are quiet as he shuffles by. He's doing his best to look his Teddy-est. It's not working.

Augie greets him at the door. "Jesus Christ, Dad." He goes to hug him but stops short. He doesn't want to hurt him. He looks like he could break. "We were worried."

Philip joins them. "What the shit happened to you? Who did that to your face?"

"It's nothing. I fell." He hobbles toward the bar. "And cut my foot."

The two men hang back, trying to make sense of Teddy's new look.

Philip joins him at the bar mid order. "How 'bout a club soda? You sure you're all right?"

Teddy is on autopilot. He can't think right now. He can't think of his sister's face or prepare the seething monologue he's going to perform for his father. The last words he'll ever speak to him. No. The only thing he can do right now is survive. He takes his whiskey without making eye contact.

"We'd better get to our seats."

The house is full. Teddy is numb to the concerned eyes trying to catch a glimpse of him. He would take his customary seat in the back corner, but his aching heel won't let him. He settles into the red velvet chair and does his best to drink without shifting the ice in his glass.

He pays no attention to what is happening onstage. Not even enough to criticize a missed beat or slow costume change. If Emily's words didn't get through to him, he certainly won't listen to his own. As *The Sins of the Father* trudges to its final bow, Teddy is oblivious to his own context. He makes sure to escape the audience before curtain call. He doesn't want to risk being called to the stage to say a few words.

He mills around the lobby as catering staff set up for a party. He catches his reflection. He should be embarrassed by his appearance, but it's the best he's looked in days. He hopes his bandage stays fresh throughout the festivities.

The audience erupts in applause. It's finally over. He's more interested in the food, which is all bullshit.

"What is this?" Teddy holds up a cracker smeared with something white and garnished with a purple petal.

A young waiter looks him up and down. "Are you . . . are you here for the show?"

"I wrote the show."

Teddy tosses the cracker and browses the next table. There's a tall red pyramid made of strawberries. He leans down to get a closer look. What happens if he takes one? How are they held together? His musings are interrupted by thin black legs. A large spider scurries up the structure. Teddy takes a hop back. Twelve more legs circle the ripe berries from the top down. Teddy calls over to the waiter, but he's drowned out by the audience rushing into the lobby.

Teddy floats in the eye of the storm. The crowd swirls around him, chatting and laughing. There are hugs and handshakes, dropped names and awkward introductions. He watches as people file by the flower-topped crackers and infested fruit. The pyramid is shrinking as fingers dig into its strawberry walls.

Elizabeth is one of the last to exit the theater. He waves across the room to her, his lifeboat.

She meets his gaze and heads to the ornate front doors.

"Dad." Augie has found him. He hands over a plate of food. "Eat something."

Teddy sniffs a cracker. "Where is your sister going?"

Augie is distracted. "Nora's in Nicaragua. Feeding elephants or something."

Philip, never far away, slides into the conversation. "They have elephants in Nicaragua?"

Trish is at the bar with a man Teddy doesn't recognize. They are standing closer than friends.

"I'm glad you're eating." Philip gives Teddy's shoulder a light squeeze.

Teddy keeps his eyes on his wife as he picks up the overpriced snack. Her face is soft. She's wearing more makeup than he remembers. The man next to her is short. Shorter than Teddy, anyway. He's wearing a sweater under a sport coat. Loafers. He smiles generously. He either has great teeth or implants. He's straight out of a hot grandpa catalog.

Something doesn't feel right. Something is moving. He looks down to find his hand covered in spiders. His food is overflowing with thin, black, dancing legs. He yells and drops his plate.

The swirling stops. Everyone is looking at him and the mess he made. Augie is quick to get on his knees to clean it up. The man he doesn't know helps Trish with her coat, and they leave. He follows them out. They are getting into a car by the time he makes it to the sidewalk.

Elizabeth is smoking by the doorway. She is the perfect distraction from worrying about his wife driving off with another man.

"Hi." He's out of breath.

She doesn't respond.

"What'd you think?"

She's not buying into his small talk and turns her head to exhale a puff of smoke.

"Look, maybe I shouldn't bring it up, but I thought we were good? Can't we move past this Jon drama?"

She puts out her cigarette. "That's cute."

"What?"

"That you think there ever was a Jon."

He yells her name as she turns her back and walks away. Augie finds him alone in the dark.

"There you are. Should I get you something else?"

"What?" He's a confused old man.

Augie is careful to remain calm. "To eat, Dad."

"No. I'm fine. Thank you."

Augie tries to make small talk out of a very big topic. "Philip said you guys talked. It's a great play, Dad. Really. It's going to be one of your best."

Teddy always considers his first drafts final. Augie suggesting his greatness in the future tense doesn't bother him. Right now, what is bothering him is the way his son keeps pronouncing "Dad." It makes him feel like he's not invited to his own party.

"He wants me to cut the whole damn thing." He digs in his pockets. He doesn't know what he's looking for.

"No . . . no. Just the Emily stuff. There's so much more there."

Stuff?

Augie continues, thinking he's on a roll. He takes a page from Philip's book and keeps it light. Breezy.

"The prop department is going to be pissed. They hate dealing with food." He laughs.

Teddy doesn't know what's so funny, but he laughs with him. It's easier.

"What made you think of ham? And pineapple? Is that a real thing?"

Teddy stops laughing. "Huh?"

"Feels real 1950s. I love it."

"What are you talking about?" Teddy is not amused.

"Act Two. The dinner? With that big ham covered in pineapple? The whole place will smell. It's great. Expensive, but great."

"That's in the play?" Teddy doesn't realize he said that out loud.

"Yeah, Dad. It's like forty pages of it."

There he goes, saying "Dad" again.

"No." Teddy is angry. "That happened. That was last week."

Augie bites his lower lip. "Has anyone checked you out? After your fall?"

"I think I should go home."

Finding out that recent dinner with his family never happened makes him sadder than it should. He's lost something he never had.

Like magic, a cab comes by. Teddy holds out his arm.

His son pleads. "No. Let me call you a car."

The cab pulls over. Teddy opens the door to the back seat.

"How about I come with you?"

Teddy waves him off and shuts the door. He breathes heavily and wills himself not to cry. Losing his mind has been painful. This is the first time it has been devastatingly sad.

The ride home is long and dark. No light shines through the windows. The dinner never happened. He's not going to question it. That would require walking back through too many moments he's trying not to remember. He adds it to the pile of evidence stacking up to prove his stale state of mind. He embarrassed himself tonight. He knows that. Maybe there's medication he can take? Maybe going to rehab, actually getting sober, could buy him a few more good years? Staying sober, that would be a hefty price. He's not sure the investment would be worth the return.

He's glad this trip is taking an unusually long time. He's in no hurry to get home.

As a child he had a recurring nightmare of being in the long back-seat of a car. He would lean forward to talk to his mother, just to find an empty seat. No one was driving. He was all alone. How long had he been sitting there thinking he was safe? That felt worse than crashing.

He's on his way to an empty apartment. He's sure Trish won't be there. If Emily isn't there, perhaps he'll kill himself. The gun in the bottom drawer is waiting for him. He should take more comfort in that. He might be alone, but he's still in control.

He's woozy. If he's debating life and death, he really needs to eat something. The physical pain of hunger and torn skin is starting to eclipse all other thoughts. The bandage on his head is growing moist. He opens the door before the cab fully stops. He rolls out, barely managing to stay upright. He's lucky he's in front of his building. He was getting out regardless.

He hopes to make it upstairs without seeing anyone but isn't certain he can do it alone. The sound in his ears is narrowing to a fine point. A high-pitched buzz. He pushes through the air like he's swimming. He drops his keys at the door. Miraculously, he doesn't pass out when he bends down to retrieve them.

He opens the refrigerator in the dark. There's nothing there but a half gallon of milk and some condiments. He chugs from the milk container. Bracing himself on the cold countertop, he rummages through the cabinets. There are two boxes of cereal. Both are mostly crumbs. He pours them into the first container he can find and adds the milk. He gulps it down without a spoon. How ridiculous of him to think there was ever anything more in this barren space. That there was ever warm food and laughter.

He consumes enough calories to keep him on his feet.

"Emily?"

He limps to his office. When he's dead, can he still be with her? A light turns on, and it spills into the hall. He picks up his pace.

She's working at his desk. She looks over and smiles. He sits down on the sofa, the least-used piece of furniture in the apartment. If he's in his office he's working, not relaxing.

"I thought, I actually thought I was a part of my family."

She sits next to him and almost sings; she's trying so hard to provide comfort. *"Opinion is a flitting thing, but truth outlasts the sun. If then we cannot own them both, possess the oldest one."*

"The truth is awful."

They sit quietly. After a moment, Emily reaches to the other side of the couch for a plaid blanket.

"I didn't know how much I wanted them. Wanted that sort of life. I don't think I've ever been happy."

Emily stands and helps him stretch out on the sofa. She slips off his shoes carefully.

She speaks softly. *"Within its reach though yet ungrasped. Desire's perfect goal."*

She covers him with the blanket, pulling it up to his chin.

"Will you stay with me?"

"This seems a home." She looks around the room. *"And home is not. I learned at least what home could be."*

"If I kill myself, will we be together?" He's close to sleep.

She smiles and shrugs. She strokes his hair and, like a mother telling her child there are no monsters under the bed, says, *"A coffin is a small domain."*

There's still work to be done. A final scene left to write. She'll make sure he finishes the play. His breathing grows slow and steady. He's safe to rest. He won't be looking for his gun or his bottle.

"Will equal glow and thought no more but come another day."

She leaves him to gather his strength for what comes next.

He's in the pantry with his mother and sister. They've made a nest on the cold tile floor with pillows and blankets. His mother is holding them close. She's smiling and singing. She's squeezing their arms a bit too tight and laughing a bit too loud for this to be fun. Teddy doesn't like being on the floor. A mouse could crawl across his legs any second. He's nervous sitting under the shelves of canned goods. What if his sister sneezes and knocks one down on his head?

His mother does a good job convincing him that this is all a grand adventure. In that dusty space in the back of the kitchen Teddy is presented a choice. Recognize that this isn't normal. That this is scary. That this is out of his control, and something bad might happen. Or, have an exciting, super fun night with Mommy. Scary things were often sold to him as exciting. Such a lucky boy to do such exciting and different things.

Abigail stays mostly quiet, but little Teddy is now having a ball camping out. He has butterflies in his stomach and squeals as his mother tickles him. She stops abruptly at the sound of a car door slamming. His father is home.

"Shhhh. Shhh. It's time to calm down."

"But Mama—"

Her smile is wide, her voice soft and firm. "We must be quiet. We're hiding from the dragon. As the prince and princess, you must keep the village safe."

His father enters the house loudly and yells his mother's name. He never enters a space without causing a disruption. Teddy begins to say something, but his mother covers his mouth. As his father's feet stomp through the place looking for his family, his mother whispers intensely, "The dragon will never think to find us here. Now, stay very still, and we'll win the game."

His father is shouting upstairs. "Abigail?"

"Shut your eyes, and in the morning, we'll surprise Daddy. But don't tell him our secret spot, or the dragon will know where to go next time."

If this game means going to sleep, Teddy doesn't want to play anymore.

"I don't care if we win. I want to play with my cars."

Doors are being opened and slammed shut.

"No. It's too late to play."

Teddy squirms in his mother's grip. "Then I want to sleep in my bed."

His young voice is threatening to get louder than a whisper. His mother covers his mouth.

"We're not leaving. Don't make another sound."

He goes to sleep promising himself that in the morning he's going to tell his father and ruin the game. He'll tell his father all their secret hiding spots so they can never play again.

The sound of women's voices wakes him. He's straddling the line of sleep and can't focus on the talking in his office. He shifts on the leather cushion. He wants to sit up, but his body is stuck. His eyes are too heavy to stay open. His mind is growing more alert as his body shuts down to rest. He hates this feeling. Trapped. The only way out is to give in. Next time his eyes open, hopefully both his mind and body will be able to wake.

He's walking through his childhood home. His last dream took place in the pantry off the huge kitchen in their beach house. Country estate. The type of place where incredibly wealthy New Yorkers spend their weekends. It was less of a dream and more of a replay from a group of memories he can only summon when deeply asleep. Now he surveys their penthouse apartment. He's a guest in this scene. An observer. A ghost. A time traveler. He doesn't like this. He doesn't like to watch.

There's commotion coming from the master suite. His mother is arguing with a child. It's him. He stands in the hall watching. He wants to wake up. He doesn't like being here or listening to his mother being yelled at. The child's voice is shrill and privileged. Why is she letting him talk to her like this?

"Teddy Bear, I'll be right there. Be patient."

Her voice is sticky-sweet, like syrup. She's racing through the bed-room, rummaging through nightstands and dresser drawers. Teddy waits impatiently in her walk-in closet. His favorite place to play.

"Mommy needs to find her pills." An edge creeps into her tone. "Do you have them?"

"No!"

She begins tossing items around the room. Teddy recognizes this level of panic. This level of need deep in the muscles for a pharmaceutical rescue. Heat rushes to his face as lace undergarments fall at his feet. He's about to step into the room and help her look when she holds up a green bottle filled with treasure.

"Found them!" she sings.

She shuts her eyes and exhales. Help is on the way. Teddy wonders what's in there. Uppers? Downers? She pops open the lid and empties the contents. Light bounces off small shards of glass in her hands. Where are the pills? Teddy is stunned as he watches her meticulously select and chew the sharp substance. Her mouth begins to bleed. It starts as a trickle and overflows as a thick current as the shards repeatedly slice her tongue. She makes a tight fist around what's left in her hand. Blood pumps out from between her clenched fingers. Blood covers her face and stains the front of her nightgown. Her son calls for her, demanding her attention. She continues to crush the glass in her mouth with brittle molars.

He sits up before his eyes open. He's breathing fast. Sweat beads on his back and shoulders. It's bright and warm in his office. He doesn't know how long he's been asleep. He's grateful to be awake but heavy with the knowledge given to him from his recent dreams. He never understood or appreciated what his mother did for him. Like so many of the women in his life, he treated her poorly. He can still confront his father. It won't repair any of the damage, but he will do his best to take any of the peace he may be holding on to at the end of his life. He owes his mother that.

He desperately needs a shower. The best he can do is peel off his clothes from the closing-night party and splash some cold water under his arms. Clothes that fit him a month ago now hang on his fragile frame. He doesn't know what to do with the bandage on his forehead. The edges of the tape are peeling. A blood vessel popped in his right eye and has painted the bottom half of the white sclera pink. It's going to be a long road back to normal. He grabs his keys and a wad of cash and shuffles out the door.

Outside, the air stings. He puts on sunglasses to stop the sun from burning. Nothing can help keep tiny needles of dirt and breeze from getting under his faulty bandage. He needs to walk fast but can't. As he reaches the bottom steps of his building, he considers giving up. He trudges on down the block.

He stops at a pretzel cart on the corner. A woman is in line ahead of him but moves to the side and gestures for him to go first. He points toward a piece of hot, twisted dough and digs in his pocket for cash. The vendor waves off his attempt to pay. He's being kind but mostly wants to limit his exposure to this man who is obviously not well and possibly contagious. Teddy doesn't have time to show gratitude. He needs to get these calories into his body. The two strangers are relieved to see him walk away.

His foot is throbbing and becoming wet in his boot. He won't be able to walk the remaining few blocks to his father. He throws the pretzel wrapper on the sidewalk and crawls into a cab. He's too busy eating to tell the driver his destination, but in minutes the car is stopped in front of his father's modern and sparse building. He tosses some cash at the driver without looking at the meter.

He wipes salt from around his mouth as he makes his way up the stairs. He never noticed how many stairs were in his life until they became such barriers. What else has been unknowingly blocking his path?

He pounds on the door, not wasting the time to locate his keys. The Polish nurse welcomes him as if she was expecting this unexpected visit.

"Mr. Teddy, you're hurt?"

She reaches toward his bandage. He sidesteps her and walks as confidently as he can to his father, who is slouched in his chair. With all the effort it took to get there, he never thought about what he was going to say. This will be the last time they speak. His arms are twitching. There is so much fury pent up in his joints, his body might snap. He needs to do this now and be done with it.

"I know what you did. To Abigail. Your own daughter." His voice is shaking.

The nurse comes to his side. "Sit down, Mr. Teddy. You don't look well."

"I won't be here long." He looks at her sharply. "Neither will you. I'm done paying for this. My father can rot in a home somewhere."

"You're upset. I'll get snacks."

"I don't want any goddamn snacks!"

He leans over his father, raining down a mixture of spit and hate. "You sick son of a bitch. You ruined everything. Everything that was good, you—" He can't stand to look at his face. He screams at the nurse. "Do you know what he did? Do you know how he tormented his wife? Ruined his daughter? Hurt her over and over again?"

Teddy is unhinged. The nurse is calm. Her voice is deep and steady. "I know everything. Do you?"

Teddy isn't sure what reaction he'd expected, but he was not expecting that. He takes a step back. Did she suddenly lose her accent? The nurse continues, wrapping her arms around his unresponsive father.

"My Sammy is a bad boy."

Teddy continues to yell. "What? What is wrong with you? He raped his daughter."

"A very bad boy."

The nurse leans down as if she's going to give her patient a kiss. Instead, she bites into his ear with her sharp, jagged teeth. Teddy backs up in shock and disgust. He falls to the floor and continues to push himself backward with his hands. The nurse laughs as she chews his father's flesh. The wounded man looks up without making a sound or expression.

Teddy screams. "Stop!"

She takes a chunk out of his neck this time. Blood squirts onto her face and the floor.

She smiles wide, exposing red-stained teeth. "Don't you want him to hurt? Like you? Like your sister? I can hurt him over and over again."

This can't be real. He must still be in his office sleeping.

He has a hard time standing, but he manages to get to his feet. "This isn't happening."

His phone rings in his pocket.

She talks with her mouth full. "We all get what we deserve, Mr. Teddy."

"Don't talk to me." He backs up to the door. His phone will not stop ringing.

"Even you."

He runs down the hallway, cursing at himself to wake up. His boot is flooded with blood. He leaves tracks all the way down the front steps. The city looks real. The people passing on the sidewalk smell and take up space. He's not sleeping. His body lurches forward and he throws up. His phone is now vibrating from a text message. He retrieves it from his pocket. Philip is trying to get hold of him. He struggles to read the screen as his eyes blur:

We need to talk.

His knees buckle, and he falls to the concrete.

Chapter 16

Augie sits in a chair across from Teddy's hospital bed. There are finally stitches in Teddy's foot. His head wound has been properly cleaned and covered. His body is stiff and bruised from another fall.

Augie comes to his bedside when he sees his eyes open. "Dad."

Teddy works hard to put his son's face into focus.

"It's Augie. You're in the hospital."

Teddy tugs at the IV in his arm. Augie moves his hand away from the tubes pumping fluid into his father.

"You need that. They say you're severely dehydrated." He holds up a plastic bag with soiled clothes. "Is this what you were wearing?"

Teddy's mouth is painfully dry. He tries to generate some saliva to help him get the words out.

"Just relax. We'll get it sorted out."

Teddy's voice is tired, but he's finally able to speak. "Where's your grandfather?"

"Grandpa? I don't know. I'm sure he's at home. Do you want me to let him know you're in the hospital? I . . . I don't think he'd understand."

"Does your mother know I'm here?"

"No. Should I call her?"

Where is Trish? Isn't she the first person they would track down?

"I've called Philip. He's—" Augie stops abruptly. It appears this isn't something he wants to discuss while his father is in a hospital gown. "He's on his way."

"Where's my phone? I think he called me."

"Yes, he's been trying to get ahold of you. He's pretty pissed, actually. You promised you wouldn't disappear again."

"I don't think I've ever promised anyone anything."

"That's probably true." Augie smiles.

It's nice to see him less worried, if only for a moment. "Can I have some water?"

Augie points to the bag of fluid hanging by his bedside. "You should have gotten checked out after the party. I should have insisted. Thank God someone found you."

"Found me?"

"You were in the elevator. Out cold. They don't know for how long."

"At your grandfather's?"

"No. In your building. Were you going to Grandpa's?"

Teddy is filled with relief. He chuckles and blinks away tears. This warm feeling is fleeting. A group of doctors enters the room.

"Hello, Mr. Maine," one of them says. "Glad to see you're awake. Are you comfortable?"

Teddy is alarmed by the number of people in lab coats. "What's going on? When can I go home—"

Augie is the acting grown-up in the room. "Dad. We need to do some tests."

Teddy recognizes a familiar face. "Katherine?"

The doctor in charge glances at Augie and prepares Teddy's bed for transport.

"Katherine?" Teddy's voice is louder this time. Demanding.

Augie leans in close. "We're taking you to get an MRI—"

Teddy is beside himself. "Why is she here? She's not this kind of doctor. She's not a real doctor!"

Teddy sees his past lover standing in the doorway clear as day. She's not in scrubs but a tight-fitting suit and heels.

She's also not concerned with her patient's level of panic. "Relax, Ted. We're all here to help you."

He's the only one who can hear her. His bed is rolled toward the door. Katherine takes hold of the rails and begins pushing him down the hall. He tries desperately to stop them as he screams for his son. It's an unpleasant scene. An intern is urgently instructed to sedate him. They hold him down as they push a syringe into his arm. The medicine works quickly. Teddy continues to protest in slow motion.

"Augie. Don't let her touch me. Augie!"

"Let the doctors do their job, Dad." He stands in the hall as the bed rolls forward. "I'll be right here when you wake up."

The bright lights above him provide a blinking road map to an unwanted destination. He's quietly begging the white coats around him to stop. He's helpless and incoherent.

Katherine is in charge. She positions technicians in the high-tech booth as Teddy is transferred to the MRI tube. She speaks into a microphone behind the glass. Speakers deliver her voice in surround sound.

"You're heavily sedated, Mr. Maine. Don't fight it. We're going to take some pictures now, and when you wake up, we'll have a better idea of what's going on. Won't that feel good, Teddy? To know what's going on?"

He tries to open his mouth to scream, but nothing moves.

His father sits up, fastening a gold watch around his wrist. Teddy is a child. He remains under the covers of his bed.

"I didn't like that."

"You will," his father replies, pulling a white T-shirt over his head.

"It hurts."

"It will feel good one day." His voice is casual.

"Why do you do that to me?"

"Because I can."

He turns to look at his young son clutching his blanket under his chin.

"We're all animals. Mommy. Me. Your sister. Sure, we can talk. Make art. Build tall buildings with fancy machines, but we're just like all the other beasts in the wild. We take what we want, when we want it. The bigger and stronger you are, the more you can take. You have been given a gift, Teddy. You'll grow up to be bigger and stronger than most. Right now, you're weak. All children are. This won't last forever. Unless you let it. Don't let anyone fool you. Life isn't that complicated."

It wasn't often that Teddy's father gave him these late-night lessons. He was always more interested in his sister. Even as a young boy, Teddy was never quite weak enough. He was quick to grow tall and lanky. Taller than his father. The memories of these few encounters lived deep in his bones and grew with him. Out of sight but ever-expanding, embedded in his muscles, coiled around his tendons, and knotted in his intestines.

Teddy wakes up in a chair next to his son. He doesn't remember what happened. He feels exposed and small.

"Are they done with all the tests?"

They are sitting in a crowded emergency room.

"What tests? Do you need something tested?" Augie is looking at his phone. He seems frustrated. Distant.

"Where are we?"

"The emergency room." Augie self-corrects and softens. "The nurse called from Grandpa's. She said you left a trail of blood down the hallway, and Philip found you sleeping outside his building."

"Where is Philip?"

"He had to get to a meeting."

Teddy feels the urge to apologize. This is rare. It comes out as a question. "I'm sorry?"

Augie puts his phone away. "Let us help you, Dad. Look at you. You look like shit. You're running around the city like some crazy homeless person. You have a goddamned open head wound. You know they won't even do anything about that here. You have to see a specialist. A plastic surgeon. They cleaned it out the best they could."

"Then what are we waiting for?"

"They're going to stitch up your foot. Jesus Christ. I should have never let you leave the party by yourself."

"What meeting?"

"Huh?"

"You said Philip was at a meeting."

"He'll meet us at the apartment. I don't want to talk about it now."

Teddy wants to ask more questions but stays quiet. He rubs his arms, searching for a mark or bandage from the IV.

Augie watches him. "What?"

"Shouldn't I be getting some fluids?"

"How long do you want to stay here?" He takes out his phone again.

Philip is waiting for them at the apartment. He's in the kitchen putting away groceries when Augie helps Teddy through the door on crutches.

Philip is doing his best to be a happy camper. "You literally had nothing to eat in this house. No wonder you're so strung out."

Teddy isn't good at accepting help. "You did all this?"

"It was delivered." Philip isn't going to play any pity party games.

"Thank you."

Augie dumps out a plastic bag from the hospital and brings Philip up to speed.

"Seven stitches. A plastic surgeon needs to look at his head." Then he turns his attention back to his father. "You can't take these until you eat." He hands him a bottle of pills.

Augie has relaxed some on the trip over but remains irritated. Inconvenience feels better than worry. Being angry is easier than being sad. It's getting to be too much. Teddy can see it on his face. Augie is a good boy, but he has his limits. Teddy knows he is becoming a burden, and he'd have to be a much better father for any son to be willing to carry this heavy a load.

Philip continues to busy himself in the kitchen. He pours Teddy a glass of milk and collects ingredients to make a sandwich.

"So? What did she want?" Augie's voice is loaded with anxiety.

Philip is quick to blow him off. "I don't know if we should talk about it now."

Augie isn't dropping it. "The meeting didn't go well?"

"Did you think it would? Their source is back."

"Bullshit."

They're talking as if there are only two people in the room. It's happening, or perhaps it has already happened. Teddy is an irrelevant part of his own life. Philip sits across from him, eating half of the sandwich he just made, pushing the other half toward Teddy on a plate. Screw him. Screw both of them. His body will heal. They'll come groveling back once the money starts coming in. Teddy will hold on to his sanity long enough to make sure they regret this. He's sunk so low, cracked so wide, unraveled so much, that he is willing to turn away from the only two people in the world who love him. In Teddy's mind there is always someone better waiting.

"Where's Trish?"

Philip and Augie shrug. No one but Teddy finds it odd that she's been missing from this whole unfortunate episode.

"Who's that man she was with, at the party?" he asks.

Augie answers, "Closing night? That was Doug."

"Who the hell is Doug?"

"Her husband, Dad."

Teddy laughs. Philip puts down the lunch he was not enjoying.

"Let's take these pills and get you to bed." Teddy doesn't appreciate Augie's non-answer.

"Seriously, where is your mother?"

Philip tries to help. "It's been a long—"

"Damn it. I'm not a child."

Being angry is easier than being sad.

"Relax, Ted. Augie is just trying to help."

Now Augie's voice is raised at Philip. "Trying? What do you think I've been doing all day? Trying . . ."

Philip isn't used to his magic touch not working. "Okay. We're all stressed—"

Teddy explodes. "Someone tell me what the hell is going on!"

Philip should be kind right now. He should use a soft voice to defuse this family drama. He should be careful and concerned for his friend. But he can't. For all his years of fixing things, he's just been lucky. He has no idea how to make his sick friend better.

"She left you! Years ago! She's gone and married to somebody else." He has waited decades to say that.

Teddy rumbles, "I don't believe you."

"I don't give a shit." Philip's voice carries a weight Teddy and Augie are hearing for the first time.

Teddy needs to quickly get back in control. "You should leave."

Philip stands, knocking his chair roughly back from the table.

Augie hesitates. "I don't think he should be alone."

"Don't act like I'm not in the goddamn room! Get out! Both of you!"

Philip doesn't wait for Augie's decision. He leaves, yelling on his way out, "You've really lost it!"

With everything he is feeling, dreading, Augie doesn't want to leave him like this. He doesn't want new patterns to form inroads to harden into an estrangement.

"Dad . . ."

"Go!"

Augie walks out slowly. He pauses by the cluttered counter. He's about to open his mouth. Try one more time. But Philip is waiting in the hallway. It's time to go. He needs to keep at least one of them on his side.

Teddy deadbolts and chains the door. He turns around and is

slapped in the face by the emptiness of his surroundings. It can't be true. Trish lives here. He's sure of it. He runs to the bedroom, dragging his foot behind him. He'll certainly find some reassurance there.

The large bed is covered in his clothes, a suitcase, random pages of research and outlines. He goes to inspect the mahogany dresser. It should be lined with perfume bottles and moisturizers. An overflowing jewelry box with gaudy, never-worn necklaces spilling out. A paperback or two with a receipt as the bookmark. None of that is there. Just dust and rings in worn varnish.

He throws open the double doors to their expansive closet. One side is bare. The other is littered with his clothes that never found their way to hangers. He walks in and pulls open the built-in drawers. Nothing. He finds a velvet loafer in a back corner. One half of a feminine-but-sensible pair of shoes. Trish has a dozen pairs just like it.

He walks out, toward the bed. With each step a lightning bolt flashes, blinding him with light.

He's in a crowded downtown apartment. It smells like weed and musk. It's summer, and too many of the men are wearing tank tops. They are much younger. This is one of their first rowdy nights out together. Shortly after making their grand entrance as a couple, he's leaving with another woman. He is sure to wave over his shoulder as he escorts a bubbly redhead out the door. He doesn't think twice about it. They talked about this. Trish didn't need any convincing. Neither one believed in the antiquated rules of fidelity. Only one of them had been lying. If he had thought twice, paused to look closer, he would have noticed his soon-to-be wife's tense expression and her eyes growing wet and weary watching her neighbor's hand moving firmly up her thigh.

A flash of light.

He's back in their first one-bedroom apartment. Trish sits pregnant and alone, reading as Teddy loudly beats Philip at chess. When she stands, the baby shifts and takes her breath away. Teddy continues to rant gleefully about his bishop's sly attack. Philip rushes to her side.

Crack. Flash. Boom.

He fast-forwards through countless dinners, as they talk to each other through the kids or not at all. So many moments of her studying him from across the room while holding Nora close. And finally, a hospital. They are holding each other in the hallway. He's keeping her upright. They are both sobbing. Her whole body is shaking. He's hardly seen her laugh in twenty-five years, let alone sob. He doesn't know what else to do but hold her up.

Yes. Yes. He knows all this. He knows he was a shitty husband. It wasn't often wine and roses, but they always managed to figure it out. Didn't they?

He walks through the front door of their current apartment. She's sitting at the table. There's a bag next to her feet. He goes to the fridge before saying hello. It's not that late, but the apartment is dark. She must have sat down as the sun was setting and never gotten back up to turn on a light.

"I was going to kill myself."

He turns to her. "What?"

"I was going to kill myself. Leave my body somewhere you would find quickly."

"Let's not do this now. I have a headache and still have work to do."

"Do you know why I didn't?"

He plays along. "Tell me."

"Every time you see my face, you hear my name, you'll be reminded of what you did. I don't deserve to be alive. I'll get what's coming to me but not until I watch you rot and suffer first."

Her chilling demeanor silences him. She leaves without another word.

That was the last time he was alone with his wife. He remembers now.

He runs out of the room and into the hall. Everywhere he looks he can see where she is missing. He replays the dozens of times he has called out her name in this empty space. He has been alone, calling out to no one. It's crushing.

Emily turns on the light in the office. Wait! There *has* been someone! He leaps toward the room like he's a child, and inside is Christmas morning. She's busy working. He watches her write at his desk. He can't restrain himself long.

His voice is regrettably desperate. "When the play is done, will you leave me?"

She responds without looking up from her work. *"The life that tied too tight escapes will ever after run."*

"You're all I have."

She puts her pen down, annoyed, and reassures him. *"No friend have I that so persists as this eternity."*

He enters the room to get a closer look at what she is working on. "Are you finished?"

She shakes her head *no*. There is one last twist to sort out. She taps her face with her pen as she thinks. *"As subtle as tomorrow that never came. A warrant, a conviction, yet but a name."*

"I confronted my father. At least I think I did. I don't really know what's happening."

Does he want it to be true, what he saw at his father's?

"It was awful. The things his nurse was doing to him. There is no way it was real. Philip's right. I've totally lost it."

He takes a seat. "Trish is gone. I forgot that she left me." He cries and laughs as he continues this rare emotional purge. "Augie. The way he sees me now? I'm sick and old. A burden. I never wanted to do that to him."

She is focused on finishing. She half-heartedly comforts him. *"While we were fearing it, it came. But came with less of fear because that fearing it so long had almost made it fair."*

"There is nothing fair about getting old."

Becoming dependent. This is the hell Teddy fears most. His phone rings. He assumes it's Philip calling to apologize or Augie calling from outside the front door. His face brightens. It's Elizabeth. Emily encourages him to answer. Finally. Someone else can tend to him.

"Hello? Elizabeth?"

"Can we meet?"

"Yes. Please. Anything . . . um, anytime."

"Tomorrow."

"Of course."

"Good. Noon at Porter's."

"Okay. I'm so glad you called."

She hangs up without saying goodbye. Emily smiles, satisfied with this turn of events. She gets back to work at his desk. He's assured she'll be here for a while and leaves to finish his sandwich and take the prescribed amount of pain medication. He has a reason to pull it together. Elizabeth called. Screw everyone else. There is always someone better waiting.

Chapter 17

Porter's is that New York lunch spot you see on sitcoms. Trendy and bland. An expensive treat that doesn't deliver. He's not surprised this is his daughter's go-to. She is disappointedly trendy and bland.

He shouldn't think like that. He shouldn't be judging the one person he might have left. Even when he's holding tight to a life vest, he'll do all he can to make himself sink.

He orders two Bloody Marys from the waiter, a professional who takes one look at Teddy and lowers any expectations he has for a tip. He doesn't offer to bring waters. Teddy's head itches. He left his crutches at home. He managed to give himself a bath and a shave. He is exhausted by what it took to look this decent. If he hadn't gone through the trouble, they would have stopped him at the door.

He's nervous. Everyone around him poses a threat. The manager keeps an eye on his section. He's the only one seated in a cluster of four tables. The waiter is taking too long with the bartender. They are talking about him. There are no women or children in the dining room. That doesn't seem statistically possible for a Wednesday afternoon. His mind spins with countless conspiracies. Was he ever able to sit in peace?

Examining the staff closer, all are men. All have short-cropped hair and are of average size. The perfect size to fit into a government-issued uniform. Their shoes are shiny. Too shiny for restaurant workers. He's walked into an ambush.

He plots his escape. There's no silverware on the table. Smart. He has no weapons, and he can't move quickly. His best bet is to wait until they are distracted. He needs to create some type of diversion. He doesn't notice Philip and Augie walking toward the table. He's calculating how many paces there are between himself and the bathroom. The moving chairs make him jump.

"Dad."

He looks up at Augie. "What are you doing here?"

The waiter returns with his drinks as the recent arrivals take their seats. He will be more attentive now that real customers have entered the scene. Philip sits and takes one of the Bloody Marys.

"Thanks. Expecting someone?"

Augie orders a beer. "Just us, I hope."

Teddy is alarmed. Why is he the only one confused? They must be in on this. They must be behind this whole operation. No one has noticed that he is on high alert. That he is on to them. He still may have a chance.

"I appreciate you coming. I know it's hard for you to get around but, you know . . . neutral territory." Philip laughs and takes a bite of celery. The long green stalk looks comically out of place at this serious standoff.

"We have a lot to sort through," Augie begins. "First, Dad, I love you."

Is this an intervention? Did they use Elizabeth as bait?

Philip is rather contrite. "I'm sorry about yesterday. We should have never left you alone. We're both very concerned and want to help. How's your head?"

"My head is fine."

"It's not fine, Dad. You're not fine, and that's okay." Augie reaches for his hand, but he can't catch it before it slips under the table.

A duo in starched white shirts flanks the table. Teddy braces himself. He grips the bottom of his chair. If they are about to drag him out of there, he is going to put up a fight. The employees deliver a breadbasket and place settings. He slides the silverware onto his lap and waits for their next move.

Philip is in a hurry to get this done. "Here's the deal, pal."

Teddy squeezes the butter knife hard in his palm. He won't tolerate being "pal-d".

Philip continues. "The book is back on. The source? He's back."

He drops his weapons. They bang on the metal table legs. Augie reaches down to retrieve them. Teddy's mind centers on the crisis at hand and stops playing the action-adventure saga.

Philip is blunt. "We're not going to fight it."

"What?" Teddy's voice is loud.

Augie tries to keep things calm. "Listen, Dad. This is a good plan."

Philip launches the pitch of his career. "We're going to take control of the story. Their little tell-all will be worthless. Old news before it ever hits the shelves. People are only going to care about you getting better. Whatever is going on, I don't know, maybe it's little strokes . . . I had an uncle . . . looks a lot like what you're dealing with . . . we're going to get it figured out. There is no more fighting it, okay? We are going to lean into it and focus on getting you better. That's the only way through this."

They are asking Teddy to bend when he has already snapped. He would have preferred his imagined kidnapping to this dismal reality.

"No one has ever helped me. Never." His voice is shaking. "There are no other writers. Why won't you believe me?"

Because it's a lie.

Time for Philip to show all his cards. "I've gone to his house."

"Who? Whose house?"

Augie jumps in. "Paul Sharpe."

Teddy shakes his head. "Not this again."

"The guy loves you. He's willing to do whatever we say."

"Philip, please. You're better than this."

"He gave me the play, Ted. The draft that went missing. He has it. It was never stolen. He was finishing it."

"This is unbelievable." Teddy stands, preparing to storm out. The sudden movement causes his stitches to stretch. He winces in pain and sits back down.

Philip lays it on thick. He needs to close the deal. "It's good. Really good. Exactly what we need. I know you did most of the work. Your voice is clear through the whole thing."

"There's no shame in collaborating, Dad."

"We get a press release out with your . . . your medical condition, and sneak in a feel-good story about reconnecting with an old partner."

Augie feels like they are on a roll. "People will be excited. After all these years, the dynamic duo is back."

"Excuse me?"

Philip holds up his hand to stop Augie from adding anything else. He's clearly out of his league here. "That girl's story will come off as cruel. I doubt they'll go through with it."

"Who cares about that twat?" Teddy retorts. "If we do this, I've told everyone I'm sick and a fraud."

Philip doesn't miss a beat. "Sick, yes. Fraud, no. You didn't cut Paul out. He never wanted any credit. He's always been more of a muse than anything. You didn't lie about anything. Nobody ever asked. He will denounce the book. It won't get any traction, and the rumors will die. It's really a win-win."

"For whom?"

"For all of us."

The trio sits silently. Teddy knows they're right. This is the best way out. He knows he's sick. He also knows he's a fraud.

The waiter passes out menus, and Teddy flips the cardstock in his hands. "What is this?"

"The menu." The waiter is patient with his explanation.

"It says River Pointe."

"Yes."

"Why?"

"That's the name of the restaurant. Want to hear the specials?"

"No, thank you." Augie is quick to get rid of an audience.

Philip and Augie study the menus as if they didn't just outline the end of Teddy's career. Like they weren't just negotiating the unfavorable terms of his legacy.

Teddy declares, "This is Porter's."

Philip has shifted into autopilot after surviving their confrontation. "What's a porter?"

"Porter's. The restaurant. I'm supposed to be at Porter's."

Augie continues to look at the menu. "Dad, that place closed like three years ago."

"Oh, Porter's," Philip remembers. "Yeah, they had great calamari. Augie, what does this say? I didn't bring my readers."

They've moved on. Check. Mate.

"I have to go. I'm meeting someone." Teddy stands, carefully this time. "I'm late."

Philip is okay with this meeting being over. It went better than expected. "I get it. It's a lot to process."

Augie waves the waiter over. "Get something to go, at least."

Teddy shakes his head. He can't talk. He needs to focus all his energy on walking out the door. The waiter puts his arms out to spot this brittle man. Teddy waves him off. He would have liked to push him down. Throw him into a table. Right now, all he can do is remain standing.

Augie and Philip are satisfied with his reaction. He'll hobble home to his empty apartment and realize the only sign of life is from them. They are all he's got. He'd better listen. Maybe he will even come to recognize this is a solid resolution. The best possible curtain call.

He makes it outside. He pauses, searching the facade of the building for a name. This has got to be Porter's. He studies the initials R.P. etched in white on the window. Under his reflection, "River Pointe" is scrawled in fine cursive. He should go back inside. He needs to eat, and he isn't certain he can make it home by himself. There's no Porter's. He doubts Elizabeth ever called.

Augie runs out as he deliberates. "Dad!" He's holding his phone. "Grandpa's in the hospital."

Chapter 18

His father looks comfortable. Alien, but comfortable. Tubes are in and out of his body, helping his chest rise and fall. Drips and beeps fill the beige room with sound. It makes for a calming rhythm. Teddy doesn't know how long he's been sitting across from the bed, listening to each manufactured breath.

He stands to stretch his legs. He isn't sure what's going on. He shuffles close to the bed to investigate his father's flesh. Any bite marks? Missing pieces? He's all there. Not a scratch on his weathered skin. What he saw at his father's apartment was horrifying. Teddy would have never hurt him like that, but he wasn't sad to watch. In hindsight, he's disappointed it was nothing but another false vision. Strange trip. Misfired neuron.

A young doctor enters the room. "You must be his son?"

"Yes." Teddy reaches out his hand. "Teddy Maine."

The doctor shakes it reluctantly. "Did you have that looked at?"

"What?"

"Your head."

Teddy quickly takes back his hand. "I'm fine. What's going on with my father?"

The doctor looks around the room. He's not sure he's talking to the most qualified next of kin. "Is anybody with you?"

"My son should be on his way."

"Okay. Good."

Why is that good?

"Can you please tell me what's going on?"

"Right. Your father, he's had private nursing care?"

"Yes. Round the clock."

"He has a respiratory infection. That, coupled with his existing COPD, makes it impossible for him to get enough oxygen on his own, and he is too weak to adequately clear his airways. We have him on strong antibiotics. It could be viral. That recovery would be longer. Hopefully, meds will clear it up quickly. If the infection resolves, I think he has a good chance of coming off the ventilator."

"Is he going to die?"

"With elderly patients like this, it's often a simple infection or even a common cold that causes a rapid decline. Rest assured he is in the right place receiving excellent care. We should know more in twenty-four hours. See how his body responds to the antibiotics."

"Thank you."

"A social worker will meet with you to review some options and the resources that are available, should you need them. Would you like to wait for your son?"

"That's fine."

The doctor gets to work recording the flashing numbers and checking measurements on the hanging bags surrounding the bed. "Oh, the cafeteria is open until five if you're hungry."

How many times a day does he deliver the news that someone is about to die? That this could be a loved one's last twenty-four hours? And then announces the cafeteria hours. Teddy envies his detachment. Do you learn that in medical school? Who teaches you how to unplug all these machines?

He looks down at his father. Each beep is pounding toward a final crescendo. Now that he knows this could be it, he's strangely sad. He doesn't have a very large puzzle. He can't afford to lose any pieces. This may be the biggest piece of all. Will he come together in a new, better shape, or with his father's passing will something always be missing? Even a faulty brick might be the one thing holding up the whole building.

It's hard to think of him as a monster while watching these machines keep him alive. Would his sister feel the same if she were here? He'll have to find her. She needs to know when they bury their father. The room is shrinking, and the air is growing thick. He is hungry. He can't imagine anything in the cafeteria will be worth eating. Beggars *can* be choosers.

He walks out, knowing he may never need to come back. It's devastating how unceremonious the moment feels.

He has no idea how to get out of the maze of trauma and sickness. Every exit sign leads to another beige floor. Each oversized elevator door opens to more hushed voices and codes being called overhead. A slow burn of panic sets in with each wrong turn and new hallway. He stops in the middle of a busy floor. People walk by as if he's a ghost. Maybe he is.

Finally, a Good Samaritan stops to help. "A little turned around?"

She's small. He doesn't realize she's talking to him.

"They sure don't make it easy."

He spins around and bumps into the source of the little voice trying to help him.

"Sorry," he says gruffly.

"Are you trying to get to the parking garage or the lobby?"

"Anywhere. The lobby." He's talking fast.

"We all make it out of here one way or the other. Let me help."

He's expecting directions. Instead, she takes his hand. It's wet. It takes a few steps for him to register the unexpected feeling of moisture. He looks down at her petite frame for the first time. Her face is sweet and wrinkled. Her eyes are dulled with age. Her hospital gown is cut down the middle. There is a dark, jagged mess where her abdomen should be. Teddy jerks back his hand.

"What's wrong? You okay, mister?"

He stumbles backward into a magazine stand, knocking it over. He turns and sprints down the hall. He busts through a side door and miraculously makes it out to the sidewalk. He has no idea how he got there. He could have sworn he was on the sixth floor. His foot is on fire. He starts to sob. Wet, round, real tears stream down his face. The rupture in his foot may have caused it. The realization that his father is dying, and that he isn't far behind, keeps them running down his chin. It's not so much his own death that is breaking him but the creeping acknowledgment that it will be a painful and lonely process. Nothing he has accomplished could have prevented this. Nothing his father did that was right or terribly wrong has stopped the clock from ticking. Absolutely none of it matters. Life really is not all that complicated.

He thinks about curling up on the pavement and never moving again. Not yet. He wants to say goodbye. He needs to say goodbye to her.

He drifts home on a tide of tears and blood. It's dark in the apartment. He stops himself from calling out for Trish. Old habits are hard to break. He needs to do something about his foot but is too afraid to take off his shoe. He's sad there's no light coming from the office. He needs to see his last friendly face. He grabs a bottle from the side bar in the front hall and goes to wait for her in the dark.

He drinks quickly, trying to work up the courage to take off his shoes. His foot is sticky with drying blood and pus. His stitches are no match for his erratic behavior. He sits on the sofa and leans his head back in the dark, shutting his eyes in an attempt to block out all sources of light. His head is fuzzy from the injection of booze and lack of food. He feels something down by his feet. Luckily, his reflexes are slow to respond, and he doesn't kick.

Emily is on her hands and knees, tending to his foot. She needs him to be able to walk a little farther.

"Oh. You don't need to do that." He's embarrassed but grateful. They both know he needs the help.

She speaks, her voice barely above a whisper. *"How firm eternity must look to crumbling men like thee."*

That could be taken the wrong way. He takes it with kindness, as she intended.

His son stands in the hall on the other side of the door. He was worried to not find Teddy at the hospital. His relief at finding him at home is fleeting, however, as he listens to his one-way conversation.

"My father is dying. He could already be gone. I don't know. This doctor, young guy, little older than Augie, told me like it was nothing. Like he was breaking the news that I needed a new muffler. I want to be that detached. From him. From everyone. I can't believe I'm actually sad."

She has slipped off his shoe and wet sock and has moved on to wrapping his foot in a fresh cloth bandage. She hums as she works.

"Dad?" Augie turns on the light, startling him.

Teddy is surprised and a little ticked off. "How did you get in here?"

"I have a key. Always have. Who are you talking to?"

Augie comes around to the front of the small sofa. Emily gets up off the floor and sits next to Teddy.

"I don't like you just barging in here."

"That's fair. Sorry. I was worried when you weren't at the hospital. I'm glad you're safe."

"Why wouldn't I be? I can take care of myself."

Augie does not want to start a fight without Philip there for back-up. "Good news. The social worker is going to meet us here in the morning. Philip will be here, too. You know, another set of ears to help with the logistics of everything."

Teddy grunts his semi-approval. He drank too much too fast. His body feels like a heavy stone that is somehow floating.

"Did you ever eat anything?"

Basic needs. That's where they're at right now.

"Looks like you got a fresh bandage on your foot. Good. Don't

want that to get infected. Relax. I'll fix you something." Augie pauses
on his way out. "I'm going to stay here tonight. In the guest room."

As he gets to work in the kitchen, Emily continues tending to her
patient. She takes the bottle that is ready to fall from his weak grip
and supports him upright with some throw pillows. She covers his
lap with a blanket. She watches him for a moment before she leaves, a
crumbling man indeed.

He wakes up to voices in his kitchen. There is a half-eaten sandwich on
a plate next to him. He must have slept in the office. He doesn't blame
his son for leaving him on the cramped sofa, but he really wishes he
had slept in a bed. His head is pounding, and he is the type of groggy
where you're not sure if you've even woken up.

He supports himself against the wall as he makes his way toward
his guests. There are Augie and Philip looking like they just had the
best sleep of their lives. Overly upbeat and perky. Perhaps it has something to do with their guest. She's a pretty, young blonde. She would
be stunning if not for an unfortunate mole on her chin. They are all a
bit taken aback by his appearance. The licensed professional does the
best job hiding it.

"Dad, this is Sadie from the hospital," Augie says. "She's a geronto-
logical social worker."

"I help old people," she adds with ease. "Please join us. I love your
place. It's not often I get to make house calls so close to the park." Her
voice is feminine but official.

"Thank you." He sits down stiffly.

Philip passes him a mug of coffee.

"We are here to discuss your father," Sadie begins. "How wonderful
you have this support system with you. There are two things we'll go
over today. Many families find great comfort and meaning in this process. First, I find it helpful to get some of the basic logistics out of the
way so when your father does pass, whether that be this week or next

year, you don't have to focus on making arrangements but can enjoy coming together in his memory."

Who's coming together? All his counterfeit friends and phony worshippers? What if they knew his secrets? The ones Teddy's memory is flirting with. If they knew, would they come?

"I'd like to keep it simple," he manages to say.

Augie and Philip look at each other, impressed that he is actually engaged.

"Are there any current plans for a service or burial? Has your father made his wishes known?" Sadie looks to Teddy.

"Cremated."

She takes a glossy folder from her fake leather bag. "Here's some information on various cremation services. Most are connected with churches or funeral homes and can be a one-stop-shop for you. Any gathering or a memorial?"

Philip chimes in. "Of course. He's a legend. We should have something at the theater. That will be easy. The PR girls can take care of it. They throw great parties."

Does a man who rapes his daughter deserve crackers and carnations?

"I love that you are thinking of it as a party. Death should be a celebration of life."

Philip seems pleased with himself. Flattery from a younger woman is never a bad thing.

Teddy wants to tell them. Tell them what his father did. How he destroyed his mother and sister. What sort of party would the PR girls plan then? He doesn't know what's stopping him. Is it his own guilt for letting it happen? Is he feeling guilty because it didn't happen to him? A strong tie that he doesn't understand is binding him to his father.

"Do I know you?" Teddy asks, like he just remembered something.

"Pardon?" Sadie doesn't know how to take him.

Philip is eager to keep this on track. "Teddy is normally the one people recognize." Always breezy.

"Oh." She's a little embarrassed but mostly confused.

Philip continues. "He's Teddy Maine, the playwright. His father is Sam—"

"Sam Maine! Yes, the actor. My mother loved him!" She quickly corrects herself. "Loves him. I remember watching *The Young and the Restless* together. He was such a good bad guy."

The most acclaimed stage actors found their way to the cash cow of daytime soaps.

"Whichever company you go with," Sadie says, getting back to the topic at hand, "call them from the hospital, and they will take care of the rest. It can be helpful to ask a trusted friend to make that call so it can be done in a timely manner. Those nearest to the deceased might not be in a good place emotionally to tend to such things."

"We've met before." Teddy's thoughts are now on their own track.

"It's possible. New York is really just a small town."

"I'll do it. I'll make the call." Philip is practically shouting. Another opportunity to score points with a pretty girl.

"Wonderful. Now, another important thing to prepare for is your father recovering. Whether it's another few days, or maybe he'll surprise us all and make it another few years, we want him to be comfortable and fulfilled."

Teddy gets back to business. "He has 24/7 nursing care."

"I saw that in his medical notes. He lived at home?"

"Yes. Not his home—our family home. We bought a more accessible apartment."

"Makes sense. Must get a little lonely for him. I understand that before he was hospitalized he was exhibiting some significant signs of dementia. Have you witnessed things like rapid mood changes, delusions, or hallucinations?"

Augie jumps in. "Yes."

What would he know? He doesn't see his grandfather outside of public events, when he's hunched over in a corner.

"All three." Augie is excited.

"That must be hard." She's very good at her job.

"It is." Augie has stolen her favor from Philip.

She takes out more glossy folders. Both men seem strangely eager to have the information. He's not *their* father. Why do they care this much? Teddy is growing more irritated with this whole meeting the more he wakes up.

"It's important for caregivers not to take the mood swings or personality changes personally. Easier said than done, I know. The person you love is still in there, but their brain has changed from the disease. That doesn't diminish who they were or the memories you have."

Can Teddy separate his father from his disease? Only a sick man would have done what he did.

"When dealing with other changes in the brain, those that cause hallucinations or delusions, it's best to go along with it in a way that makes everyone feel safe and your father feel validated."

"Really?" Augie is taking notes.

"You're going to want to correct them, fix them, but remember, the goal of end-of-life care is comfort and quality time. You don't want to spend precious moments arguing or trying to explain something to a person who no longer has the capacity to understand. It is often rather scary for them, especially when the hallucinations start. It creates a lot of conflict in the brain as they question what's real."

Teddy snaps his fingers. "The pharmacy. That's where I know you from."

The pretty social worker seamlessly switches gears. "Possibly. I've certainly been to a lot of pharmacies. I understand your father doesn't talk much? Does he respond in other ways?"

"It was the CVS on the corner."

She makes eye contact with Augie before carefully responding. "Sure. Yes, I've been there many times."

"Thank you. I've been meaning to come back and thank you properly. You really went out of your way to help me."

"Well, helping people is my job."

Augie reaches out his hand. "Can I get your card?"

"Absolutely. I know it's a lot to take in, and I've left you with quite a bit of homework to do."

Teddy is over this. "Are we done? I should get to the hospital."

The room nods in agreement. Philip and Augie stand. Teddy would, but he doesn't want to appear any weaker than he already does.

"This was wonderful information. Thank you so much for coming out to the apartment." Philip extends his hand.

She responds with a shake and a hand on his shoulder. "Of course. When Mr. Maine is settled at home, we can arrange another visit. I'd like to see his setup and talk to his nurse directly."

Teddy was going to break the news that the nurse is fired, and he is moving his father to a facility, but if he survives this hospital stay, maybe home with his nurse is exactly where he's supposed to be. That woman and her sharp teeth know better than anyone how to take care of him and offer him quality time. He smiles for the first time in a while.

Augie shows out the pretty girl. "Thanks," he says in the entryway. "This was really helpful."

They are standing close. Her voice is less professional. "My cell is on my card. Call anytime. Really."

Once the door is closed behind her, Philip raises an eyebrow. "You'd better call her." He's proud of him like a father would be seeing his son with a nice girl.

"Wonder if she likes Italian."

"Everyone likes Italian." Philip chuckles.

Again, Teddy is a guest in his own home. A spectator. An afterthought. The other men don't expect or understand his sudden anger.

"Jesus. A man is dying."

Philip begins to lightly protest. Augie interrupts him. He's always been a fast learner. "You're right, Dad. Sorry. Grandpa should be our priority right now."

"Yes, he should be. If you will excuse me, I'm going to go see him."

Teddy looks pathetic attempting to walk out in a huff, trying to exit with any sort of superiority. Augie and Philip are quiet and let him leave without a fuss. They have a lot to talk about once they are alone.

Teddy pauses outside the door before trekking to the elevator. Should he ask one of them to go with him? No. He will die independent. Even if that's what kills him. He doesn't really want to see his father. He wanted to be done with that meeting. Is that how they'll talk when it's about him? Nobody seemed to struggle.

It's an uneventful trip to the hospital. He is confident he will be able to leave without any drama. This time he studies every sign and leaves a trail of mental breadcrumbs so he can find his way out.

Everything is the same in the room. The rhythmic beeping. The bags with their dripping. But this time his father has a visitor. It's Elizabeth. She is sitting close, staring at the old patriarch's face.

"Elizabeth." Teddy smooths his hair.

She doesn't look at him. "I'm glad you're here. Are you avoiding me?"

"What? No, never."

"You missed lunch."

"I was there. I tried. There is no Porter's."

"Hmm. There was the last time I checked." She stands and grabs her bag.

"Don't go. It's so nice that you're here. I'm sure your grandfather would be touched."

"I came to see you." She leaves the sick man's bedside. "To give you this." She hands him a large brown envelope.

"What is it?"

"I think it will help you fill in the blanks."

He opens the flap and pulls out the first page. It's a script. His script. The version that went missing.

"No. No. Elizabeth, how do you . . . where did you get this?"

"From my client." She starts to walk out.

"Stop. I know we've had our problems. I'm sure I've done a lot of things wrong, but you can't possibly have anything to do with this."

She doesn't turn around. She never does.

"I'll see ya."

He is dumbfounded. Did Philip and Augie know about this? Is Elizabeth the source? Does she have something to do with the book? He can't trust anyone.

He only assumes the worst of intentions. His mind can't stretch to see this coming from any other angle. Like the possibility that his children and best friend are working hard to save him from himself. From succumbing to his own sickness and pride. That they are all doing their best to ensure a graceful exit.

Or, maybe, it is something else entirely.

The machines in the room start to demand attention. They scream a warning in unison. Teddy is in the way. A flurry of professionals in scrubs flood the room, pushing him to the side. They are shouting to each other in a foreign language consisting of numbers and abbreviations.

"What's going on?"

"Sir, you need to step into the hall."

Teddy backs out of the room, watching this group of strangers put all their energy into saving an old man. A bad man. A man who has outlived karma and does not deserve any sort of heroic or even ordinary intervention.

"Stop."

No one can hear his half-hearted call over the blaring machines.

He tries again. "Stop!"

A hand goes up. "Wait. Is there a DNR?"

The room stops spinning for a millisecond and turns to Teddy. He doesn't answer. A gloved hand grabs a clipboard at the end of the bed.

"No. Nothing."

They get back to their life-saving work. A few faces linger long enough in Teddy's direction for him to feel judged.

He races down the hall, carefully and correctly reversing his path to the exit. He almost forgets what he's holding in his hands. He doesn't struggle getting home. Pain and discomfort are becoming his norm.

He feels his heart beating with each quick step, but he is numb to the throbbing in his foot and the pulsing in his head. The different ends of him are demanding attention, screaming out warnings like the machines at his father's bedside.

The apartment is dark. He starts to tear open the envelope at the kitchen island but stops. He is too exposed. What if Augie barges in? He cannot give him and Philip the satisfaction of following their plan, not yet, not until he reads it at least. He stops at his office door. Can't hide in there. Emily is the last person he wants to see right now. He quickly sneaks into the master bedroom. He shuts and locks the door. Still not secure enough. He goes to the half-empty walk-in closet.

He takes out a page. Wait. This isn't what he saw before. He doesn't know what this is. The paper is old and faded. The font is from an actual typewriter. He dumps out the contents of the envelope, letting dozens and dozens of mismatched pages fall to his feet.

It's a medical report of some kind. He gets down on his hands and knees and rifles through them too quickly to make sense of the written notes, typed reports, and is that a child's drawing? He is making a mess. Stalling. He slows down and begins to smooth out the pages and divide them into stacks. He recognizes a perfect circle made in crayon. It is the gleaming bald head of his father.

He remembers the place he drew this picture, his father's portrait. He and his sister were shuttled over to this strange, loud building. Abducted from their posh, private, day school and taken downtown to this yellow maze of tile floors and unfamiliar faces. He remembers seeing police officers and men in suits. They only talked to women. Most were older and smelled like stale perfume and smoke. They were kind. Rushed, but gentle. They gave him saltine crackers and apple juice to make him feel more comfortable. They asked him lots of questions and scribbled down the notes that are now stacked in front of him. Their observations. Suspicions.

Some of the questions were silly, and they would all laugh a little. Some of his answers seemed to make them sad. They were a good audience. He liked telling them stories. If only his mouth weren't so dry from the crackers, he could have talked for hours. He didn't notice when they were done asking questions. He was more worried about the cracker crumbs he left everywhere. They told him it wasn't a problem and had him wait in the hall with his sister. The two sat on uncomfortable green plastic chairs, waiting for their mother.

"Oh, my God," he says to no one.

He scans the typed reports. Words like "genitals" and "penetration" jump from the page. His sister was wrong. He didn't lie to the authorities. They didn't believe him. Or worse, they did. All of this was quickly filed away in a special place where things that are meant to be forgotten go. Money is good at solving problems.

The handwritten notes are far more graphic and detailed than the typed reports. Despicable acts narrated by a child. He doesn't read much. He doesn't have to. He remembers the smells. Raw and hot. He remembers the pain and not knowing if he was allowed to cry. And every memory is his father not bothered at all by his young son's confusion. Refusal. Tears.

His body is overwhelmed with emotion and revolts. His stomach spasms. He makes it to the bathroom just in time to vomit and weep into the sink. Mucus and bile hang off his chin and drip from his nose. His body is wrecked from such a violent purge, but there is no relief. He isn't emptied or cleansed. There will never be a moment of reprieve again. Not from pain. Anguish. Guilt or shame. This truth is not a welcome explanation but a heavy sentence.

His broken heart does not dwell much on his father and his thick fingers. He is dizzy with the misplaced rage he feels toward his mother. How could she have let this happen? To her baby? To her boy? How could she be with a man who hurt her children?

Being angry is easier than being sad, and his mother is always the safer target.

These are the unknown currents that have flowed beneath

everything in his life. He can't bear the weight of this revelation. He finally feels at home in his skin, and he wants to rip every inch of it off.

No one can know about this. He wipes his mouth and takes off for the closet with determination, moving his aching muscles like a superpower.

He gathers the pages documenting the secrets of his past and holds them close to his pounding chest. He will burn them. Yes, that will fix this, but this panic, this need to purge, it will stay with him for the rest of his life. He will always feel like he is running in quicksand away from a burning building. He will always be waiting at a hostile border with the wrong passport.

He crosses the hall to his office, where there is a metal garbage can and a lighter waiting. With any luck, his father is dead. If his luck holds out, he will be close behind him.

He keeps the lights off. Enough is shining up from the streetlamps. He finds his ceremonial Zippo lighter. Seems an appropriate tool for the task at hand. He flips over the textured metal garbage can, spilling random bottles and wrappers to the floor. He doesn't look down at the pages as he prepares them for cremation. He refuses to read another word. He buried it once. That didn't work. This time, he'll burn it.

The edges curl and turn black. He moves the lighter around, waving his hand to help the little flame take flight.

Emily joins him and looks down at the fire. *"He keeps his secrets safely."*

He is glad she's there with him. He never wants her to know about Paul, if there even is a Paul. No. She is his only co-author, whether that's the truth or not. But this is something she should know. This is something they share.

They are quiet for a moment, enjoying the crackle of the fire. He asks her without moving his face from the warmth of the flames, "Did you know?"

She also keeps her eyes on the fire. *"To break so vast a heart required a blow as vast."*

Teddy was right all along. She is the only person who understands him.

She isn't there to offer him comfort, but she can't fight her nature.
She edges close to him and takes his hand. *"I rose because he sank. I
thought it would be opposite, but when his power dropped, my soul grew
straight."* She doesn't want to feel this connection to him, but it's real.
She continues to offer support. *"The harm of years is on him."*

They watch the fire die out.

Augie busts through the front door and calls for him.

"Dad?"

Apparently, barging in is his thing now. Teddy finds it sweet and
comforting. He got his answer. If he dropped dead alone tomorrow,
Augie would find him. Augie would weep and wail in the hallway as
they rolled his body away. He would then bring the pretty social worker as his date to the funeral.

"Yeah," Teddy answers as the last red ember flickers out.

"What's going on?" He can smell the remains of the fire. "Jesus.
What are you doing?"

Teddy doesn't answer. Augie delivers the news. "Grandpa's dead."

Good. He nods. "Thank you for being here."

Teddy kicks the garbage can to make sure there isn't anything left
but ash. He is quickly drenched in panic. Does Augie know what's
just been turned to dust? Did Elizabeth tell him? Show him the awful
proof? No. He would have seen it on his face. Elizabeth is keeping this
secret. Why?

"I think I should lie down," he says.

"Absolutely."

Augie leads him to the bedroom. He is gentle with his father in a
way that is intimate and new. After the worst moment of Teddy's life,
this may be the best. He is so grateful and unworthy of his son's love.

He sinks into the bed. The mattress curls around his body, pushing him deep into the center of something. He smells vanilla and smoke. He is home. His home when it was filled with his family. Trish was always burning vanilla candles.

"Daddy, read one more."

He sits on the edge of Elizabeth's pink bed. She is surrounded with pillows and stuffed animals. It is a lovely, cozy memory.

"I've already read too many. Time for bed." He leans down and gives her a kiss on the forehead. Soon she will be too big for this. "I love you."

"Love you too, Daddy." She rolls over to snuggle a unicorn.

This is wonderful. But it isn't right. Something is missing.

He leaves the room quietly. Augie is waiting for him in the hall. He is just becoming a teenager.

Teddy pauses. "What?"

Augie doesn't say anything. He doesn't have to. There it is. That's what's missing. Disappointment. It is dripping from the lanky boy's face. It darkens the color of the walls.

"Go to bed." Teddy does not appreciate the way his son lingers, judging him. He is about to raise his voice when the boy slips back into his bedroom.

The warm feelings have left, only the usual nag of mild discontent remaining. Teddy sighs as he picks up a scarf from the floor. He opens the hall closet to add it to a pile of winter gear. His sister's body hangs from a rope, next to raincoats and fleece jackets. Her body is limp. Her eyes are open. Her limbs dangle as she gently swings. Teddy screams for help as he grasps her legs, trying to hold her up.

"Trish!"

Teddy keeps screaming. He is no longer in his hall closet but in his sister's dark and bare studio apartment. The ceiling fan groans from the weight of her body. He attempts to slide a turned-over chair closer to him with his foot. It's no use. Even if he could cut her down, she has been dead for hours. As he loosens his grip, the plaster above him cracks and splinters. He manages to pull her body out of the path of the falling fan and ceiling debris. It is loud and dusty. This is how she died.

"What are you yelling about?" Trish is next to him in the hall. "Ted?"

"Nothing." He tosses the scarf into a basket and shuts the door.

His face is wet from tears and sweat. His head is pounding. He isn't ready to be awake.

"Augie?"

There is no answer.

He does not want to get out of bed. He is afraid and doesn't trust that his body is strong enough to keep him upright. He half-heartedly calls out for his son again. His weak cries aren't loud enough to carry into the guest bedroom. He is alone in the dark. He reluctantly shuts his eyes and travels to his next destination.

Chapter 19

He sits on the balcony of a grand, historic church. He doesn't bother trying to fill in the gaps or piece together how he got there. It feels real. He is grateful that, as his grip on reality unravels, he's being spared the hardships of bathing and getting places. He's clean and in a wrinkled suit. Emily is next to him. He didn't know she could leave the apartment. Neither did she. She is soaking in her surroundings, leaning over the railing like a child, watching the mourners in dark suits file in below.

Philip joins them. His shoes echo on the marble floor. He sits down next to Teddy.

"So, I guess the old man made some arrangements."

Teddy doesn't reply.

"I'm sorry. I know you wanted this small. It's good of you to come."

Was not being here an option? Too late to escape now. Best he can do is hide out on the balcony.

"Don't worry about a thing." Philip pats his back as he stands to leave. He takes Teddy's silence as a win. Best leave while he is ahead. "He was a remarkable man."

Emily studies Teddy for his reaction. He smiles tightly. She understands the burden of knowing a remarkable man's secrets. She knows many. This will not be an easy day. Maybe it is too much. Maybe she shouldn't have brought him here.

She squeezes his hand. *"He lived the life of ambush and went the way of dusk. And now against his subtle name there stands an asterisk."* She did not anticipate feeling this softness toward him, but nothing is ever as simple as it seems.

The massive cathedral is buzzing below. The pews won't all be filled—he was an entertainer, not a foreign dignitary—but it's a respectable showing. Teddy spies Augie and Nora toward the front. Trish and his replacement are nearby, fulfilling the family duties of shaking hands and accepting condolences. No one looks up. Are they giving him his privacy, or do they not care if he's there?

A flash of color walks down the aisle, surrounded by somber suits and sweaters. It's his sister. She is wearing a dark pink pantsuit fitted more for a cocktail party than a church service. She is carrying herself with such ease and grace that she doesn't stand out as garish. Her radiance is both enviable and contagious. Happy tears flood his eyes. He is so relieved to see her. There's also a stab of embarrassment. His wounds may be fresher, but she has clearly come through their shared trauma better.

As if their thoughts are connected, she stops mid-stride and turns to look up at him. He sheepishly waves. She nods and smiles confidently. This is a day of liberation.

The service has all the theatrics of a grand funeral. His father thought religion was for the weak. He must be pleased seeing all these sheep gathered there to honor him. Teddy's ears are filtering out all the accolades. Groundbreaking. Brave. A rare talent. His attention is focused on the shiny waxed railing in front of him. It's beautiful and ornately carved with twisting ivy. The architects chose design over function. This railing was never meant to keep anyone from falling facedown onto the marble floor below. A body could easily slip through or tip over. A person doesn't need to jump. Just stand and lean.

Emily grabs his arm. He did not realize that he was standing. How long would he fall before hitting the stone below him? What would it sound like? He wants it to be loud. He wants the sound of his bones cracking and skull splitting to drown out every last lie, every prayer and hymn being wasted on this awful man. Let his blood filling the cracks on the gleaming floor be the only thing these mourners remember.

Emily's grip is firm and keeps him on the balcony.

He planned to sneak out before the organ processional, but here they are, surrounded by people on the main floor. Acquaintances file by, attempting to give their sympathies without making eye contact. A bright voice calls over the crowd. It's Katherine. She makes a beeline for him, but he is not the one she embraces.

"Emily! So good to see you."

Teddy is stunned. He looks around breathlessly. Katherine and Emily continue with their pleasantries.

"Still with Teddy?"

Emily smiles broadly. *"Incredible the lodging but limited the guest."*

The women laugh at his expense.

Teddy interrupts them. His voice is low and rushed. "You . . . you can see her? You know each other?"

"Of course." Katherine pauses and looks to Emily for permission to continue. "Emily is a patient of mine. Former patient. She's graduated." She winks affectionately.

Emily shares her appreciation. *"Confirming all who analyze in the opinion fair. That eloquence is when the heart has not a voice to spare."*

Katherine's mood quickly changes, dripping with sympathy. "Teddy, I'm so sorry about your father. How are you holding up?"

He is too preoccupied with his realities colliding to hear what she's saying.

Like a good partner, Emily answers for him. *"Of his peculiar light we keep one ray to clarify the sight to seek him by."*

Katherine nods. "You've got a good friend here."

Teddy responds late and flatly. "I'm fine."

Emily gently chastises her date. *"How happy is the little stone that rambles in the road alone."*

Both women look at him as if he is a child.

"I hope you find the peace you deserve, Ted." Katherine kisses him gently on the cheek and exits into the crowd.

The exchange was so ordinary it leaves him dizzy. His head is starting to throb. Philip finds him in the crowd. Teddy's eyes are sticky. He blinks in an attempt to focus on his face.

"Lovely service. You all right?" Philip puts a firm hand on Teddy's shoulder.

He continues blinking. He can't tell if Philip and Emily are occupying the same space. Should he introduce her? As whom? As what?

"Teddy, you good?" Philip moves unusually close out of concern.

He should have knocked Emily over, but she remains at Teddy's side, gazing up in amazement at the huge stained-glass windows.

"Yes. Sure. Thank you."

Philip is not convinced. "You're coming to the reception?"

"Of course."

He is not. He's going with his good friend to the family's storage unit. He needs to take advantage of being with her out in the world. He wants to take a look through the family dumping grounds now that he knows what sort of garbage to look for. He will keep his father's secret, not out of honor or love, but out of pure self-preservation. He is not prepared, physically or emotionally, to do any sort of deep dive or a proper sweep for incriminating relics, but he's got it in his head that he has to go now, so that's what he's going to do.

He takes Emily's hand to guide her through the crowd. He wants to leave before he has to talk to anyone else. They climb into a waiting dark sedan. Emily is nervous. This is her first time in a car. He wishes he were the one driving, and they were in his Porsche. That's something to look forward to. Teddy is suddenly overwhelmed with exhaustion, like a pill he doesn't remember taking has kicked in. It will be a long drive to the outer boroughs. He doesn't fight the losing battle and leans back to sleep. He holds her hand as he drifts off. She's grateful. His heavy breathing and slowing pulse are comforting as a foreign world zooms by.

When he wakes up, it's dark, and they are far away. The car is running in an alley flanked by uniform storage sheds. Streetlights, along with strategically placed floodlights, offer security and an eerie glow. It takes a moment to adjust to his surroundings. He gets out of the car, wondering if he is still sleeping, but the damp air and smell of exhaust convince him he's actually at his destination. He stretches and walks closer to the large garage doors. The car door slams and Emily joins him. The unexpected sound of the sedan driving away grabs his attention and shakes him out of any last remnants of sleep.

"Hey!" He yells and attempts to run after the car. "Shit."

It does not occur to him that Emily instructed the driver to leave. He pats down his pockets to find his phone. No need to panic. He has a few bars and plenty of battery. Nothing left to do but get to work.

The door is heavier than he expected. He hates looking weak in front of anybody, especially Emily. Oh, well. It's not like this is the first time she's seen him struggle. The door rumbles as it finally rolls over his head.

It's almost empty. He's initially relieved. He didn't have a plan or even a flashlight. This was always a fool's errand. He reaches for his phone to call back the car. To call Philip to call back the car. His helplessness will get him in trouble once again. He will need to explain where he is and why he's not at the reception. A shape in the back corner of the concrete cube catches his eye. He fumbles and turns his phone toward it. He can barely make out the outline of a person sleeping under a frayed blanket. Great. Squatters.

"Hello? Hey, you can't be in here."

The mound is unresponsive.

"Buddy. Wake up. You gotta go."

He walks closer. Slender, polished toes peek out from the blanket. "Hello?"

This time he's asking a question, not barking a demand. Whoever is under there is going to need help, and he's in no position to help anyone. More random objects come into focus. A shoe. A small notebook.

A collection of used needles. A familiar-looking backpack raises his heart rate. He hurries to the body and crouches.

"You all right?"

His gentle shaking slides the blanket off a bit, exposing the back of her head.

"Hey. Hey, wake up."

He rolls the girl over. It's Elizabeth. He doesn't believe it at first. He rips off the blanket. She's in her private school uniform. Her nails are painted black and bitten down to the nub. Her arms are a roadmap of pain. Scabs and punctures from needles, and carefully placed slices from a razor blade. A needle hangs from her right arm. Her body is warm and limp.

"Help!" His howl echoes, reaching no one. "Elizabeth! Wake up. Help!"

He awkwardly drags her small frame out of the garage to the street. In the harsh floodlights her condition looks dire. Her tears have dried black on her face from mascara. Teddy screams and frantically tries to resuscitate his daughter. His previous CPR training has only been prime time cop dramas. It doesn't matter how much he fumbles or how soon an ambulance arrives. She's been dead for years.

Emily stands over them. He'd forgotten she was there.

"What do I do! What do I do!"

He pounds on Elizabeth's chest. Accepting that it's pointless, he pulls the body onto his lap and rocks it. He looks down helplessly and furiously tries to smooth her hair out of her sticky face. He doesn't notice a woman has joined them. A young woman dressed in gray with a serious haircut.

"Hi, Dad."

He raises his head slowly to find Elizabeth standing close to Emily. Teddy tries to speak, but it's all panicked gibberish.

Emily calmly steps forward. *"We apologize to thee for thine own duplicity."*

He carefully stands, leaving the body curled on the pavement. He addresses Elizabeth.

"You died."

He remembers now. He remembers getting the call from Trish. No words, just sobs. A nurse took the phone and gave him instructions. By the time he got to the hospital, she was gone. They had spent a good hour working on her. Trish was motionless in the hallway as he burst through the emergency room doors. He ran to her, and they both wept, holding each other up. He could see the nibbled black fingernails of his seventeen-year-old daughter hanging limp over a gurney.

Trish screamed like a wounded animal. Teddy did his best to calm her.

"Don't you ever touch me again," she hissed, pushing him away.

She left him standing alone in the hospital and later left him forever.

"You're a . . . a . . . ghost? This whole time?"

"She could not live upon the past. The present did not know her and so she sought this sweet at last and nature gently owned her."

It makes sense that Emily interprets for him. The women hold hands.

"Am I dead?" Teddy is apprehensive to touch them. He inches closer, hoping they will touch him.

"Almost." Elizabeth hands him another brown envelope.

"What's this?"

"Something that will help."

"I don't need any more help. Please. I just want to be with you."

"Read what's in there. That's a start."

"Elizabeth, I'll do whatever it takes, but I can't . . . I can't take any more surprises. What you gave me, about Grandpa? That is nothing I needed to know. I didn't remember it for a reason."

Emily interjects with a tone of authority. *"You cannot make re-membrance grow when it has lost its root. The tightening the soil around and setting it upright deceives perhaps the universe but not retrieves the plant. Real memory like cedar feet is shod with adamant. Nor can you cut remembrance down. When it shall once have grown, its iron buds will sprout anew."*

He begins to unlock the envelope's bronze clasp.

"Don't open it here."

He takes advantage of the silence. "Can I hug you?"

Elizabeth doesn't answer. He takes that as consent and wraps his arms around her. "I've missed you so much." He cries into her shoulder.

She has never had a chance to see him this way. It's strange but nice. Emily was right. Sometimes people can change. And sometimes they can't. She gently pushes him away. She studies him for a minute. She could take back the envelope. Spare him more pain. They could move on together and start anew. Emily takes her arm. She understands more than anyone how hard it is to write the truth.

It is time to go. The women turn and walk away. Their shoes crunch on gravel and then click on the pavement as they disappear into the dark misty air.

"Wait!" Teddy yells after them.

Elizabeth answers without looking back. She never looks back. "We'll see you soon."

The body is still at his feet. He sits down and examines the lines on her small arms. This is how she died. Alone. In pain. Crying. A father's worst nightmare.

A car slowly rolls up, and he is blinded by headlights. He holds up his arm to shield his face and moves quickly to get out of the way. The body is gone. He is alone in the street.

"Teddy Maine?" the driver yells as he gets out of the car.

"Yes?"

"Here's your car."

The man holds out a set of silver keys.

"What?"

"You're here to pick up your car, right? Sorry it took so long. It's like Tetris back there. I gassed it up for ya."

It's his Porsche.

"Oh. Thanks."

Teddy circles the running vehicle. He forgot how much he loves this car. He wants to blame someone else for forgetting it out in storage all these years, but it is his fault.

"Get her a wash and wax, and she'll be good as new."

"Thanks."

He takes the keys and slides into the driver's seat. It's been so long he hopes he remembers how to drive a stick. Emily was right: some memories are made of iron. It feels good to be in control of something again. It is hard to believe he was sobbing a minute ago. He thinks about driving out of the city. Driving all night until he runs out of gas. For as little as he cares about others, he has never just taken off, intentionally disappeared. It's tempting, but he can't. He needs to get through whatever is in that envelope so he can finally be with his girls.

The car is a mess. He balls up food wrappers left on the passenger seat and tosses them out the window. He drives home from Queens like it's his regular commute. He makes it to his building in record time, but then, time hasn't meant much these days. He parks in a loading zone. The city can tow it. Probably cheaper than keeping it in storage. All of Teddy's favorite things end up disposable.

Chapter 20

He feels lighter walking up the steps to his apartment. Younger. Maybe it's a boost from being behind the wheel or relief from not needing to work so hard to manage his existence. He doesn't have to make sense of everything anymore. Elizabeth said it, it's almost over. He comes through the door and walks quickly to his office.

"Emily? Elizabeth?"

He turns on the light. The room is empty. He is uncertain and cautious about what he's holding in his hands. Elizabeth has never been the bearer of good news. But he is also excited and impatient to be done with it. Life. If this is the final hurdle to being with them, he'll jump it. He'll do anything.

He opens the envelope to find a small notebook. It's Elizabeth's journal. One of them, anyway. It is small and delicate, with the weight of one of Emily's carefully bound collections. He smiles, enjoying this invitation to get closer to his daughter. He casually flips through the book, causing random notes and photos to spill out.

He bends down to gather them and falls through the floor. He lands silently on brightly polished wood. He is in a white room with gigantic walls and ceilings. It's a museum. There isn't much hanging on the walls, just a few large and heavy golden frames.

"Hello?"

He spins around the room. His shoes echo as he tries to identify his surroundings. In another room that looks exactly the same, he sees a man and a young girl. They are studying the wall behind an empty frame. The man leans down and whispers in the little girl's ear. He rubs one of her shoulders, and they move on.

"Excuse me?" Teddy's voice should boom in the empty space, but it hardly reaches his fellow visitors. "What is this?"

The man nods and smiles. The little girl waves. He takes their responses as welcoming and moves quickly toward them. He recognizes them, but they don't seem to know him. The little girl hides behind her dad's legs. It's Elizabeth.

"Sorry. I didn't mean to scare you."

The younger version of himself pushes her forward. "It's okay, honey. You can give it to him."

She reaches out and shyly passes him the journal that was left on the floor in his office.

"Thank you."

He looks down to study the handwritten treasure. When he looks up, they are gone. This must be where he is meant to learn all his daughter's secrets. He sits down on a padded bench in the center of the room and begins to read.

He is in the back seat of his prized Porsche. It's a gorgeous day for a drive with the top down. Elizabeth sits in the passenger seat. He's driving. Their past incarnations don't notice that they have a visitor. The car is in tip-top shape. He is cramped in the back seat that is best suited for children, but he doesn't mind. He smiles as he runs his hands along the fine leather.

Front-seat Teddy is relaxed, with one hand on the steering wheel and the other resting on the gearshift. He moves it occasionally to bring a silver flask to his lips. Elizabeth is dressed in one of her infamous white dresses. Her hair is pulled back. Blond strands whip her face. Her hands are tightly crossed at her waist and are of no help keeping the hair from beating her cheeks.

He enjoys being with them. They are on their way to the Emily Dickinson Museum. A special daddy-daughter birthday trip. He remembers this fondly. He doesn't remember drinking so much while driving.

He is standing on his boat. Elizabeth is older now. So is the other him. They are sunbathing. Elizabeth fills out her bikini. Something is off. There are too many empty beer cans. Where is the rest of the family? Didn't Elizabeth hate being out on the water?

Back in his private museum, he flips through the pages of the journal. He wishes Elizabeth were here with him now. He could use a friendly face. He is enjoying this, though. For the first time, he is not worried about going crazy or growing old. His mind is not broken. It's operating on a whole new level. He has tapped into a superior part of his consciousness. He is figuring out how to exist outside the confines of his body. Of time. This is a gift, for sure, but he could still use some reassurance.

He stands in the kitchen. His family is at the table eating dinner. All his friendly faces are there. Even Philip appears to be visiting. Emily wouldn't be in this scene. This is long before he committed to studying her. Augie has grown into a handsome high schooler. It's painful to see Elizabeth entering her sullen years. She is in a hoodie with her head down, staring at the food she refuses to eat.

Little Nora interrupts the silence. "Do you need a Band-Aid?"

Her big sister isn't listening.

She tugs on her sleeve. "You're bleeding. Mama, 'Lizbeth is bleeding."

Trish's head snaps up in alert. Teddy passes by his disinterested self, seated at the head of the table, to get a closer look. A pink scratch on Elizabeth's collarbone is creating a thin, beaded red line.

"Bitsy."

Trish's voice is soft but fierce. She motions for Elizabeth to zip her sweatshirt. She quickly complies, absorbing the blood with her finger and pulling the zipper up under her chin. The edges of older pink scratches peek out from her long sleeves. Out of habit, she tugs them down and balls up her hands inside.

This catches Augie's eye. "Why are you always wearing that stupid hoodie? It's like a thousand degrees outside."

"Augie." This time Trish's voice is just fierce. "Leave your sister alone."

Philip looks tensely back and forth between Elizabeth and Trish. He has been very quiet, spending more time drinking than eating. He looks much more serious than Teddy can ever recall, and years older. Breezy Philip must be having an exceptionally bad day.

Augie is right, though. Teddy remembers Elizabeth often wore layers year-round. It bothered him, but he chalked it up to adolescent dramatics. He was surprised it didn't bother his wife. She was the one who always cared much more about the way things looked. She wasn't a vain person but strived for a carefully curated life. Sweatshirts in July would definitely have pushed her buttons, only they didn't. Teddy didn't think much of it in real time. Now that he's noticed these pink edges, he regrets not being more curious.

He blinks, and he is gone. Elizabeth sits alone outside her school principal's office. It's a sunny day, and her fancy academy has excellent natural light. Her head is down, arms crossed tightly at her waist. She doesn't look defiant but small, like she is trying to shrink. There's red smeared all over her white dress. Some red paint has dried on her arms

and neck. Her hair is wild. Ah, yes. Her brave butcher-bird presentation. He smiles, remembering how proud he was of his spunky girl. He
doesn't remember the ordeal ending up with her so sad. He's sure it's
just the dread of sitting outside the principal's office.

He positions himself close to the frosted glass door. He can hear
the murmured voices of himself and his wife inside. Can he just walk
inside? Why not.

Trish sits in a shrunken state similar to her daughter. Teddy is
spread out in his chair and appears to be half in the bag. That's a bit
embarrassing. These walks down memory lane include some uncomfortable twists.

The principal's voice is measured and concerned. "We are all for
students freely expressing themselves, but—"

Teddy rudely interrupts. "Really?"

He does not have to say much. His posture is dominating the room.

"Elizabeth's teachers are concerned. She has been withdrawn. Have
you noticed her acting differently at home? Have there been any big
changes? Perhaps a death in the family or some other stressor?"

Trish opens her mouth to speak. Teddy beats her to it. "No. She's
a teenager. I shouldn't have to tell you that thirteen-year-old girls
are moody."

"She's missing quite a bit of work. That's unlike her. She's always
been an incredibly conscientious student."

"I'll make sure she does it. Are we done? Is she suspended? What?"
Teddy is both combative and ambivalent.

"Mr. and Mrs. Maine, I didn't call you down here for a disciplinary
matter. I'm concerned about your daughter's well-being."

"Thank you, but that's *our* job."

Teddy stands and offers his hand. The principal reluctantly shakes
it. Teddy takes no note of his wife and leaves the office.

Trish smiles apologetically and gathers her things to leave. The
principal quickly walks around her desk to speak privately. She stops
Trish from leaving with a soft hand on her forearm.

"Mrs. Maine." Her voice is barely above a whisper. "I don't typically get involved with family matters, but here." She hands her a card to a women and children's shelter. "My home number is on the back."

Trish nods, not making eye contact. She stashes the card deep in her coat pocket.

"Elizabeth is a remarkable young woman."

"I know." Trish's voice cracks.

She leaves before she starts to cry. She is afraid if she starts, she'll never stop. She has got to keep it together for as long as she can. She has to figure a way out of this, and tears won't help.

He sits, angry and alone, on his bench in the museum. This is not right. No. It didn't happen like that at all. Trish was pissed, but she wasn't on the verge of a breakdown. There was never a need for a secret exchange of phone numbers. He didn't take it seriously enough, and Trish gave him the silent treatment for the weekend.

He puts the journal down.

"I'm done!" His voice echoes.

He doesn't know who, if anyone, can hear him. He doesn't care. He walks into another empty room.

"I don't want to do this anymore. Elizabeth?"

He spins around, startled by the reverberations of his voice.

He rushes through an archway into another room. A red exit sign hangs over a chalky white door. The handle doesn't budge. It isn't locked. It's not real.

"Damn it."

Every room he scurries into is the same. Then, he spies another way out, an elevator. He pounds the down button. Or does he need to go up? Both light up yellow. Nothing happens. He slams his palms on the door.

"Emily!"

Finally, he hears women talking.

"Hello?"

He follows the sound and weaves his way through dozens of rooms. The noise is coming from somewhere.

He walks into what appears to be a screening room. It is a black box with a large rectangular screen. Oversized square chairs are randomly placed around the floor. The film is filtered, like a graduate student thesis. His family fills the screen. He bypasses the overstuffed chairs and stands with his nose to the screen. Trish and Elizabeth are packing in Elizabeth's room. He is watching them mid-conversation.

"No, no. Grab the other white one."

Trish is micromanaging their barely pubescent daughter. Elizabeth rolls her eyes and stomps back to her closet. She throws a bright T-shirt on the floor and pulls a white dress off its hanger.

"You know I'm over this." Her voice is thick with sass.

"I know." Trish's voice is thick with patience.

"I never liked those stupid poems or these stupid dresses." She jams the dress into a duffel bag. "It was, like, a two-week stupid phase, and he can't let it go."

"You are lucky to have a father who loves you so much. Supports your interests. And . . . it was a bit longer than two weeks."

"Whatever. You said it was creepy."

"Elizabeth, please. Can we finish?"

"I want to see my friends."

"You will. I told you, we'll have a sleepover next weekend."

Elizabeth sits on the bed. She thinks for a minute about what she is going to say and how she's going to say it.

"Mom?"

"Yes, love?"

"I don't want to go."

Trish sits next to her.

"I know. I don't want you to go, either."

Teddy backs away from the screen.

Wrong again. A stupid phase? Clearly what transpired at the

storage unit is proof it was not a phase. Emily wouldn't be with them now if it were ever just a phase. Trish and Elizabeth never talked like that. Never talked about him like that. Elizabeth loved her birthday trip to the Amherst Homestead. It was one of the happiest days of his life. Their life.

He doesn't have much time to stew over the past's inaccuracies. Another clip is spliced in. It's a shaky handheld home movie. He can hear a congested cough from the cameraman. Whoever is filming is sneaking around his boat. It looks like a hot day. Elizabeth is alone, napping in her bikini. Next to her are bottles of Hawaiian Tropic and vodka. The magazine she was flipping through apparently fell from her hands when she dozed off. Her arms and random bits of exposed skin are covered in Sharpie doodles. Black swirls and hearts. Flowers and mandalas. It is disturbing and beautiful.

There are suppressed chuckles from off-screen. A masculine arm comes into frame, holding a red plastic cup. The cup tips, and water splashes on the teenager's bare midriff.

Elizabeth screams and jumps out of her chair. "Jesus Christ!"

The camera shakes with laughter.

"Very funny, Dad."

Elizabeth shoves him, making the picture go sideways. The screen goes black and then starts on a loop. He does not want to see any of this twice. He leaves the screening room. The conversation in Elizabeth's bedroom spills into the cavernous halls, following him.

"Mom?"

"Yes, love?"

"I don't want to go."

He covers his ears like a defiant child.

"I know. I don't want you to go either."

He doesn't know where to direct this anger that is making his skin boil and his bones crackle. He doesn't know who to blame for blowing it all up and leaving this gaping hole of regret in his guts.

He howls, "Get me out of here!"

He is suddenly in a theater lobby. It is buzzing with the who's who of the city's arts community and all their rich friends. He stumbles down red-carpeted stairs toward the golden lobby doors. He bobs and weaves his way through the crowd. No one appears to notice his underdressed body pushing against the current.

He cannot wait to get outside. He thinks he will be safer there. He makes it to the sidewalk and takes a moment to catch his breath. He looks up at the glittering, colorful show poster. He's at the Met. It's opening night of *The Magic Flute*. His stomach drops. He is still trapped in the past. Stuck in Elizabeth's questionable recollections.

Should he leave? Will he end up somewhere worse? How is he going to find his way home? He decides to test his surroundings by attempting to talk to a fellow patron who is lighting a cigarette nearby.

"Bum a smoke?"

The man pays no attention to him and ashes the cigarette at his feet. A dark sedan pulls up. Elizabeth falls out of the back seat, laughing. She is clearly drunk or high. Probably both. She wipes her nose and stands up with a slight tilt. Teddy wants to run to her and cover her up. She's in a long, beaded dress that is both too big and too tight. She is busting out of the sweetheart neckline. Teenagers are masters at manipulating push-up bras. Rows of beaded fabric hang loosely over her torso and drag on the ground. She is wearing a gauzy, ill-matching cardigan to keep her arms covered. Her hair is stacked high on her head like she's playing dress-up. Her makeup is heavy and sparkly, which was the trend back then.

He watches himself roll out behind her. He grabs her waist, practically knocking them both over. It looks like he slept in his tux. How could Trish let them out of the house like this?

The car drives away. The two find a dim section of sidewalk. Past Teddy lights a cigarette for her. Present Teddy can't help himself. He steps between them.

"What are you doing? You can't let her smoke."

He can't hear him.

"Elizabeth." His voice is parental. He hopes she can hear him. Maybe they are riding the same wave of consciousness. "Button your sweater. Is that Grandma's dress?"

She doesn't answer. They take turns drinking from a flask. Elizabeth is trying hard to be a grown-up, but she can only manage small sips. This makes her father laugh. Teddy does not find any of this funny.

He cannot believe he is acting like this in public. He follows them inside. He wants to leave, but Elizabeth isn't safe.

Wait. He freezes. Elizabeth isn't safe with him?

He runs next to them. He is unnaturally close, studying their every move. How is this happening?

He observes people as they hurry by, everyone trying to avoid eye contact. No one is interested in making small talk with them. Opening night is filled with major players. There are no fans here to suck up to this train wreck. Finally, another couple stops. They are a similar pair. An older man with a questionably younger woman. Eyes heavy from what looks like days of pre-partying. Both men laugh too loud and allow their hands to linger too low on their dates' backs.

The man is Simon St. Claire, a dirtbag real estate developer who sometimes dabbles in producing. He is not handling middle age nearly as well as Teddy and looks even more disgusting next to a young girl. But is that girl his daughter?

It's time to go in. Teddy follows the group to their box seats. He's not done being shocked. He can't fathom ever willingly being somewhere out and about with Simon St. Claire, yet here they are, cozy, sharing box seats. He wants to call Philip. He needs him to fix this.

Simon drapes himself all over his date. Elizabeth's head bobs. She is fighting to stay awake. Simon gives her arm a little pinch, and she snaps up with a squeak.

"You don't want to miss the pretty costumes, sweetheart." His voice is narrow and smoky. Teddy always hated listening to him talk.

She excuses herself and stumbles over her dress. Teddy follows her. She takes small, careful steps and uses the wall for support. They push through the doors leading to the restrooms. This is where he leaves her. He walks through the door into his white-walled museum. He quickly tries to get back to the other side.

"No. No!" He pounds on the door. "Elizabeth? Anybody!?"

His cries are pointless. He trudges back into the barren exhibition halls. The frames are now filled with large oil paintings. Formal portraits from the past. There's Austin and Vinnie. Edward Dickinson with his wife and, of course, Emily. Teddy looks up at her sly smile.

"I'm ready. Whatever comes next, I just want to go home." He is begging now.

Laughter is coming from the screening room. He rushes to the dark space, hoping to find a friend, or a way out.

The room is empty just as before. His eyes open wide to take in the happy scene playing on the screen. Yes! Yes! It is her birthday trip, exactly as he remembers. Elizabeth gliding through the garden in her long white dress. Both excitedly climbing the stairs to Emily's room. Walking hand in hand from the Dickinson house to the boutique hotel in town. Elizabeth is laughing and talking a mile a minute. This is how it was. How it should be. A father spoiling his daughter with an over-the-top birthday weekend. A father supporting his daughter's budding literary interests and fostering her searing intellectual wit. Her bare arms are soft and clear, left free to soak in the sun. She smiles often and stands tall, taking up all the space she can.

He sits down, relieved. Finally. Somebody got this right. Music underscores a montage of their evening in Amherst. It is lovely to watch. Then the screen goes dark, but the film isn't over. The action has moved to a poorly lit room. Teddy squints and leans forward. He doesn't want to miss a thing.

The music has stopped. There is no longer sound. He can barely make out the image of a man sitting up in bed. This must be their hotel room. Teddy is in the bed, waiting. His shirt is off. The rest of his body is covered by blankets.

Why is there only one bed? They must have gotten separate rooms. Elizabeth was a brave girl to stay by herself across the hall. The bathroom door opens, spilling light into the room. She takes a tiny step onto the carpet. Her hair falls down her back in long curls from being in braids all day. She tugs at the T-shirt hardly covering her pink underwear. She curls her toes deep into the shag, hoping to stay planted in her spot. She rolls her body inward, trying to disappear.

He takes her in from across the room. "You look cold."

She keeps her eyes on the floor.

"Come to bed."

After what feels like years, she lifts one foot and then the other, inching toward her father.

The screen goes black.

Teddy sits still in the dark.

Everything in his body stops.

He is back on the water. Frozen. He can't stop himself from breathing, so he takes the shallowest breaths possible. Elizabeth is alone, leaning over the railing, smoking. Holding a burning cigarette in one hand, she picks at a scab on the inside of her arm with the other. She's been out in the elements for too long. He's starting to sweat just standing there. The sun is baking everything on this boat.

"Elizabeth!" Her father calls for her from belowdecks.

"What?" She answers with the typical tone of a teenager.

"Get in here! You're going to get burned."

She looks out at the ocean. How far could she swim? Augie's the athlete. She wouldn't make it far. That could work. She's going to end up there sooner or later. Why not today?

"Elizabeth!"

"Fine!" She throws the cigarette overboard.

Teddy's body begins to reanimate.

"Don't." He rushes toward her. "Don't go down there."

She walks past him.

He grabs an empty liquor bottle and smashes it. "Stop!" He grips the jagged weapon tight in his sweaty hand. "I'll kill him."

He jumps down the stairs behind her. He throws his body into the door, anxious to confront himself.

He lands on the floor of his artist's prison. His hand is bleeding. He punches the wood panels beneath him, and drops of red spray onto his face.

"No. No. No."

He crawls to the bench where he left the journal. He grabs it roughly and begins to rip out the pages. He would never hurt Elizabeth. Not like that. Not ever. She needed more help than he ever realized. That is a mistake he will own. She was clearly very troubled. But no. Never would he do something like that.

Denial is a powerful drug. Unfortunately, he doesn't have enough to make it to his next fix.

He is in the back seat of a dark sedan. He's not visiting. He's not watching or observing. He is there, alone, waiting for Elizabeth. She walks down the building steps, awkwardly holding up her beaded dress. He yells playfully from the window.

"Move your ass!"

She flips him the bird and continues cautiously to the car. A few more steps and she slides in next to him. She scoots in close.

"Your mother see you in that dress?"

"Of course not. I snuck out while she was giving Nora a bath."

"Well, I think you look gorgeous."

She shrugs. "Whatever. Whatcha got?"

He opens his suit jacket, revealing a mini-pharmacy. "Pick your poison."

"Don't mind if I do."

She leans into him and rubs her hands on his chest. Chipped fingernails make their way to the inner pockets of his jacket. She pulls out a small baggie of small round pills.

"What are these?"

"Let's take 'em and find out."

He is ready to cut loose. It has been a long week. Nora had an ear infection, and he thought this was going to be a painful date night with his wife. Philip is out of town. There isn't a babysitter in sight.

He pops the cork on a bottle of champagne. She pops a pill. He passes her the bottle, and she washes it down. The sequence ends with a hiccup. Teddy laughs and drains half the bottle in one gulp.

"Hey, driver. Take us around the park a few times." He turns to his daughter. "We have some time to kill."

She takes the bottle and sips what's left. He unbuttons the top of his shirt. He's not wearing a tie. He leans over her and tosses the empty bottle on the floor mat to roll at her feet. He grabs her face and kisses her hard. His hands quickly move down her body and up her dress. She's doing her best to keep up and hold herself under the weight of his body. He buries his face in her cleavage, and she robotically runs a hand through his hair. She keeps her head turned toward the window and counts the streetlights as her body complies.

He holds what is left of the journal and stands. This happened. This is true. He can feel it deep in his body. He can feel it, and it feels good. He releases a scream that is both painful and primal. He knows everything now.

He is back in his office, surrounded by torn, bloodied pages. It's dark. One dim lamp knocked on its side casts grim shadows on a desperate man. His hands still tingle from massaging the peach fuzz on Elizabeth's thighs. He smells champagne and gasoline.

This is the ending many expected. It will be no surprise that Teddy long enjoyed abusing a young girl. It may shock some that it was his daughter. No one has to know. He can burn the evidence, turn any record of his past into ash, just like he did before. He digs around in the mess for the metal garbage can. He finds it and frantically scoops up the journal pages. He is sure to pick up every last incriminating note. Destroying the evidence will save him. Will it save her? She doesn't want to be remembered as a victim, does she? What does she want?

It's a little late to worry about that now. He has to get out of there. He has to do something. Burning the proof is not enough. He dumps the pages into his worn leather bag and snatches up random items from his desk drawers. He is sure to take a bottle with him, and his gun. He won't be back.

He sprints from the safety of home. He doesn't feel any pain. No sharp jabs from his injured foot or drops of blood from his freshly cut hands. The open wound on his forehead hasn't dripped in a few days. He hasn't had time to notice his steady healing.

He's surprised to see his car still parked illegally out front. Anything that happened more than ten minutes ago might as well have happened a decade ago. His brain is a fractured mess.

That's right, he was at the storage unit. He drove his own car here. It's all coming together.

It does not take long to get out of the city. He can hardly see the yellow dashes on the road through the dark, a light sprinkling, and his dirty, cracked windshield. The wipers squeak and smudge with each pass. There isn't quite enough rain to make them useful. The old convertible top no longer closes correctly. Inside, the car is damp from the drizzle and loud from the rushing air. Once gorgeous and vintage, his prized Porsche is now old and useless.

He doesn't know where he is or where he's going. He's frantically following someone else's plan, but they didn't leave him a map. They left him a gun. He was happy to find that safe and sound in the bottom drawer of his desk.

His phone keeps buzzing as he speeds farther from home. Philip must be looking for him, wondering why he's not at the theater celebrating his late father, or maybe Augie has noticed his absence. Is it still today? For all he knows, the funeral was a month ago.

Philip was a good man who was ill-equipped to spend his life with Teddy. The truth is going to validate his worst fears. One more person left decimated in Teddy's wake. Perhaps it's a well-deserved punishment. A good man would not have associated with the likes of Teddy Maine. A good man certainly wouldn't have become his right-hand man. His fixer. He can try to convince himself he was there to protect the girls. That he did all he could to rein Teddy in, manage his vices. But he knows he never did the one thing that mattered. He never stopped him.

Teddy squints, trying to read a neon sign flashing outside the passenger window. It's for a motel. There's a vacancy. He pulls into the banged-up parking lot that has more potholes than cars. He shuts off the engine and breathes in the silence. He is about to ring a bell, and he knows it can't be unrung. He doesn't have another option. This is how it ends.

This no-name travel lodge, which looks like it caters to meth dealers and adulterers, is about to become famous. This is where they'll find him. This is where he'll take his last drink and write his last line.

It's raining harder now as he walks toward the office. He doesn't care and makes the trip slowly. His shoes fill with water. He feels nothing, a mercy he doesn't deserve.

The shabby lobby is the color of the inside of a garbage can. The young blonde behind the counter knows better than to make conversation with guests who check in this late. She's pretty, with an unfortunate mole on the side of her chin. She slides him the key to his room. *The* room. His fingers linger on the desk.

"Thank you."

She nods without looking up from her book.

"For everything."

He heads back out into the rain. There's no overhang. The rain pelts him from every angle.

His room is only a slight improvement from the lobby. The walls are freshly painted. The bed is covered with an itchy burgundy quilt, and the mattress is dented in the middle. The carpet is stained and flat. It's all perfect.

He dumps his bag out onto the bed and rummages through his supplies. He opens a bottle of vodka. He's never been picky, but wishes his last drink were brown. So far, this isn't all that different from his usual nightly routine.

He knows what he needs to do. She will have the last word. His final act will be her story. He collects the damaged journal pages and spreads them out on the dresser. He doesn't try to put them in order. People will dissect and study them in their own way.

He shuts his eyes. He waits a moment. Maybe, just maybe, when he opens them he won't recognize the face in the mirror. This isn't him. This isn't who he is. There's another way out of this.

He takes in his reflection. This is exactly who he is. Who he's always been, for lifetimes, maybe. He digs through the mess on the bed and finds a pen. He's constantly looking for a pen. He rips a piece of yellowed stationery from a pad kept by the phone and writes one last line:

"It's all true."

Elizabeth and Emily are there. He doesn't know how long they've been watching him. His body quakes with everything he wants to say.

"I'm sorry."

Elizabeth responds calmly. "I don't have a speech prepared."

"You don't have to say anything." He motions to her words littering the dresser.

He sees her for the first time, not covered in scars or through the tinted glasses of his obsession. She's not some hardened creation of his imagination. No. She's small, like the wren. Her hair is bold like the chestnut bur in Emily's poem. Her sad eyes shimmer like the sherry at the bottom of a glass left by the last departing guest.

"I love you. I've always loved you. I hope you know that."

"I do."

She stands close to him. If she were breathing, he would feel it on his skin. She studies the creases on his face. She knows he was hurt. She knows his soul tried its best to right a wrong. To be better. She also knows, more than anyone, that he failed. Miserably.

"I don't hate you. I loved you, too. When I could."

"I'll do anything to make this right."

She shrugs. "It's done."

Emily hands him the gun. *"They say it doesn't hurt."*

She takes Elizabeth's hand and leads her to a safe distance. Not that they are in any danger. He can't hurt them anymore.

He wants to hesitate. He wants this to be hard. But it's not. It's inevitable. It's necessary.

In one smooth motion, he puts the gun to his head and pulls the trigger. He falls backward, joining the bloated, bloodied corpse on the floor.

Epilogue

They stand in a barren field. Emily has taken Teddy here before. He is not filled with dread or fear this time. There is no color or light. They are floating in a waterless tank. Teddy's body is healed. His skin is smooth and new. Emily and Elizabeth are equally refreshed and serene. The sound of wind whistles, but there is no breeze. Teddy studies his hands. Is this real?

He speaks, piercing the void, not sure what his voice will sound like. "Are you okay?"

Elizabeth can finally be honest. "Yes." She savors the truth and continues. "Goodbye, Dad."

"Where will you go?"

Emily answers. *"Two butterflies went out at noon and waltzed upon a farm and then espied circumference and caught a ride with him. Then lost themselves and found themselves in eddies of the sun."*

"Can I go with you?" He knows the answer but makes Elizabeth say it. "No."

The place they are going is not for him. Not yet. Maybe not ever. They are going to a place where they are nowhere and everywhere at once. A kingdom with no king. A garden with no bailiff. They will be home in a house with no master. Elizabeth can feel every cell in her body that was once bound by the earth now buzzing through her like the sun. She is ready to leap into the unknown that is now so comfortingly familiar. There is a part of her that remains tethered to her father. All of us move through the universe, connected for better or worse. In this moment, she has managed to untangle herself and has the freedom to float at a greater distance now that their rope has one less knot. She can be pulled farther and farther away by the tides of the moon and the sparkle in each star.

She wants to touch him. Embrace him as his loving daughter. But some pieces can never be put back together. When certain things are broken, they are never safe to touch again. Certain things will always be sharp and dangerous.

The women turn to leave as a car pulls up.

A large, grotesque, and friendly man steps out of a dark sedan. It's Charlie.

"Teddy Maine?" he calls out one last time. "Your boss sent me."

Teddy appreciates the callback. He smiles at the familiar face.

Charlie joins him as Teddy watches Emily and Elizabeth walk away. They are headed toward a horizon with no color but a growing white light. He can rest now, knowing that she is safe. He will roam in a space where pain comes from within. His spirit will repeatedly be inflicted with an unforgiving chill and darkness, the absence of sound or touch. He's not afraid. He is ready.

"I'm glad she's happy. My Elizabeth. She deserves this."

"Some say we all do."

"Even us?"

Charlie chuckles. "Even us."

Teddy strains his eyes to stay with them for as long as he can.

"Emily tried hard to help me. I failed her."

Charlie does not waste words. "She was never here to help you." He nods toward Elizabeth. "She was here for her."

As they walk, two become one. Teddy will have another lifetime, or many lifetimes, to make this right. If he ever can.

Before she is absorbed into the brightness, Emily stops and looks back. *"His heart was pure and terrible, and I think no other like it exists."*

Eden Francis Compton

(Biographical and Historical Fiction)

ISBN: 978-1-646300-52-5

Death Valley is a story of how far you can push someone until they finally strike back. It's about love, greed, and a wide-open desert where men mostly end up dead.

ISBN: 978-1-646300-54-9

Hedy is the story of an unlikely partnership between the arrogant, avant-garde composer George Antheil, the brilliant and underestimated movie star/inventor Hedy Lamarr, and the unpredictable aviation tycoon Howard Hughes, in a time when America desperately needed the very hero they were too frightened to embrace.

ISBN: 978-1-646300-58-7

A heart-stopping thrill ride from beginning to end, Catch and Kill is about abuse by the powerful, those who conspire to protect them, and the dangerous path required to reclaim the truth.

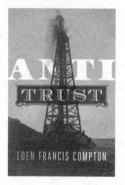

ISBN: 978-1-646300-70-9

Based on a true story. When Rockefeller ruins her father during the Cleveland Massacre at the turn of the 19th century, a determined young reporter sets out to destroy one of the nation's most powerful men.

ISBN: 978-1-646300-74-7

Inspired by a true story. In Victorian-era Indiana, Belle Gunness has it all. A lavish lifestyle on a large estate, three kids, and a man who will do anything for her.